To David

The imag...

And the ... imagined -

Tiger Tiger:
Underlying Crimes

Joann Mead
2-8-17

JOANN MEAD

Tiger Tiger: Underlying Crimes is a work of fiction. Names, characters, businesses, places, events and incidents are either the products of the author's imagination or used in a fictitious manner. Any resemblance to actual persons, living or dead, or actual events is purely coincidental.

For Jim

TIGER, tiger, burning bright.
    In the forests of the night,
What immortal hand or eye.
    Dare frame thy fearful symmetry?

The Tyger - by William Blake

~ PART 1 ~

Hong Kong & Shenzhen, China
&
Rhode Island, USA

1 HONG KONG HOTEL

"I know just enough to be dangerous." Mei purred in Kahliy's ear as he caressed her.

"I love when you talk sexy to me, Mei." Excited by her warm, moist breath, Kahliy ran his tongue along Mei's slender neck.

"It all depends on temperature. The tiger cage needs to warm up before it opens." Mei softly panted. Kahliy twisted a long lock of her jet black hair around his index finger, tugging it tight.

"You make me so hot, Mei. Tell me more." Kahliy lifted his head and stared into her chocolate pudding eyes. Her smoky gray eye shadow and black liner pencil accentuated the natural tilt to her epicanthic eyes.

"Tell me about your tiger cages, Mei." Kahliy was equally intrigued with the "tigers" that she designed in her lab, training and coaxing them to do her bidding.

"When they open, the DNA tiger-cages can release medicine." Mei's eyes widened, she feigned a grin of kindness and compassion. "Kahliy, the tiger cages will benefit health and humankind!"

Mei's expressive face then morphed to another

theatrical mask, one of menace and sinister evil. "Or they can release deadly viruses." Mei's wicked sneer transformed again, laughing at her own melodramatic histrionics.

"Oh Mei, you do excite me." Kahliy was captivated by Mei in more than one way. "Mei, what do you know about the Tiger flu?"

"Oh, I know all about the Tiger flu. After all I am your little pussy, Kahliy." Mei teased Kahliy relentlessly. She knew what men wanted.

Kahliy buried his head on her chest, his light brown hair smelled of lemons.

"Your scientists are reckless like you, my little tigercat." Kahliy slid his hand between her legs, prodding with his fingers, he caressed her inner thigh just high enough to make her wet.

Mei closed her almond eyes and moved her hips to Kahliy's massaging motion. "Oh Kaaah–Leee!" Mei groaned with pleasure.

It was an unusually stormy afternoon. A mix of torrential rain and pounding hailstones punctuated the thrusting, the probing, the manipulating, heightening the intensity of their lovemaking. Mei throbbed with pain as Kahliy thrashed hard, plunging as deep as he could. But Mei did not want it to stop. Not until she could take no more.

~

When Mei first met Kahliy, they were students at Hong Kong University taking graduate courses. Their mutual interest in microbes, especially the viruses, initially drew them together. But their mutual lust thrust them into bed at every opportunity.

Mei often visited Kahliy at his comfortable hotel in Kowloon. They shopped at the trendy malls where Kahliy indulged Mei with fashionable clothes and expensive jewelry. Mei never seemed to have enough of anything. Today, their shopping was sabotaged by an intense storm.

Golf-ball sized hailstones broke the glass ceiling and flooded the Festival Walk shopping mall. Kahliy thought it a perfect opportunity to explore what else Mei could offer him.

Kahliy rolled off the bed. He returned with a tall glass of ice water that he slid into the opening between Mei's thighs. "This will cool you so you do not swell. You *do* like it too much, Mei. You are a greedy girl."

Mei held her breath from the shock of the icy cold on her heated inflamed skin. Her thin fingers lifted the tall glass from between her thighs, bringing it to her lips. She sipped slowly, exhaling with a sigh of relief.

"Tell me more about the Tigers, Mei."

Mei told Kahliy that Tiger Flu originated in a Thailand zoo when the tigers were fed carcasses of birds and dead chicken. Many tigers became infected with bird flu, H5N1. Over a hundred tigers had to be killed to stop the contagion. In the past, the big cats never got the flu, ever. Not until Tiger flu made then vulnerable.

Kahliy wanted something else from Mei. "Mei, are your scientists even more reckless than the Dutch and Americans who created the deadliest strains of bird flu?"

Mei laughed as she replied. "Reckless? We are all reckless. As the Americans would say, who are they to call the kettle black?"

Mei kissed the back of Kahliy's honey brown neck as he turned his attention to her small breasts.

"Your English is much better than mine. The American way of saying things often confuses me. But we agree. They are so arrogant." Kahliy's mood changed abruptly from laughter to solemn and pensive.

"What can you get for me, Mei?" Kahliy flicked his tongue on her erect nipple, for emphasis. He then rolled over on his back to distance himself from Mei's nubile allure.

Mei ran her fingers along the tightly strung muscles of Kahliy's legs. His erection still prominent, his libido at times insatiable, she wondered what Kahliy wanted next. Climbing over him, suspended like a bridge, Mei playfully peered into Kahliy's spherical green eyes, the flecks of gold, like sparkling glitter, fascinated her. Mei was enamored by Kahliy's handsomely chiseled face, his strong, lean body.

By Mei's assessment, Kahliy was a fine male specimen. His huge "member", a new American word Mei had learned, complimented the bulging wallet he carried when wearing his stylish jeans. By Mei's definition of "usefulness", Kahliy fit the bill entirely.

"Please Mei, my little pussy cat. Where do they keep the Tiger Flu viruses?" Kahliy implored.

"At the animal research laboratory, scientists took the bird flu virus from a dead Bengal Tiger. They infected fury ferrets, small slender rodents. Like toys, they played with the virus DNA, the genes, changing the bird flu viruses to Tiger flu mutants that are very, very deadly." Mei paused for effect.

Kahliy raised one eyebrow, gesturing with his hand, he encouraged her to go on.

"The viruses were made more contagious. They now spread easily in humans. Airborne!" Mei blew on Kahliy's face and displayed her mischievous grin.

Kahliy read how scientists created new highly contagious, deadly flu strains. These new "Tiger" strains were hyper-lethal, very infectious in people and capable of spreading a global pandemic. They were "superbugs" that could wipe out humanity.

Kahliy sighed. He knew Mei could give him what he wanted. Given enough money, Mei would do anything for him.

"Kahliy, what else do you want?" Mei too could manipulate both microbes and men to get them to do what she wanted.

For now, Kahliy decided, he would just give her more. His hands firmly grabbing hold of her hips, he penetrated her like a precision boring tool, drilling a deep well for oil.

2 URBAN VILLAGE

Mei remembered the first time she peered down the long metal tube of a microscope. She could see tiny red beads strung together and dark purple spheres clustered like grapes. The mix of beads, round globes, long rods, and springy spirals, enthralled Mei. A virtual treasure chest of tiny jewels revealed an exquisite beauty to Mei's young eyes so unaccustomed to a new world of secret gems.

Mei's father often longed for his childhood, when he could still see the sky in Shenzhen. In the Shenzhen of today, when his daughter Mei looked out the window, she could only see into the windows of the shabby apartments next door. As the megalopolis of Shenzhen sprung up, so did the Urban Village of "handshake" or "kissing" buildings. You could do either with buildings this closely packed together. Beyond looking into the windows of crowded neighbors, Mei could see only slivers of grey sky and reflected sunlight.

~

Father opened a worn gray plastic garbage bag. He retrieved a small tatty cardboard box. Shaking it lightly the box made faint tinkling sounds. Mei hoped the box was filled with jewelry. But to Mei's disappointment, her father revealed an assortment of glass slides, some broken, others intact.

"But Father, I hoped you would bring me precious jewels. Even broken bottles are more beautiful than these." Mei whined, frowning in disappointment at father's gift. From an early age, Mei knew she could soften her father by playing on his guilt.

Father then carefully lifted a black microscope from the bag. He routinely brought home old plastic trash bags filled with a jumble of used wallets, wrist watches, and assorted scrap metal. All were tools of his trade. None of these items remained in their tiny apartment for long. Always something different, the old trinkets barely got Mei's attention. But today her curiosity piqued.

She asked her father, "What is this odd machine, what does it do?"

With his long boney fingers, he grasped an unbroken glass slide and placed it under the tubular lens. Peering into the eyepiece, he could see nothing but darkness. But Mei caught a glimmer of joyful glee in his eye as he remembered to tilt the circular mirror to reflect a sunbeam. A simple microscope he had used in his village school was shared among many. It all came back as he expertly fingered the focus knob.

"Mei, look into this tube, you will find what you want." Father suggested, grinning in anticipation.

Mei's pout became a grin as she peered into the tube. Strings of red beaded necklaces, elongated purple bangles and silver spiral bracelets made Mei squeal with delight.

Mei hoped Father would bring her more sparkling jewels. Perhaps he will find some pretty jewelry, like the microscopic beads of purple and red, but ones she could string around her long neck? Or perhaps some treasures lost at sea, odds and ends, bits and pieces, unlike those useless things he collects in his plastic trash bags.

Mei begged Father to please not sell her microscope.

He conceded with "Only if we need to eat." Half teasing, half serious, one never knew when their luck would change. The Urban Village brought risks along with opportunities, and the risks could be quite dangerous. Some say the Chinese symbol for opportunity is the same as the symbol for danger. Or perhaps it is only a catchy expression for wishful thinking.

When Father did not return home one evening with his usual cache of trinkets, Mei was disappointed. She wanted to show him her collection of shiny satin fibers of black and gold lace and her assortment of other tiny colorful threads, a strand of her black hair, and a beautiful filigreed fly wing, its golden interior surrounded by dark patterned edges. Mei collected fashionable fabrics and glittering jewelry on a microscopic scale.

~

Mother never told Mei what really happened when Father disappeared. Only that he drowned. His body found in the Pearl River Delta, washed up on the shore. Like debris from a shipwreck washed up like the flotsam and jetsam; Mother only had contempt for the wretched wreck of a man that he was. She knew she must now support both herself and Mei.

Mother recently found a job as a maid in a Shenzhen business district hotel. With Shenzhen's explosive growth in technology, especially computers and software, business men from Hong Kong created a demand for these newly built hotels. Mother saw opportunity where Father always went after the more risky, shady endeavors of pickpocketing and pawning. But now Mother must seek more risky opportunities to support herself and Mei. Mother knew that the higher the risk, the better the pay.

Mother's housekeeping services stretched later into the night. Mei was long asleep before Mother arrived back home from work. The influx of Hong Kong businessmen brought more opportunity than Mother expected. Besides the Cantonese language they brought with them to

Shenzhen, they also brought a hearty appetite for exotic flavors. Mother both spoke their language and brought spicy tidbits to their rooms. The spicier the offerings, the more money she made. Mother learned how to serve up a veritable feast for her voracious and hungry clients.

Mother would never let Mei see what was in her knapsack, a small backpack that she carried to work at the hotel. Mother seldom let it out of her sight. But when Mother slept, Mei stole glances and pawed at the soft and silky fabrics mixed in with Mother's ordinary day clothes. A small plastic zip bag contained Mother's cosmetics, smoky colored pencils to line her large tilted eyes, pink and red lipsticks, powders and a small mirror. But Mei was most enamored by a hidden necklace of purple glass beads. Mei resisted the urge to adorn herself. Someday she would, but Mei did not want to stir the wrath of her mother. She would keep mother's secret life hidden.

3 BAMBOO

Ever since Father's drowning, Mother's temper flared often. Mei kept her head low and her eyes averted. She stared deeply into her microscope at the red and purple beads her mother took no interest in.

Those early years were always dark and damp – the squalor, the overcrowding of the Urban Village in stark contrast to the new high tech district with skyscrapers mushrooming around them. Mei's mother spoke Mandarin, but unlike the migrants who came to Shenzhen, she also spoke Cantonese, the language that opened doors with the new businessmen. Mei and Mother spoke both languages, easily switching between the two.

Mei explored the contents of Mother's knapsack when the opportunity arose. Mother, exhausted from her work, often fell into deep slumber. Mei found the contents continually changing, like the contents of Father's trash bags filled with wallets and watches. The silk skirts and lacey lingerie made her ponder, but not for long.

Curious. Mei wondered what Mother might do when all dressed up. Mei sometimes fell into dizzying dreams, imagining Mother dancing, her neck draped with purple beads, her bangled arms swaying, her silk robes flowing, while businessmen clapped politely for more.

One day, while exploring the knapsack, Mei found a pair of lacey black panties that both shocked and amused her. She rubbed her fingers on the silky patch at the crotch that had been soiled with a dried glistening film. Mei, thinking about the men who might have touched Mother there, felt a tingling sensation between the lip-like folds where dark pubic hairs had started to grow. Mei's long fingers explored the folded skin, stimulating and awakening something new, a sensation she liked, a lot. Reaching deeper, rubbing gently, her fingers moistened and dried with the same glistening sheen as the film on Mother's black lace underwear.

On another day, her favorite find was a strand of heavy red-orange beads. Carnelian red agates the same color as the blood that now began to flow, spotting Mei's synthetic grey panties.

Mei conjured a long dream of how, someday, she too would wear black lace panties like the filigree of fly wings she saw in her microscope. She would string around her neck big purple glass beads like the spherical gram negative bacteria on her microscope slides. She would stuff them all into her own knapsack along with silky blouses and skirts. Just like Mother.

She dreamed her special kit would transform her – a metamorphosis from an ugly grey larvae to a resplendent black fly with opaque gold and black lacey filigreed wings. Mei had never seen a real butterfly.

While Mother slept, Mei was exploring the backpack again. Feeling the fabrics, she extracted a pair of dark nylon stockings, wondering how they attached to the suspender hooks on a red lace garter belt. Mei imagined pulling the stockings up her legs. She rubbed her thighs, higher and higher, dragging her fingernails against her skin. Engrossed trancelike in her sexual fantasy, she slipped her fingers between her legs and fondled herself until she exploded with excitement.

"Mei, what are you doing?" Mother peeked through bleary eyes, half asleep, until she could make out Mei's silhouette, Mei had her head tossed backward holding Mother's garter belt and nylons in one slender hand, the other buried deep between her upper thighs.

When Mei didn't answer, Mother leapt from the rumpled bed, rushing towards Mei in a rage. Mother grabbed the knapsack as Mei hurriedly tried to stuff the nylons and red lace back in. In the struggle, Mother's cosmetic bag spilled on to the floor along with her maid's uniform. A pile of lace and silky lingerie were strewn in disarray.

Mother swung her hand around and forcefully planted a loud slap on Mei's pale left cheek. The stinging pain merged at once with Mei's intense arousal. Mei suffered the fiery, urgent, burning and tingling sensations generated by her sexual experimentation, that coupled with her feelings of humiliation and embarrassment at being caught by her mother. Mei had never felt so many conflicting emotions all at one single moment. To Mei it was an oddly confusing awakening.

Tears began to stream down Mei's face, momentarily cooling the heated inflamed skin of her left cheek. Mother stuffed the spilled contents back in her knapsack, still shaking with anger. She could see red welting up on Mei's face. Taking hold of Mei's right arm, Mother pulled Mei to her feet and spun her around. Mei cowered. Mei knew what was coming next. Mother's bamboo rod.

This was not the first time Mother lashed out at Mei, but the striking of blows to her legs, thighs and buttocks continued longer than any beating Mother had inflicted before. Mother's fury was unstoppable, reason totally eluded her. Mei's embarrassment at being discovered by Mother was overwhelmed by the burning, searing, cracking whacks on her lanky legs. Mei tightened her muscles to defend against the blows. She had learned the technique, pulling her legs in close and stiff, squeezing her thighs, buttocks and groin muscles as taut as she could. From that moment on, Mei's sexual urges were intimately tied to the perverse pleasure of an abusive beating.

Once Mother's adrenaline rush dissipated, her concern turned to the red handprint on Mei's face. Mother tried to focus, thinking how she could disguise or explain the markings. The legs are always easiest to hide under clothing. But perhaps Mei's facial redness and bruise would need a cosmetic concealer stick or light beige foundation make-up?

Appearances are important, as Mother often told Mei. As she regained her calm, she sat in silence, composing an explanation for Mei on what she must learn. Beatings were always part of learning. "It is my strong love that makes me do this, Mei." Mother screeched in Mei's ear.

After canning Mei so viciously, Mother pulled her away from the windows to a far corner of the room. Mei barely made a yelp, she only faintly whimpered once the canning had subsided. Mei knew that if she cried aloud or objected in any way, the thrashing would only get worse.

"I work hard, many hours, to get money so that you can go to school. Mei you are a selfish girl, too curious for your own good. Someday, you must take care of me. You know I take care of my mother. It is the obligation of a good and dutiful daughter. Someday, it will be yours too." Mei's grandparents lived in a rural village where Mother and Mei traveled by train to visit and celebrate the Chinese New Year. Mother ingrained the indebtedness owed to parents. The filial obligation went without question.

"Now, it is your duty as a daughter to study hard for the *goa kao*. You are useless if you do not score great marks." The *gao kao* test pretty much decided if a child in China would succeed in life. Mother expected that Mei would spend most of her childhood studying. All parents knew that their children might be their only source of income for them in their old age.

"It is your only way out of this dirty, grimy place!" All

parents hounded their children on the essential importance of education. Perseverance, diligence, dedication and self-discipline were words all children learned from an early age. The pressure to succeed was unrelenting.

"If you want to get rich, you must work very hard!" Mother adamantly pounded the message. She pulled hard on Mei's ponytail for emphasis, staring deeply into Mei's dark brown eyes. "Your pudding eyes must read and study and learn. Otherwise you will end up in hotels, a maid like me!" Mother underscored her lesson with one last swipe of her bamboo rod against Mei's skinny bottom.

Mother took a deep breath, her voice softened. "You must get a good job in the new buildings. High technology they call it. You study hard, your science and your math, and some day you can do technology work. And you can find rich men, not with stupid jobs but *careers*. You must take care of me when I am old."

"Yes Mother, I will study hard. I will be a scientist and work for the rich men in their technology buildings. My microscope will help me get there. I have been told there are big powerful microscopes in those buildings that will show me the secrets of life."

Mei mused over the promises and goals she had set for herself. Mei knew what Mother meant, that it would take hard work and studying. But she could find the men to make things easier for her. The men who would help her get what she wanted. The trendy clothes and jewels, the slinky short skirts and lace underwear like Mother used.

"I will not be young forever, Mei. Youth fades, but money is forever," Mother grinned at her superficial eloquence. "Stay diligent and do whatever will make you stand out above the rest of the girls. You need the highest achievement in school to bring great wealth in life." Mother felt the lesson had made its way into Mei's head. As Mother's own mother once told her, "There is nothing like a good beating to focus the mind." And Mei's mind was now clearly focused.

Over the next few days, the swollen red welt on Mei's face did not linger long but her body continued to ache after Mother's administered "lesson". Mother only had to make the mere threat of a "lesson" and Mei's body would throb with pain, and the pings and pangs of her erotic daydreams. The sensations, the anticipation of a hurtful thrashing and heightened sexual arousal became a familiar pairing. It became harder and harder for Mei to dissociate the two.

Mei learned Mother's lessons well. First and foremost, the road to riches must be travelled with a well-equipped knapsack.

4 LEPIDOPTERAN

Shenzhen was not the hilly village it once was in the past. The "zhens" or drains in the rice paddy fields had all but disappeared. Migrants from inland China left their villages to live in factory dormitories. On the weekends they would return to their home cities. Foreign investment gave way to a boom in manufacturing, services and high technology.

In 1997, Hong Kong reverted back to Chinese rule. Whereas the British and other internationals called it a "hand over", the Chinese called it "the return". Prince Charles delivered the farewell speech for the Queen, ending over 150 years of British rule. Shenzhen became more and more integrated with Hong Kong as high tech, biotech and pharmaceutical companies exploded exponentially.

As Mei grew up, Mother continually stressed their Cantonese ancestry and the advantages of being bilingual in the Urban Village. "Mei, you will have opportunities to advance. But first you must be the top student in school."

The competition in school was fierce. Mei learned her lessons and she studied hard despite the distractions of the Urban Village. School totally absorbed Mei, demanding her constant attention for nine hours a day, six days a week, followed by homework and more studying during most of her waking hours.

Mother, resigned to her lot in life, knew that Mei would not have to live in the grimy Urban Village forever. There were new work-study programs between Hong Kong and Shenzhen that would allow Mei freedoms Mother never imagined. But it was Mother who made it all possible with her successful entrepreneurial side line. With that extra money, Mother bought access to better schools. And her pressure on Mei never let up, vowing to cane her to death if she ever slipped up in her grades.

Mei had no close friends at school, but beyond being lonely, Mei grew up being bullied. She worried how she would survive the endless harassment. Her long lanky body was always a source of ridicule and embarrassment. When she walked between classes, a popular group of girls constantly harangued her. "She is a spider. Look at those long skinny legs." Blatantly giggling and laughing, their nickname "the spider" stuck and Mei became the butt of many jokes. The girls, in her classes were aggressive and competitive, constantly testing Mei's mettle. But Mei, a shy, serious student, kept her head low and her anger deep.

Despite the persistent badgering at school, Mei took pride in her diligence and resilience. Excelling in the sciences and her passion for microscopic beasts, she used her slender hands and ability to gently coax the tiniest creatures to do her bidding. She found an intimacy with all things small that she could probe and manipulate. They became her closest friends. Little did Mei know that her dexterous hands and svelte body would one day transform her life and help her to escape from the Urban Village.

Mei pursued her goals; someday she would work in the skyscraper buildings. But for now Mei's only escape was indulging in her sexual fantasies. It was the only reprieve she had from her studies and her dreadful surroundings. The noises, the smells of garbage, rancid foods and excrement all added to a heady mix. Mei gazed out at the colorful clothes that hung between the buildings so that she could imagine exciting daily lives of people that went beyond the squalor they were tethered to.

Mei awoke one morning hearing muted moans coming from their tiny bathroom. Mei spied through a crack in the door as Mother showered. Her black hair soaked, her face grimacing, Mother seemed unable to open her swollen, blackened left eye. A marble of black and blue rings encircled her upper arms and wrists. Her shoulders were covered with scrapes and scratches, two red lashes trailed down Mother's back.

Mei could not contain herself as she pushed open the door and cried out in horror. "Mother, Mother!! What has happened to you!" She emoted aloud, "Mother, did you have an accident? Did you fall?" Her mind raced looking for a reason. Was Mother hit by a trolley? A bus?

This time, Mother did not anger. She turned off the shower, pulled a towel around her small shoulders, and with a look of profound sadness and despair, sighed in resignation. "Sometimes you get more than what you are paid for, Mei."

Mei learned another lesson. With opportunity comes risk. And with risk comes pain and punishment. Yet Mei was convinced that someday she would emerge a beautiful butterfly able to fly wherever she wanted.

5 NANOLAND

Mei's life was full of lessons and mantras. Mei's mantras guided her through life's quests and perils.

Mei repeated the mantra, "Work hard, get rich." All students knew that was the only way to get ahead. But Mei was not so naïve to think that there couldn't be other ways of getting around the system beside diligence.

Affluent families sent their children abroad to foreign universities, but Mei would not have that advantage. Her advantage came with her ability to absorb science and speak multiple languages. And Mei's English was key. It would open more doors than Mother's useful Cantonese.

At school another common mantra that Mei repeated was "The best to do is do your best", at least that is how Mei translated it into English. Jobs in biotech now required English as mandatory. After all, science journals were published mostly in English, and most scientific advances came from American and European universities. But China had been catching up in leaps and bounds and began to surpass other countries in many ways. Mei knew that a premier college focusing on the biological sciences would put her on the fast track for a job in the science laboratories of Shenzhen.

Her personal mantra morphed to "Work smart, get rich." Working "smart" did not apply to the job itself. She collected people who could help her along the way, those easiest to influence, those with the money and the power. And they were almost always men. Unlike the men in the hotels that Mother had to please, Mei would find men in academia, in industry, and in the research laboratories where Mei's combined skills and offerings were incomparable.

In the laboratory, she manipulated the microbes. And "smart" men, easily succumbed to her charms. Compared to Mother's hotel businessmen, the men of science were gentleman. Not the greedy, vicious businessmen who used Mother in degrading ways. The scientists were naïve, unaware of the hot spots of urban sin in Shenzhen. Mei's lab-coat sexuality appealed to their limited imaginations. Everything was clean and sterile and efficiently executed. Mei would offer herself up as an exciting lab experiment. A diversion from the many tedious procedures they churned out during their waking hours.

For those researchers with repressed urges, Mei could awaken new sensations they forfeited for much of their lives, always deferring women for science. In turn, they had the power to give Mei advantages, favors, privileges and hopefully, someday, an avenue to a new life in the West.

~

Some years later, Mei's memories came flooding back with the captivation she felt on her first day in her new laboratory. Mei, absorbed and engrossed, stared mesmerized into the scanning electron microscope. It was a far cry from the optical microscope her father brought home. The equipment purred like a tiny kitten, honing in on the tiniest details, far beyond the power of any light microscope. In the world of infinitely small viruses and strands of DNA, Mei could escape from her surroundings. Mei lived in a microcosmic world that contained the secrets of life. Her world was so peaceful, organized and sparkling clean in stark contrast to the noise and chaos and filthy passageways of the Urban Village.

Mei knew her science, both the yin and yang of it. Her diligence and curiosity in all things invisible to the naked eye secured her a coveted job at World Genomics. Mei delved into the world of nano, the smallest elements making up life. Her ability to manipulate tiny strands of DNA landed her in the research lab affectionately called "nanoland".

The gargantuan labs of World Genomics controlled the global market for the sequencing of human DNA. The company was efficient and cheap. A person's DNA blueprint, their entire genome, could be revealed at a fraction of what it would cost in the US. It was often said that China now owned the DNA of Americans, perhaps someday the entire world.

World Genomics Inc. literally took care of its employees. Mei was housed along with other scientists and technicians in the spartan but free dormitories on the Chinese mainland. Unlimited meals were served in cafeterias. Best of all, dating was encouraged. All this was given in exchange for people working a minimum of twelve hour days.

Mei knew she was privileged to get a job in a top security lab with DNA nanobots that could one day be delivery vehicles for medicines and drugs. As Senior Technician at World-wide Genomics, she had more perks compared to other technicians. She pushed to attend the advanced genomics courses in Hong Kong. Ambitious, she applied for fellowships that would take her to Europe. And maybe someday she would find a new life in the West. Mei wanted it all. But at the Yuan equivalent of $600 a month, she would not be experiencing a lavish lifestyle any time too soon. Only one person could help Mei get what she really wanted. And that was the director of her Shenzhen laboratory, Yi Lo.

Yi watched Mei meticulously cocooned in her full-body white Tyvek bunny suit. Her gloved hands had an adept and confident air, her subtle moves coaxing the DNA strands, the nanocages, to do exactly as she pleased. She opened and closed the strands to create the cages that would one day deliver medicines directly inside the human body.

Yi's elevated status meant he could influence how his underlings could advance. He was strict, officious and demanding, not a cell out of place, not even one errant microbe. After all, it would only take one microbe to contaminate the scrupulously clean lab. He demanded that protocol be stringently adhered to. Harshly admonishing any lapse, any breach of standard operating procedures. Any ideas or opinions to the contrary were not tolerated. The lab, its gleaming stainless steel benches, the negative pressure flow, ensured no bioburden, absolute sterility.

All staff showered in and out. With the strictest attention to detail, electronic access, log in and log out, he controlled the comings and goings of his staff, their schedules, their assignments. He commanded loyalty to him and the nanoland goals. And for the loyal, trusted staff, those who might do for him, Yi knew he had the power to control their destinies.

Yi whispered small praises to Mei, her exquisite hand movements. "As you advance, I will give you more freedom to learn". His message was obvious to Mei, she could be given extra time for exploring, experimenting.

"I do want to advance, Lo." Mei addressed Yi Lo by his first name when no one else could hear. Familiar, suggesting the intimacy they might soon enjoy. Mei could show him her appreciation for rewarding her ambition.

Along the sterile white hallways, everything was monitored from Yi's office. The hallway cameras, the lab access room cameras where gowning and hand washing, ten minutes scrubs, were timed. Yi could observe the most private of places, even the showers were monitored. Full-body scrubs, no quick rinses, Yi watched Mei's meticulous cleaning of every orifice, massaging her shaven mons, her long fingers disappearing high between her thighs. Mei's body scrubbing went well beyond the mandatory ten minutes.

Mei, who suspected Yi was watching was suggestive in every way, let him know what she wanted. What she expected – a promotion to Research Scientist, where she could set the schedules and assignments, the flow in and out of the lab. Access. It was all about controlling access. From Yi, Mei wanted access to his office.

It wasn't long before Yi scheduled brief but efficient interludes. Yi was discrete, always ordering Mei to his office at the end of her shift, after watching her shower-out.

For lab technicians, short hair was enforced to all except Mei. Yi allowed her to grow her luxurious black hair long if she kept it wound tightly under a head wrap. In the hallways, staff roamed only as necessary, still cocooned but in less stringent protective wear.

Yi made exceptions for Mei when he ordered her to his office. It was there that he indulged his fantasies, his wildest desires, which were pedestrian by Mei's standards. Vigilant, Yi's eagle eyes made sure that no one else roamed the hallway when they entered or exited.

Eventually, he gave Mei the access code where she could prepare herself for their encounters so that no time would be wasted. Yi did not believe in foreplay and he would not take the risk of unprotected sex. Always those government-issue condoms that Mei hated. Not like the silky smooth hand latex in the gloves they used in the nano lab. The forced, selfish sex required by Yi was *quid pro quo* for what Mei could get in return.

Over time, Mei would masturbate beforehand and bring herself to orgasm before Yi arrived at his office, releasing her natural juices before his hurried methodical penetration. Yi applied the same efficiency in his office as he did in his lab. Encounters lasted only minutes. Perfunctory. Expeditious.

Mei serviced Yi regularly, always with her requests for special privileges, no money exchanged hands. And when a fellowship to the West – rare indeed – materialized, Mei responded even more vigorously and added oral favors, before Yi might move on to another conquest in his lab. A married man, Yi only wanted one thing from his serial flings with female underlings. Cocooned, there could be beautiful butterflies within. Once they emerged, he would trap them, spread their wings and add them to his Lepidoptera collection.

"Oh Lo, Copenhagen is my dream. Please make my dream come true." Mei begged.

Yi would release Mei and let her fly off to Copenhagen, once she finished her coursework at Hong Kong University. For Yi, there was an unlimited supply of newly emerging Lepidoptera and it was best not to arouse suspicion by keeping them around for too long. Trap and release. That was Yi's personal policy when it came to his underlings.

6 TIGERS

Mei lay dreaming, half in and out of slumber, after a sweaty heated sexual marathon.

Kahliy repeated, insisting on an answer. "Mei, what can you get for me?"

"Kahliy, I could get whatever you want, but it will cost. Our Tiger flus are much more powerful than the Dutch and American flus. Our bird flu viruses have every type of new mutation you could want. And they can be designed, custom-made, to suit your needs. We have changed the little birds into powerful tigers!" She laughed at her humor.

Between the glint in Mei's dark eyes and her self-satisfied smile, Kahliy could see she was tempting him, taunting him with something seductive, sinister and down-right evil. He reflected for a while on what Mei revealed to him. And what she had to offer.

"Mei, tell me. How do your nanobots work? How do they let the Tiger Flu out of the cage?" Kahliy coaxed Mei to divulge more. He stroked her long arm from shoulder to fingertip.

"Ahh, the nanobot tiger cages like it very warm, at body heat. The DNA doors are like little arms. They will open at 37 degrees Celsius or at 98.6 degrees Fahrenheit …for Americans." Mei enticed Kahliy with a throaty sigh, she stretched her arms around him latched tightly around his neck. "Like this." Her grinning lips turned to a devious sneer. Mei knew she was clever; she could use her sexuality to tease men, to manipulate them, to make them do what she wanted. She toyed with men the same way she manipulated DNA.

Two could play at that game. Kahliy twisted Mei's thick luxurious hair around his fingers. He tugged hard to get her attention. "What more can you tell me." He insisted.

"The tiger cages release the Tiger Flu viruses in a warm, wet mouth." Mei poked out her tongue between her lush lips. Kahliy was doubly seduced by her science and blatant sexuality. He wondered what else she could do with her wet pink tongue.

Mei chuckled at herself and went on. "Four or maybe five days will pass before the fearful tiger brings a deadly fire to the brain. Tiger Flu is not the same beast as the ordinary bird flu."

Kahliy startled. His gold-speckled green eyes widened. His mouth dropped before he could muster a reply. "A deadly fire? Do you mean it is neurologic? It attacks the brain? Oh what terror that would generate." Kahliy paused to muse. Mei pursed her lips and kissed his cheek as a small reward.

"But Mei, has it been tried? Tested?" Kahliy was unconvinced that the Tiger Flu could infect people.

"No, Kahliy, of course not." Mei peered into Kahliy's round inquisitive eyes. She could see an intense desire, beyond anything carnal. Mei wondered what he would be willing to pay for the Tiger Flu? Mei hesitated and tempted him again. "But it *could* be tested. I know a way."

"Yes, we must test the Tiger Flu. We need proof that it will work." Kahliy's voice pitched higher, his words came faster, excited about the prospect. But Kahliy was skeptical of Mei's ability to pull off something so audacious. "We must have proof of the concept."

"But of course, like all good scientists, Kahliy. Would you have money for my first experiment?"

Kahliy argued. "But how could *you* test the Tiger Flu, Mei?" He would not let her play with his gullibility. She needed to assure him that it was possible.

"I often meet with people from the West. Visitors who come to our labs."

"But how will you find the right person to test with Tiger Flu?" Kahliy was still skeptical, but intrigued.

"Western scientists often come to collaborate at World Genomics. And I am their favorite tour guide. We have receptions. And meetings too." Mei fingered her plump lips as she contemplated the possibilities.

Kahliy encouraged Mei to continue. "Mei, I love you. You are beautiful and brilliant. But how do you get the Tiger flu viruses and capture them in your nano-cages?"

"Kahliy, My little brother works in the high security veterinary labs. He oversees the animal viruses, the bird flus from chickens and ducks. And that is where they keep the Tiger Flu collection. The lab has samples of the bird flu viruses collected from infected tigers and leopards."

"I didn't know you had a brother, Mei." Kahliy thought with China's one child policy that she would certainly be an only child. "Why didn't you tell me?"

"Oh Kahliy, he is not my parent's child. We often call our cousins and close friends 'Little Brother' or 'Little Sister'. And I think of my friend as a brother. I know that he loves me, but I let him know he is only my friend. But he will do whatever he can for me, his desire is very strong. I have always thought that he might be useful to me in some way."

Kahliy understood. Mei labeled her friends as "useful" or not. Wasn't that just what Kahliy thought of Mei? She was useful? Useful for the sex she so generously offered? Useful for her knowledge, her expertise with microbes and DNA? And she had her access to the resources of World

Genomics.

"Yes, Mei, tell me how you will cage Little Brother's ferocious tigers in your lab."

"My lab has tested drug delivery with our DNA nanobots. Some of the drugs can be carried by nanobots to fight cancer, they are targeted to destroy the cancer cells. But the little DNA cages can *also* hold viruses like the H5N1 Tiger flu. The viruses are tiny enough to fit inside the DNA cages."

"Interesting how they can be used in different ways." Kahliy pondered the thought. "But what will you do to the visitor?" Kahliy was not sure about how the experiment would work. He tugged again on Mei's long dark strands, to help her focus. A little pain to concentrate the mind, he thought. He jealously thought she might try to infect a drunken scientist in bed.

Mei registered the sharp pull. She even enjoyed the intensity. The mix of science and sex punctuated with pain. But she preferred to be the one inflicting pain. Sociopathic perhaps, Mei had little empathy for others. Ultimately, people were important for what they could do for her.

"Oh, meow Kahliy, your little kitty wants to be petted."

Kahliy eased off, pulling only on one single strand of her hair. "Tell me more."

"The DNA tiger cages, when they are warmed up in the body, the cages open and release their captives. The cages can have medicines or maybe Tiger viruses? The tiger cages open in a warm mouth. The Tiger virus then claws its way into the palate, the airways, and travels through the blood vessels to the deepest parts of the body. They will travel all the way to the brain."

Kahliy watched the subtle motions of Mei's tongue, but he stayed focused, contemplating the possibilities. What she described fascinated him. "How will you infect our test person? You must carefully infect your subject without arousing suspicion."

"Yes, it must be perfectly timed. The incubation for

bird flu is usually three to five days. So this western visitor must soon be travelling on a plane back home. I would choose one of our visitors from somewhere in North America." Mei explained.

"Ah, I see, and your DNA tiger cages will release the Tiger Flu and infect your selected person." Kahliy thought it ingenious.

Mei's almond eyes widened. She was absorbed, thinking about her "brilliant" experiment. She wondered aloud. "How can I deliver the tigers in the cage? Maybe I could make a pill but that is difficult to persuade the visitor to take? So better, give them something to suck on, like a sweet? Perhaps a hard candy would be best? I will think about this. First I must get Tiger flu samples. 'Little Brother' will be very useful. But I need money to buy his…services. He does not come cheap."

Kahliy was ready with his offer. "We can start with $500,000 up front for your 'research' expenses. When you are ready for action, there will be much, much more."

Mei was awed by the mere suggestion of so much money. She tried not to show her astonishment on her face. She bit her bottom lip before saying, "Oh Kahliy, together we can control the world."

7 MEI AND KAHLIY

What immortal hand or eye, Dare frame the fearful symmetry?
......Did he who make the Lamb make thee?
The Tyger - by William Blake

Kahliy would leave Hong Kong at the end of the spring semester. He would be going "home", wherever that was. To Mei, it was never clear, but why should she care? The mystery intrigued her, so it was better left unsolved. Kahliy told her he had family and friends in multiple cities and countries. Was it Abu-Dhabi? Or was it Abruzzi? A man with Kahliy's golden-skin could have come from any number of countries. Mei imagined his origins to be Latin or Mediterranean. Her fantasy man of the moment, Mei thought of Kahliy as multiple flavors, like a box of exotic chocolates. She would nibble the corners to find out what was inside. She was not surprised to find Kahliy was multi-lingual, he knew Latin and spoke English, Italian, and a mix of other languages. He could easily pass for a multitude of nationalities. Mister Multiplicity, Mei had nicknamed her lover.

On one unguarded occasion, as Kahliy drifted in and

out of slumber, Mei explored the contents of his leather computer backpack. In a corner pocket Mei found a treasure trove. She fingered through an assortment of more than a half dozen passports. Most were red, green, others dark and light blue. She glimpsed the top one. Italia. Ah, no wonder Kahliy speaks Italian. Before she could explore any furthers, Kahliy had roused himself. She slowly zipped the pocket shut, hoping Kahliy would not hear. But Mei mused, speculating on the opportunities that multiple passports could bring. She marveled at the ease at which Kahliy travelled the world with multiple nationalities. How useful, Mei thought, if she too had different colored passports, like accessories to match her wardrobe. Colors like deep red the color of burgundy wine, the dark blue the color of the sea, the light purple, the color of amethyst. Anything but the purple grape of the Chinese passport she held now.

Mei wondered what other secrets Kahliy hid from her. His air of mystery all heightened her desire for the man named Kahliy. A name similar to that of a great Indian wrestler or to the Greek Kaliy. It was a name used for both boys and girls. My name is not Kahlil, Kahliy would remind Mei. Kahliy is the only name I was given.

Kahliy was not a typical student, but a microbiologist on a mission. He knew he must be careful not to expose his real objective to anyone. Kahliy kept his innermost secrets hidden. Buried deep within was a fanatical hatred of America. Despite his university education, he preserved his true convictions. Kahliy naturally absorbed the languages and culture codes of American society and purposely downplayed his visceral hostility towards all things Western. Not even Mei knew what he really wanted. But Kahliy would willingly expose himself to Mei, down to life's most intimate detail, in bed.

Two people could not be more diametrically opposed than Kahliy and Mei. Mei had a passion for all things modern, the clothes, the jewelry, and the fast cars. She was driven by all the extravagances that money could buy. In Kahliy, Mei saw possibilities. Not for marriage. That was far from what she wanted. But Kahliy always had plenty of money and someone else paid his expensive tuition at the University of Hong Kong. And Mei had her motives. Kahliy could help her open doors to a life of freedom in the West.

Once there, she would meet wealthy "useful" men who could help her acquire the lifestyle she wanted. Her combined talents, unique skills and beauty, could bring opportunity. But "Opportunity does not come without risk." A mantra Mei repeated to herself. She often added a corollary, her justification for what she was willing to do. "Opportunity does not come without sacrifice." She just wanted the sacrifice of others. Mei's self-made aphorisms were her personal subjective truths. Her personal philosophy, that every man had his usefulness.

In addition to money, Mei knew she must have a knapsack pocket full of passports. And Kahliy had his sources for all colors of the rainbow. Like Kahliy, Mei could transmute her identity, be anyone she wanted to be, assuming different personas. She could be a chameleon forever changing colors to blend in with her surroundings. She didn't want to be found by Chinese authorities, should they choose to come looking for her. She would need a means of escape. One day she would be free to live a life of indulgence, a life of lies and manipulation of men.

Mei thought she held all the keys, but so did Kahliy. To him, she presented a fortuitous opportunity that had come his way. Mei could help him bring down the society she desired and the values she mimicked. Kahliy planned the demise of the society Mei emulated. He constructed the grand plan. He drove Mei. With sex, he would dominate and coerce her. With money as the lure, he would fill her knapsack full of dollars. He would reel her in. He believed she would do anything for him given enough money.

Mei bargained for more. "I need passports to elude the

authorities, Kahliy."

Kahliy angered, but did not let Mei see through his thick-skinned exterior. He calmly agreed.

"And I will need more money in euros when I am in Copenhagen." Mei's requests kept coming. "Ah yes, and accounts with more millions, once I deliver the Tiger Flu. It is the most vicious and aggressive flu ever created! And it attacks with a cough or a kiss." Mei kissed him lightly on the lips.

Kahliy agreed. "If it is what you say it is. Then I must have it. Promise that you can get the Tiger Flu for me."

"Kahliy, you will have in your possession the father of all bioweapons. Kahliy, I can do this!" She insisted.

Kahliy knew that someday, he could just as easily kill Mei as he could fuck her. Once she delivered on her promise she would be needed no longer.

Kahliy, adamant that Mei demonstrate the "proof in the pudding", he demanded, "You must show me how you have earned your seed money for your research. Present me with your first sacrificial lamb to the tiger, your deadly Tiger Flu creation."

"I will get the vaccine for us both. We need to be protected." Mei would make sure she would not infect herself. She would self-inoculate and inject Kahliy with the H5N1 vaccine before he left Hong Kong. The vaccine was available to those working in highly secure labs at World Genomics, especially for those in the veterinary and infectious disease labs, like Little Brother. A simple request, easily procured, Mei had her perfect source.

Mei and Kahliy would meet up again in Hong Kong two times. They planned to reunite next year in Denmark. With Mei's fellowship at the University of Copenhagen a timely gift, Kahliy thought it fate, auspicious in some way. Little did he know what sexual favors Mei exchanged with Yi Lo for her privileged fellowship in the West.

8 LITTLE BROTHER

Mei was not unusual growing up in a world with no siblings. Reproductive rules were dictated by China's one-child policy. Mei never questioned her lack of a "brother" or "sister" but she used those terms loosely to describe friends who might someday be useful to her in some way. She often met with her "Little Brother" in the cafeteria at World Genomics. A veterinarian and research scientist, Little Brother stood two inches shorter than Mei and, by Chinese standards, he was quite plump. Little Brother mooned over Mei and her lean, lanky figure. Mei knew he would do anything for her.

As a senior technician in a high-security veterinary lab, Little Brother worked with the virulent animal pathogens he kept securely locked under refrigeration. He controlled the deadliest of microbes and pathogens, their comings and goings were electronically monitored with secret identity codes tied to their unusual, newly designed characteristics. Many of the microbes were strains created at a veterinary lab in the north of China.

Recently, zoo tigers and leopards died during an outbreak of the virulent bird flu. Specimen were collected from the dead tigers and sent to the Chinese veterinary lab.

Lab scientists worked frantically to create every mutation and aberration possible on these already lethal viruses. During the international rush to create new flu strains, laboratory scientists in the United States, The Netherlands and now in China manipulated Bird Flu viruses to create the most highly contagious, extremely deadly combinations possible. Airborne in humans, they were easily transmitted by breathing. The scientists were accused by many of playing god. Rightly so, many feared that these deadly flus could create a world pandemic, should they accidentally escape.

Despite global calls for moratoriums on these so-called "gain-of-function" experiments, the research continued and actually accelerated for some time. Eventually, some labs temporarily stopped the risky experiments. But not China, and now many mutant strains, including the brain targeting Tiger Flu, were stored at World Genomics, housed in Little Brother's lab.

~

While Mei was away at her courses in Hong Kong, Little Brother pined away in her absence. He missed Mei beyond words; she was the light of his life, a bright bulb. On the upside, he spent less time in the World Genomics cafeteria, eating and waiting for Mei's chance visits. There was no longer a reason for Little Brother to spend long hours hoping for a few fleeting moments with Mei.

Love sickness prevailed, but over those four long months, Little Brother took to the fitness center, starting with the treadmill, trimming the fat, dropping the pounds, graduating to free weights and machines to sculpt and tone his muscles. What drove him was the potential bonus that Mei might see in him a new man, muscular, strong and virile. No longer just the man of science and animal viruses, Little Brother thought, "I will become the man of Mei's desires."

When Mei returned to Shenzhen, she did not recognize Little Brother, not until he smiled his toothy grin. She saw

35

that his face was less round, more handsome, his shoulders broader, buff, bordering on brawny.

"Little Brother, look at you!" She was pleased to see him, Mei knew she needed his help procuring samples of flu viruses from the veterinary lab. Little Brother beamed with pride for what he accomplished. Mei had took notice of his new physique. Her eyes scanned him up and down.

"Oh Little Brother, my Hong Kong courses are so grueling, so much to learn. But I see that you too have been disciplined. It is our mutual *gong fu*." Mei knew he understood what she meant.

Mei referred to the *Gung fu* or *Gong fu*, the diligence required for learning, the patience, the practice needed for acquiring academic expertise, or finely tuned skills, or the strengthening of mind and body. It could be any skill that took hard work. Only in the West did Kung Fu become associated with the martial arts. Little Brother had found the excellence that comes from lengthy practice. Mei too practiced long hours honing her skills. She manipulated her Tiger nanobots and her men.

"You are now a man, no longer my little brother." Little Brother startled at Mei's compliment, a quiver went through him, and for once he felt pride.

Mei could see him reacting. "Tell me about your work in the laboratory. Do you have the newest strains of bird flu? You must have the H5N1 Tiger flu, my handsome man?"

Mei flattered and probed, men always tell so much more when excited, stimulated. Mei knew from experience how to disarm, make men pliable tools to make them "useful". "Ah, the utility of men" Mei pondered under her broad grin.

"Yes Mei, the newest avian strains have arrived, all 127 varieties of H5N1." Little Brother displayed his gap-toothed grin. Not to lecture, he tried to capture her interest. "Ferrets, the small furry rodents, they were infected with H5N1 in the veterinary research labs. They now have many new mutant strains. I keep them safe and secure in my biosafety lab."

"And the tigers?" Mei probed. "Tell me about the tiger strains, they do so interest me."

"I also have the feline flu viruses. The samples were collected at the zoo from infected tigers and leopards. The tigers became so ill. So sad they had to be killed." Little Brother looked tearful, he was a sensitive soul.

"So very sad, Little Brother." Mei sighed in feigned empathy.

"But I understand why the zoo health director ordered the tigers and leopards to be put to death. We now know that the big cats can infect each other. Some strains are highly contagious among the cats." Little Brother shook his head showing his concern.

The feline world fascinated Little Brother, but Mei captivated him far more than any seductive science. He would do anything to win her over.

"And the new Tiger trait, the one that attacks the brain? The tigers have high fevers and stagger as if drunk, I hear." Mei prompted.

"Yes Mei, these are very alarming infections. The zoo tigers were fed on carcasses. Dead chicken. The H5N1 flu crossed over from birds to mammals. When infections cross from one kind of animal to another, it makes you wonder."

"But you have been immunized against H5N1 to protect you? I hope you have had your Bird Flu shots, Little Brother, haven't you?" Mei prodded.

"But of course, Mei. We have refrigerators full of vaccines for people working in the labs, especially those who come in close contact with these highly virulent strains. Anyone in contact with these samples must be protected. Despite our safety protocols, one can never be too cautious."

"It is better to be safe than sorry. And the families of the technicians, they too must be protected if by chance traces of the virus are brought home?" Mei's prodded. She intended to get what she was looking for.

Little Brother nodded, "But of course, Mei." not realizing where Mei was going with the conversation.

Mei decided it was time to tempt and titillate. "Perhaps we can be together more, my handsome man, I find you very appealing." Mei reached her arm across the table and lightly touched his arm, her graceful fingers then rested on his hand.

Momentarily silenced, Little Brother wondered if he heard Mei correctly. He didn't know what to say. He then ventured a daring request. "Would you like to go to a movie theater together in Shenzhen?"

Mei tilted her head, her lips turned a seductive smile. "Or perhaps we could have a quiet evening tomorrow night in your dorm room? Pick your favorite film. We could get to know each other in different ways."

Little Brother froze, he could only nod and mumble. "Yes, yes." The mere suggestion of "knowing each other in different ways" sent his imagination reeling. His heart thumped faster, blood rushed to his most sensitive parts. Breathlessness overcame him. He could not utter another word.

Mei knew how vulnerable Little Brother was to her charms. How smitten with her the first time they sat across from each other at the communal cafeteria table.

Mei, still gently stroked his hand. Overheated and perspiring, Little Brother was unaccustomed to Mei's scheming ways. He melted like the fat he had shed over the past months.

9 KUNG FU

The next evening could not come soon enough for Little Brother. He prepared his special noodle and rice dishes for Mei in his simple kitchen closeted in his cubicle of a dorm room, keen on impressing her with his domestic talents. He would be someone she could rely on to take care of her. Someone she would want as a constant companion. Someone she could love. "Love", a word now used more commonly in describing relationships in China. Not "obligation" or "convenience". Young couples in the new China now dreamed of "love" and larger families not limited to the one-child policy of the past.

Mei picked lightly on her plate. Mei was absorbed in thought with a faraway dreamy look, she lined up loose noodles on her plate, bending and stacking them, designing compartments. Little Brother asked her what work of art she was creating. She explained the art of DNA origami similar to what she constructed in her "nanoland" lab.

Mei sipped a dry white wine Little Brother mustered up for the special occasion. Wearing a simple woolen frock, she did not want others who might see her in the dormitory to think that her visit to Little Brother was anything but platonic. After all, they were friends and work colleagues, often seen chatting together. How could Mei possibly think any different about short, round Little Brother? She did not want to arouse suspicions.

Little Brother cleared the plates. Before he could fire up a movie on his computer, Mei stood up, edged in closely, and whispered a breathy sigh. "Let me see you."

Mei held him by his shoulders, feeling the muscles in his new build, inspecting his framework. She dragged her fingers against his chest over his blue tee-shirt, a knock off of the rock band "They Might Be Giants". "How appropriate that you should wear this Nanobot tee shirt, but I don't think they have toured in China."

Mei teased as her hands crept steadily up his chest to his beefy, well-shaped shoulders. Little Brother froze stiff at her touch. Walking her fingers playfully down his arms, Little Brother felt the slight scrapping of her short fingernails on the goose bumps she created. New sensations for an unworldly young man inexperienced with women; he had no idea of what to do or what might come next.

Mei toyed with Little Brother as a fun control experiment. She would teach him the art of making love. He would need practice and learning. He would never truly understand Mei's real desires. For Mei, sex was a means of molding men, shaping, manipulating, and folding them like origami birds and flowers. But what Mei really wanted was Little Brother's Tigers.

Mei kept up the teasing, stroking her hands down over his tight thighs. "Your muscles are so taut, so hard, you have become a man of steel my handsome man." When Mei reached the worn buttonhole of Little Brother's jeans, she unfastened the brass metal disc with only the slightest effort, leaving her to explore his rippled abdomen, lower, until she could feel his erection at the tip of her fingers. Mei unzipped his jeans, sliding her hand lower, she wrapped her fingers around his meaty member. Firmly holding him in a Kung Fu grip she rapidly brought Little Brother to share his fluid filled DNA. But he would need to share more than semen with Mei.

"You are my powerful, strong tiger now. Before we become more intimate, you must protect me…with silky smooth rubber sheaths and…I must have the ultimate protection. I need vaccines for me and my family. Protect me from your H5N1 tiger flu." Mei demanded.

Little Brother hesitated; he didn't think the vaccines necessary. But he vowed. "Yes, I will find the smoothest condoms for us. I want you so much. I will protect you always! You can always rely on me, Mei. You are my precious flower, a delicate blossom I will always cherish." Little Brother pointed to the bouquet of wildflowers he bought special for the occasion.

"Yes, you will always be my protector. And the vaccines, I will need them too." Mei gently ordered Little Brother to prove his love.

"But why, Mei? You should be at no risk. I follow protocols closely." Little Brother was confused by her request. She was certainly not at any risk.

"I want to test your tiger flu with my DNA nano-cages. I will destroy them, I promise you, but please help me with my research. And one day soon I will be entirely yours." She grabbed hold of his right hand, guiding him up her woolen frock, helping him find the unknown territory, dampened by desire. The possibilities excited Mei. She forced his fingers inside, like a bear in a honey pot, rubbing and riding his thick paw, she exploded like a Chinese firecracker on New Year's eve.

Mei promised Little Brother more. "When I return from my Copenhagen fellowship, we will marry. And have beautiful children together." She lured him with her willingness to depart from the outdated one-child policy. "Together our family will grow in size." Something she knew, this would further tempt Little Brother. He wasn't interested in riches and wealth, she knew him well enough.

He confided his love of children, his dreams of a family. He never honestly thought the beautiful Mei would be his. He knew he had to make her happy to keep her.

~

Two days later, Little Brother invited Mei to his room. Stashed in his refrigerator, was a six-pack of H5N1 flu vaccines. He gently cradled Mei's graceful arm, sliding a thin needle below her skin, careful not to cause bruising, he inoculated her against any potential risk of Tiger Flu exposure.

"Mei, I have the Tiger virus samples for you, but you must wait for the vaccine to take effect." Little Brother warned.

Mei dipped her hand into her frock pocket, revealing a foil packet with a high quality condom. She came prepared to seal the deal with a kiss and to teach Little Brother, rewarding him to make sure he complies with all her demands. Keep him focused on delivering. Little Brother mustn't have any second thoughts, any qualms, nor have any questions as to Mei's real objectives. Mei explained in detail why she was preforming these experiments for precisely that reason.

"Little Brother, I must prove my experiments are effective. I want to show that someday DNA nanocages might be delivered into someone to trap deadly viruses, to rid the body of infectious agents and pathogens. We do not know when nature itself will release new strains of viruses. We must fight with every tool, every weapon available. My nanocages could save humanity from newly emerging diseases. Like any dual use experiment, this is the good that could rescue mankind."

"I understand, Mei. You want your work to make the world a better place." Little Brother crooned, singing her praises. To him, Mei was not only beautiful on the outside but also within, her dedication to science and altruistic proclamations convinced him of her compassion for humankind.

"We want a better, safer life for our children. A man with your virility and integrity is what I want." Mei took little time unwrapping Little Brother's package. Unrolling, slipping on his thin rubber raincoat, she pulled him on top of her as she reclined on his single bed. She directed him under her hiked up dress, rubbing, stirring, circling, progressively smaller rings, directing him to the targeted opening, the receptive orifice, waiting for him to take the plunge.

Hesitant, Little Brother inched deeper. "I do not want to hurt you, Mei."

"Do not be afraid, my handsome virile man. Give me everything you have. Push more. And more. It is only you who will have me." Mei panted.

Little Brother exploded in nanoseconds. He thought Mei's sigh was an expression of the passion she felt for him. He would be her slave, he would do anything to keep her, whatever she asked, he would abide. He could set no limits, no boundaries, no questions. He trusted her completely.

Mei was pleased indeed. She smiled with relief and satisfaction that it did not take too long to please him and the Tiger flu viruses and Little Brother were hers.

10 DEAD DROPS

Mei's brain buzzed with excitement. She had what she needed from Little Brother, protection for herself and a variety of strains of H5N1 Tiger Flu. Little Brother included strain #127 only when Mei insisted. He realized the danger of including the airborne, contagious varieties, but Mei promised they would be irradiated with high doses. Inactivated, the deadly Tiger Strain (#127) couldn't possibly pose a threat.

Mei had her work cut out for her, continuing to service Yi Lo, the lab director, in exchange for more access to the lab. Off hours, she gently coaxed her DNA nanocages, at first, by trapping plant viruses harmless to humans.

It was all about the techniques: layering the strands of DNA, her origami, creating small compartments, folding, unfolding, enveloping viruses, releasing them, heating and cooling to make them magically respond. Mei grew the nanobots. She could make them behave.

Singing little made-up songs, she toyed and played and dreamed of the power and control that she had over the basic units, the DNA blueprints that defined all life. "Ah, my little tiger cages, some day you will unleash the tiger that I trap in you."

Mei's brain raced on overdrive, thinking hard about her trip to Hong Kong tomorrow. She needed Kahliy to help her develop the next phases of the plan. Phase 1, to deliver the Tiger Flu to their chosen "test cases", their victims. And Phase 2, how to carry and conceal the final batch of "Tigers" held captive in the DNA nanocages. The deadliest and most contagious strain would be transported from Shenzhen to Copenhagen.

Mei thought, "Now that I have my tiny tigers, I must protect them."

Mei's classes at Hong Kong university were nearing the end of term. She and Kahliy had few opportunities left to finalize a plan to execute such an audacious scheme.

After class, in Kahliy's hotel room, she pushed his advances away, insisting they talk first, play later. Time was short, they both knew the priorities. Lying adjacent on the bed, both starred at the white ceiling, keeping their heads clear of diversions, including each other.

"I have the vaccine Kahliy, next time we meet I will inject you. I have been inoculated; my immunity will soon be effective. I can work on my ferocious beasts without them devouring me!" Mei laughed her familiar chortle. "But Kahliy, how will we protect the tigers as they travel from Shenzhen to Copenhagen?"

"They must be kept safe and very dry." Kahliy added.

"Yes, somewhere that they can't escape." Mei hummed as she considered the possibilities. "Or possibly leak out!" Mei gasped at the possibility.

"You will keep them in your suitcase, your checked luggage, so they won't arouse suspicion."

"Yes Kahliy, but how can we make sure they will not be found? Perhaps bury them somehow in my jewelry, a broch perhaps, with a compartment?"

"Mei, how do you contain your nanocages, do you keep

them in test tubes?"

"Not in glass test tubes but in smaller metal cylinders, they can be refrigerated to keep them active or frozen to preserve them for future use."

"Mei, I think there is a much better way!" Kahliy exclaimed. "Ah, brilliant. We need a dual purpose container for keeping them safe and for delivering them in secrecy."

"What do you mean, Kahliy?" Mei's curiosity piqued.

"Dead Drops." Excited, Kahliy repeated. "Dead Drops!"

"You make me laugh, Kahliy." Mei smirked, her nose crinkled. "So who is dropping dead other that our sacrificed animals?"

Kahlil reprimanded Mei with a scowl. "Don't laugh at me. Listen hard, you silly girl!" He calmed himself and explained. "We can use dead drop spikes."

Mei cowered from Kahliy's harsh outburst, but she had never heard those words used with any other meaning. She shook her head. "Kahliy, just what are you talking about?" She would not take his criticism. She had no tolerance for insults.

"Mei, you say you have narrow metal tubes to contain you tiger viruses in their nanocages. Correct?"

Mei mumbled a yes. She closed her teeth tight, resisting the urge to strike back with words. She listened.

"In the past, dead drop spikes were commonly used for hiding secret messages. They were a vital tool of the trade for spies or secret agents. You've watched those types of movies, haven't you?"

"James Bond, perhaps, but only the beautiful rich women interest me, Kahliy, their fashions and their jewels." Mei shrugged.

"Now, everything is electronic, secret messages are often hidden with encryption. But spikes still have their uses." Kahliy paused as Mei started to catch on. Both were as tech savvy as others in their generation.

"Interesting Kahliy, please tell me more."

"Espionage. The word *espion* is French for 'spy'. In old Italian it is *spione*." Kahliy was well-versed in the word derivations. "In the early days of espionage, dead drop spikes, usually metal, were often left in soil, in a planter box or perhaps a ceramic pot. Somewhere, most often in plain view, spies would deposit their secrets. Buried, the metal spike would not arouse suspicion. The spike would penetrate the soil with only a small handle exposed."

Mei nodded, staring at Kahliy, she grinned broadly, beginning to appreciate the possibilities.

"Ahh, Kahliy, they must be disguised, as in a thing of beauty. These dead drop spikes." Mei suggested.

"Like you, Mei, your beauty disguises the evil within." Said Kahliy, unable to resist the jibe, he had Mei pegged. But Kahliy wasn't sure where she was going with her comment.

Mei took no notice of Kahliy's quip. She sat up, raised her arms and with both hands grasped hold of the two shiny red and gold beaded chopsticks that held her hair up in a knotted bun. Her luxurious long black locks cascaded onto her shoulders.

"Perhaps, Kahliy, they will be hidden in something like this. But plain, not jeweled." Mei handed them to Kahliy. He ran his fingers over the beaded sticks, inspecting the details and the size, their width and their length before giving them back to Mei.

"Yes, plain ones, tan colored would not be noticed when planted deep into a pot of soil. But these are too narrow. Still, quite ingenious." Kahliy stroked his smoothly shaven chin, then gave Mei an affirming smile.

"The metal cylinders I use with my nanocages are impermeable, they have tight fitting screw caps. No moisture can get in. No viruses can escape. I will fill the cylinders with small pills that keep the tiger viruses in their nanocages."

"Mei, you are quite wonderful." Kahliy stroked her

long silky threads and wrapped them around his fist. "I'm sure you will find the perfect width and dimensions." Finally, he let out a single laugh that ended with a wry smile.

"Kahliy, you will someday soon know what evil I am capable of. I will do it for you. Unleash the beast. The plague will eliminate those ruling the world, and then we will have it all. The future belongs to us."

"Yes Mei, as we both wish for. And you will deliver the drop spike to me in Copenhagen?" Kahliy asked.

"Yes, I know a craftsman in Shenzhen. I am sure he can fashion hollowed bamboo spikes that will fit the empty metal tubes. I have many of these cylinders in my lab, they will not be missed."

"Mei, you do think of everything, don't you."

"I have a vivid imagination." Mei smiled her feline grin as she drew closer. She ruffled his shaggy highlighted brown hair that framed Kahliy's handsomely chiseled face. "Show me what you can do with your spike, Kahliy."

"I will spear you with my mighty spike." Kahliy tempted Mei. "I have more imagination than you could possibly imagine. There are things about me you do not know."

They hastily removed their clothes. Kahliy grabbed Mei's hands and pulled her up to standing.

"First, I must show you how to bury a dead drop spike, Mei."

As he lifted her hips, she wrapped her long shapely legs around his thighs. Pinning Mei against the hotel room wall, Kahliy pierced and stabbed with his dead drop spike at the same time thinking how one day he would need to kill her.

11 SPIKE

Back in Shenzhen, Mei couldn't help thinking about the dead drop spike, what a clever device, it would suit her purpose. To construct the special containers, her spike chopsticks, Mei found her craftsman in Shenzhen, a carver of fine wooden ornaments. Mei explained to him how she must keep her sweetener pills in hollowed out bamboo chopsticks. The long void must be impermeable to water, she instructed him. She paid him well so he would not inquire any deeper. He must take no interest in what could be hidden or smuggled in those hollowed out tubes with her inner metal cylinders. Mei insisted that the contents be kept dry. She supplied water tight seals with a rubber ring, a lab quality stopper that allowed no moisture to seep in. The craftsman made other similar devices before. He knew what nefarious uses they might be put to.

A skilled carver, he delivered to Mei two identical chopsticks. A perfectly matched pair. Always thinking ahead, Mei wanted a backup, a second dead drop spike also with a hollow metal cylinder. Just in case. You never know when you might need one.

~

The next week, Mei and Kahliy met up in Hong Kong

for their final visit before Kahliy would leave for Europe.

With her knapsack filled with cooling packs and the H5N1 vaccine, Mei rode the MTR subway from Shenzhen to Hong Kong. She also brought her bamboo spike tightly wrapped in plastic bubble wrap.

"I have your vaccine. And I have the tiger drop spike." Mei hyperventilated from her fast trek from the train station. She carefully removed her knapsack from her right shoulder, set it down and placed the vaccine kit in the small refrigerator.

Mei handed the spike to Kahliy, who gingerly unwrapped it. Mei could see Kahliy admiring the smooth bamboo finish, it was quite simple, with a veneer of hardened waterproof sealant. Fine inlays of white bone, with two vertical stripes, were the only ornaments placed at the handle end. Kahliy seemed pleased with the exquisite craftsmanship as he rubbed his fingers along the light brown chopstick. He untwisted the screw-top end and swirled his little finger around the opening.

"The metal cylinders fit perfectly within, Kahliy." Proud of her accomplishment.

"How elegant." Kahliy swooned, so pleased with their ingenious plot. Closer and closer to refining their sophisticated plan. The future was no longer just a dream in the distance.

As Mei rose to her feet, Kahliy wrapped his arms around her.

But now it was time for the less pleasant but vital vaccine, Mei opened the refrigerator as she spoke. "The vaccine might hurt. I had some swelling and redness, it is not unusual. But in one day or two the red welt subsided." She looked back at Kahliy. "I will inject you now." Kahliy took hold of her hand, pulling her away, he kicked the door closed.

"My injection can wait. But I can't wait for you. This is the last time we will be together, for a while." One week had passed since he had last been with Mei. His lust, his yearning, his anticipation for a goodbye fuck. He handed her a gift bag from a lingerie shop with an exotic red lace teddy with nylon stocking suspenders. He insisted she wear the black fishnet stockings. "Now!" he ordered her. "Go dress."

Mei, hot and sweaty from the journey, motioned, pointing to the bathroom. She dutifully showered and dressed in an outfit suited for a cheap prostitute. Not her choice, it reminded her of what her mother wore as a "maid". Open on the bottom, her buttocks cheeks protruded below.

Kahliy imagined her every move as she squeezed into the tight teddy, waiting until she pushed open the door and emerged. Kahliy stood outside the door, fully sheathed in his best animal skin condom. Mei walked towards the bed, but he stopped, running his hand on her exposed double protrusions.

"Smooth like your ass, Mei." He said. Then pushing her back, he bent her over a brown leather chair. Mei was shocked he would take her this way. But, she rationalized, there is always a first time.

"I must get my money's worth, must I not, Mei?" Kahliy uttered. It was quid pro quo.

A plastic bag lay open on the bed with stacked dollar bills. Mei stared at the bundles of cash. Mei thought about the money, whether she could carry it all in her knapsack. She wondered aloud. "Will it fit?"

"I will be very gentle, Mei. I have always wanted you this way. You do excite me Mei."

He put on his sheath and indulged himself, changing his approach multiple times. "Today, I will take you around the world, Mei." Mei didn't resist, compliant sex slave that she had become.

With Kahliy, who knew what to expect. Expect the unexpected, she thought, pleased to have remembered the English saying. Mei liked the element of surprise, and Kahliy kept on surprising her. She mused about what other new worldly adventures Kahliy had in store for her. He was useful to her in so many different ways. Unlike any of Mother's useless degrading Hong Kong businessmen, Kahliy would help her get ahead in this world. Mei wanted Kahliy. She desired him. But love? I don't think so.

"In Copenhagen, you will have much more cash, one million. I will set up a bank account for you in Europe. Three million euros will not fit in your knapsack. Also, a new identity."

"More than one passport, Kahliy, promise me. Three at least: red, blue and green. But no dark purple." Mei demanded what she wanted, multiple identities in case any of them became compromised.

"Oh Mei, you are such a greedy girl." Kahliy smirked and rolled his eyes at her. He was convinced she had already spied his collection of passports.

"Kahliy, they are not only useful, passports are essential. To avoid the authorities. To make sure that I'm not caught. I will not be a caged animal." Mei rolled her eyes back at him. He could detect a threatening glint in her eyes. "Three passports, deep red the color of burgundy. Two, deep blue like the sea. And one green, like the color of your eyes. I must be able to hide, Kahily."

Kahliy wouldn't let Mei compromise him in any way. He had to make sure no Chinese authorities would find her, had they come looking for her, the research fellow who did not return from Copenhagen. World Genomics had a network of global feelers. But Kahliy had already come up with a plan. Mei was his tool, a means to an end. There is no freedom without death. Her death would set him free. He could just as easily kill her as fuck her. He reminded himself over and over, that ultimately she must disappear into a sea of green.

"We have work to do here, Mei.' Kahliy chided her, but Mei laughed at the task they had at hand. Together they stuffed a mix of US and Hong Kong dollars into Mei's backpack. "If I gave it all to you now, it would not fit,

Mei." Kahliy explained. "There will be much more to come. After you deliver your first experiment. As you said, your sacrificial lamb."

During the next task, Mei said little as she injected the H5N1 vaccine deep into Kahliy's arm muscle. She understood their attraction, their bond, their devious plans would sustain her. For now she would do as he wished.

Mei and Kahliy planned to "talk" via twitter. Her handle, @XOXOXMay. His handle @YOYOYSpiko. They would portray themselves as two star-crossed lovers, separated by distance. Their tweets would reflect an "until we meet again" theme. Their cryptic euphemisms would be known only to them.

@XOXOXMay I miss u. Want to show u the proof of my love. Someday, we will be together again. But now I must find a way.

@YOYOYSpiko Someday soon, please show me what you can do.

12 TOUR GUIDE

Focused, Mei repeated to herself. "I must find an opportunity. Where is the opportunity?" She hoped to find one that afternoon when a group of visiting scientists from the United States arrived at World Genomics.

Mei's boss Yi seemed more anxious and hurried than usual as she passed him in the hallway on her way to his office. She would be ready for Yi, receptive as usual. As she waited she pondered possible scenarios. Who would she choose as her first test subject, her first trial specimen? She needed to test her hypothesis. Yi would unwittingly help her execute her first experiment, a "proof of concept", that her meticulous DNA origami would unfold and release from the cage the captive Tigers to attack their prey. The golden honey sweet that Mei crafted would seduce and entice, like a honey trap laid to lure an unsuspecting victim.

Mei perfected her special recipe for honey-filled hard candies that went from crunchy to chewy to a soft ooze. Mei mixed the honey, the highest quality, she found in a specialty shop in Hong Kong, with vanilla extract and vinegar to form the hard shell. Inside, the pure liquid clover honey enveloped the beads of Nano tiger cages and their captive Tiger flu viruses. They would melt in your mouth with a tantalizing burst of gooey gold.

Nearly an hour passed as Mei lapsed into a daydream. Reflecting on the "gong" of her achievements. All the practice, honing her skills, the many hours she dedicated towards perfecting techniques. And the "fu", strengthening her mind and body, acquiring excellence in both. Between Kahliy, Yi and now Little Brother, her inner muscles gripped hold like an Anaconda. Only Kahliy with his manly drive could satisfy her voracious appetite. She thought his stamina impressive, the way he brought her to multiple orgasms. It was not just the physical romps that excited her but, most of all, it was his delivery of seed money and the promise of more millions in a backpack full of euros in Copenhagen and bank accounts in Europe.

To amuse herself, Mei imagined her knapsack brimming full of cash and how she would need a suitcase, …no, a *set* of suitcases,… and a footlocker… or a *huge* trunk to contain her newfound wealth. Mei chuckled to herself until her ludicrous thoughts were rudely interrupted by Yi pulling the office door shut behind him.

Yi switched on the hallway surveillance camera by keying in his password. Careful to keep an eye on the comings and goings of lab technicians, he always made sure no one would see Mei exit his office. Yi unzipped his brown trousers and speedily peeled them off. Mei wasted no time going to work, pulling and prodding to make him hard.

Mei badgered Yi as she rolled a condom over his small stiff dick. "I am your best tour guide. My English is much better than the other bench scientists. The visitors and their wives find me sweet and engaging." In his state of arousal, Yi nodded in agreement.

Mei had perfected the technique to his liking, a sexual ritual of quick thrusts, very fast, as Yi liked most things. Mei leaned over his desk so that she did not have to look at him. A white towel draped on the table for his dribbling and drubbing. It never lasted long and he kept his thrusting in the conventional places. Thank goodness he had no imagination, thought Mei.

As Yi pulsed an expedient rhythm, firmly pressing between her thighs, Mei's thoughts dwelled on her "gong", all her diligence, practice and repetition in the lab. The ingenious way she packed her DNA nanocages as she folded them into intricate origami cranes and dragons. Her masterpiece, the DNA tiger cages were exquisite boxes that held tightly the Tiger Flu.

Mei thought of Little Brother who procured the lethal viruses on her promise. "Yes, Little Brother, when I return from Copenhagen, I will have your baby. Or maybe babies!" It was a promise that Mei never intended to keep. "Little Brother, I have destroyed the Tiger Flu strains. It was only an experiment, I used great care. Don't worry, you can trust me."

~

That afternoon, Mei dressed in a professional navy-blue knee-length skirt and matching, loose-fitting jacket to greet the guests. Yi caved in to Mei's request to be a tour guide as quickly as he succumbed to her enticement. Mei arrived in the foyer to gather the group for the World Genomics facility tour. A long corridor with windows allowed visitors to glimpse row upon row of washing-machine sized DNA sequencing machines, most purchased from US companies. The seemingly endless display of instruments hummed away as they sequenced the DNA of every living thing imaginable.

"From the smallest microbe to the largest mammals, our goal is to read the DNA of the world." Mei intrigued the visitors with the sheer computing power. "We have the largest processing capability on earth. We have completely sequenced the DNA of hundreds of thousands of people. The first human genome sequenced in the United States cost three *billion* dollars! We will someday soon read your DNA for just a few *hundred* dollars." Impressed, the visitors let out a loud vocal "Awesome!"

The group, scientists, business men and a handful of wives, chattered like chipmunks, as they bantered among themselves. Sometimes Mei had to clap her hands and boost up her volume, but she soon got their attention.

"Someday we will sequence the DNA, the entire genome of *every* living thing. We can identify every gene, the full blueprint of DNA instructions that make us who we are. And with that we can help you with your research on discovering the genes that cause cancer or in developing the drugs to treat diseases." They nodded, enthusiastic with the potential technological resource for their research.

Yi Lo reminded Mei earlier in his office to never mention her research with DNA nanobots. And she must avoid any questions on their projects looking at human intelligence genes. She also must not bring up the "editing" of DNA in human embryos. It posed an ethical dilemma to Western scientists that many Chinese scientists did not understand. They knew there was great potential. They had no qualms with the human embryos they had been tinkering with using the new CRISPR technique. Why wouldn't they want to work on improving the human race and editing out those inherited traits that made some people ill or mentally deficient?

Yi warned her that visiting scientists often wondered how DNA information like "intelligence" genes might be used. She must deflect any questions and turn the conversation to curing diseases or to the popular panda or big cat projects.

Mei exclaimed to the now attentive group. "My favorite projects are the big cats… the tigers, leopards, cheetahs! Ah!" Mei enamored the group with her sweetest kitten-like grin. She wore no make-up, her hair in a bun; she propped a pair of dark rimmed glasses across her nose to project a studious image. She acted her part as a scientist. Cute, sweet and very smart.

After the tour, the reception room at World Genomics buzzed with more visitors, scientists and business contacts. Collaborations with US companies for their expanding markets, DNA sequencing expertise, medical services and agriculture had grown exponentially. From medical markets to global pharmaceutical companies, the possibilities seemed endless.

Mei meandered through clusters of mostly men, dotting the large atrium at World Genomics. She spotted one of the wives standing on her own sipping a carbonated beverage. No alcohol was served at this event. Alcohol consumption was reserved for later at the various dinners they would disperse too.

The young woman was about the same age as Mei. Her husband, one of the younger academics, was engulfed in a conversation with other scientists.

"Are you a scientist?" Mei initiated a conversation, full knowing the woman was not. Judging by her simple black and white patterned A-lined dress, Mei thought her style American. But her ancestry was obviously Asian, easily Chinese.

"Oh, no. Not me. But my husband is a scientist." The woman's North American twang confirmed what Mei was thinking.

"My name is Mei. Where are you from?" Mei had tucked a hard candy into her cheek.

"My name is Lian. I'm from Seattle, Washington. My husband is a professor and researcher at the University." Lian welcomed the attention.

"So good to meet you." Mei offered a hearty handshake in traditional western style to make her feel at ease. "Are you here for long?"

"We fly back home on Friday, we have had such a wonderful vacation and my husband has visited with his university colleagues." Lian explained.

Mei, sucking hard on her candy, apologizes, "Oh, sorry, this sweet is so irresistible. Please have one?" She offers

Lian a wrapped candy she holds in her open palm. "Try one, it is China's best. Filled with honey."

Lian, grateful not to have been left on her own, graciously accepted the offering. She always had a sweet tooth. She unwrapped it, popping the offering on to her tongue, finding the flavor to her liking.

"Oh, do let the Honey Sweetie melt in your mouth so that it slowly releases the honey filled center." Mei continued to babble incessantly, mostly re-hashing the successes of World Genomics, its spirit of collaboration, working with researchers, all to better understand and improve life by understanding the DNA of the world.

"Oh, the honey just oozed! A very tasty treat, thank you." Lian pursed her lips and licked the sweet residue left on the rim of her mouth.

"Lian, you must tell me more about Seattle." Lian needed little prompting, she was happy to share. Mei nodded and took in the sweet aroma emanating from Lian's mouth. But as she half listened, Mei thought perhaps she did not want to know too much about Lian. She wasted no time in gathering other untethered wives to bring them together, engage them in conversation. Mei reminded herself that everyone is useful in some way. The opportunity must be taken. There is no life without sacrifice. The sacrifice of others. Mei repeated her adage, her mantra as if a refrain from a song. Perhaps a fitting chorus.

Mei thought she would feel conflicted, wondering, had she gone too far? Is it guilt I am feeling? But only for a fleeting moment did she dwell on any doubts or misgivings.

Lian's usefulness had quickly come to pass. Mei now wondered if her "excellent" experiment would be fruitful. She let Kahliy know about her "test case" soon enough in her next tweet.

@XOXOXMay I am ready for you. Just wait and see. I

am always your little kitty. Your tiger is now out of her cage.

@YOYOYSpiko I await arrival of the most magnificent creature known to man, my Tiger cat. You are all I have ever wanted. My life's desire.

Later that evening as Mei readied for bed in her tiny dorm room, she mused. "Opportunity is fleeting. I seized the moment." Mei appeased herself by justifying her actions, that life for Lian would be short. Borrowing another aphorism from Hippocrates, she morphed it to an adage of her own making. "Life is short, art long, opportunity fleeting, experience is useful, judgement is easy."

Mei twisted another subjective truth. "There is no life without the sacrifice of others. Or is it sacrificing others?" It was all one and the same to Mei.

Before leaving Shenzhen for Copenhagen, Mei visited Mother in the Urban Village. Mei believed strongly in obligation and duty. She was indebted to Mother and she must repay the debt. Life in the Urban Village would be a thing of the past for Mother. She would no longer suffer at the hands of manipulative men. Mei bought Mother her freedom from her oppressive life. Mei proved that she was indeed a dutiful daughter.

13 MEANWHILE IN RHODE ISLAND

Jo woke up obsessing. She had done her homework. She knew she was on to something. Jo returned from the kitchen in her fuzzy pink night robe, waking Jeremy up with his usual British morning cup of sweetened milky black tea and two "biscuits". Cookies by Jo's definition. She placed them on the nightstand.

"It's H5N1 Tiger H9N2!" Jo blurted out of nowhere. "I'm pretty sure of that."

"I love it when you talk sexy to me." Jeremy playfully replied. He raised his enormous mug to his lips.

"No, really, check it out. Google it! I'll write it down for you." Jo insisted, grabbing a pen and notepad she kept on her side table for sleepless nights when she needed to purge her nagging thoughts.

"Look Jeremy, you've heard the news about the woman who died from an unusual strain of bird flu. She flew into Seattle from Hong Kong. It wasn't a common variety flu that killed her. This one isn't natural. It was created. Designed by somebody, somewhere! This poor woman's flu came from a Tiger in a zoo."

"I'd rather you come back to bed." Jeremy raised his

eyebrows and comically displayed a deviant smile.

Ignoring Jeremy's comment, Jo blurted out. "But I am *sure* of it this time. It's a biological weapon. A WMD, a weapon of mass destruction!" Jo paused to catch her breath.

"So, we are all doomed. We are all going to die." Jeremy teased in his usual droll fashion.

"Don't tease me!" Jo snapped back. "You know that there are rogues out there!" With Jo's constant manic harping on the risks and danger, "It's those global village idiots. They are bent on creating new bioweapons and pandemic superbugs!"

"Oh, and don't forget the others, the hostile actors and nations!" Jeremy egged Jo on facetiously. Jeremy, the eternal optimist thought Jo an alarmist. Too often the fatalist. But he also knew that sometimes she could be "spot on".

"Look, Jeremy, in a world of hostile actors, there are plenty of fools willing to cross red-lines." Jo bantered.

Jeremy chuckled. "Oh, and don't forget the nihilists among us!" He had studied Fred Nietzsche along with his favorite Wittgenstein.

Shaking her finger at him, Jo reprimanded and gave a warning. "Pandemics do not respect borders." She loved Jeremy for indulging her in her fears and paranoid delusions. Because, every so often, she got it right and she was convinced she was right now. "What do you think could happen if some terrorist group got a hold of these lab created bioweapons, Jeremy?" Nonstop, Jo went on and on, hands on her hips, as if lecturing a naughty child. "And all you need is one lab accident and millions of people could die if one of these super-lethal flu bugs gets loose."

"Well you are right about that one Jo. Even the CDC labs and the Pentagon have had a few mishaps. Like misplacing Anthrax and sending out a few dangerous strains of bird flu." Jeremy added some fuel to the fire.

"And don't forget the live Anthrax they mistakenly sent around…to uncountable labs …Oh, yes to a *plethora* of labs in the US and other countries all over the world." Jo accentuated the "plethora". Repeating the word, mispronouncing it with an intentional slur, "Pl-re-thora, pl-re-thora. What a pretentious word that is." Jo never knew when to stop.

"Come back to bed." Jeremy coaxed Jo. "I need to give you something to take your mind off all the world's problems." He coughed and cleared his throat, grinning theatrically with the bug-eyed stare of a sexually crazed maniac.

Jo rolled her eyes at him. "Only if you promise to look into a few things for me. Do a little research, Mister Aggregator." Jo was oblivious to the fact that her bath robe had distractingly fallen open, exposing her assets to him.

"So is this a bribe?" Jeremy asked, his face beaming a mischievous smile.

"Yep, quid pro quo." Jo quipped back.

Jeremy did not hesitate with his reply. "Ok. I'll look into it for you. Trend it for you."

Jo flashed back a grateful smile.

"So come back to bed." Jeremy tugged on Jo's arm, meeting with little resistance.

~

Jo let Jeremy sleep as she sorted through news posting and scientific articles. She kept thinking, "This just shouldn't have happened."

Jo scribbled down the key words all in upper case: FATAL, RARE, ATYPICAL, UNUSUAL SYMPTOMS, NO COUGH, NO SNEEZING, FEVER, UNUSUAL BRAIN DEATH, NO KNOWN SOURCE, NO REPORTED CONTACT WITH POULTRY

What's the medical school adage? Think horses not zebras. Ah yes that's it, Jo thought. But this one is not a horse. Surely, it has to be a zebra. This woman's case of lethal bird flu did not have a simple explanation. It was not a common disease found in nature.

She pondered and mulled over the incident, described as an isolated case. "Was it really just an anomaly? Or a harbinger of what was to come?" Jo wondered if she was on to something.

A series of articles that Jo sorted through had made the headlines. "First H5N1 Bird Flu Death in the United States." And "Woman Arriving on Flight from Hong Kong to Seattle Dies from Bird Flu."

When Jeremy woke, Jo instructed him. "Jeremy, you have some aggregating to do." It was, yet again, his turn to perform.

Aggregators like Jeremy had come a long way since news gatherers like the Huffington Post and Google News spawned them. Nuanced, they now catered to specific interests. Jeremy trolled the social network aggregators to find out in seconds what people were saying.

"Come on Jeremy, help me find the clues. Jo badgered him, often to the point of exasperation.

If something was trending on Twitter, a #hashtag or a @handle, Jeremy looked for cryptic clues from seemingly innocuous tweets.

Jeremy had plenty of tools. He used these tools to organize stories, for Jo to speculate on, to analyze, to synthesize and to create something new. Or just making the connections. Jeremy helped gather the data for Jo the scientist, Jo the investigator. He teasingly called her a "super sleuth".

For Jeremy, much of it was obscure but not encrypted. He looked for obscure euphemisms, but they could be hidden in plain view. There were messages, hidden in broad daylight, but still buried in the dark. Terrorist communications were often so subtle they would go unnoticed.

"Just what does it all mean?" Jo asked Jeremy. He constructed the algorithms to find the nuggets she needed.

Those tips and tricks, life hacks as they were sometimes called, saved time. Jo needed those novelty methods for getting what she wanted with the least expenditure of time and energy. Whatever topic Jo tossed at him, Jeremy generated the algorithm to find trends. Sometimes they led to blind alleys but others times they helped cull the internet tsunami of mostly irrelevant junk.

Jeremy helped Jo find clues, construct possible scenarios, project ahead to discover the evil intentions of idiotic rogues and terrorists. To follow events as they unfolded, in real time. Or better yet in pre-real time. If early clues were not definitive, Jeremy would vary the tactics. His algorithms were in constant flux, evolving as new clues were revealed.

As Jeremy liked saying. "Let's mash it up a bit."

~

"Jeremy, find the zebras, not horses." Jo demanded.

"Jo, you are so damn bossy! I *know* what to do." Jeremy snapped back.

Jo and Jeremy sorted through seemingly unrelated mounds of information. They searched for peculiar words, alpha-numeric combinations, obscure publications, news, blogs, and odd tweets.

Jo complained to Jeremy that the so-called "experts" seldom talked to each other. "It's inane, the way they insist on staying in their silos. Why do they go down deep wells and stay there? They seldom emerge to see the light of day."

"Fools!" Jeremy arrogantly proclaimed.

Jo scratched her head, thinking. "Except for the Partners." She mumbled. Jeremy nodded in agreement.

Experts in their respective fields, the Partners were adept at tying together disparate subjects. Only their methods differed. A partnership, they worked as a unit, they could stitch together the fabric of the threat quilt.

Jo loved puzzles, as a kid spending hours assembling just enough pieces of a jig saw to see the whole picture.

Jo thought, "Maybe it's like weaving a tapestry? No, wrong metaphor." Confused by metaphors, often scrambling them, Jo was the master of mixed metaphors. She knew she was no literary genius. But she knew she was good at connections and obsessive-compulsive enough to leave no stone unturned.

"Ah, another stupid metaphor." Jo chided herself. She amused herself for hours on end gathering pieces, puzzling out riddles, comparing, extrapolating, synthesizing, analyzing and using all those other hierarchical mind games of Bloom's Taxonomy.

She liked mysteries that were deep enough but with broad implications, they could be local or span the globe. Ever since Jo uncovered an egregious act of corporate bioterrorism, one that sickened and killed children, Jo interests shifted from local to global threats.

Just the next morning, Jo exhumed a buried message from a list of dates, times, and venues on an obscure website the Partner's used for communication. The message: The Partners would meet tomorrow at the designated time. The location was, a private facility that was now closed, giving no access to the public. The message: Tomorrow they would meet and Jo had better be there.

14 PARTNERS

Odd, Jo thought, the way the Partners were notified, not by standard e-mails, never by traceable cell or landline phone calls. As instructed, Jo checked the pseudo website every day. It was really just a shell that posed as a virtual company, a publisher of nothing concrete, just intangibles. Nonexistent books by unknown writers, imaginary musicians and unheard-of artists. Nothing you could actually get your hands on, just a long list of venues and times for gatherings of mutual interest groups and offbeat performers. It was all about time and location. Who you met with was an unknown to anyone who stumbled onto the site.

Jo descended the stairs into the basement of a now defunct Shriner's hall, cunningly hidden in a remote corner of Rhode Island. Jo thought it strangely funny, the creative ways that people now communicated in the post-Snowden era.

At the first meeting of the Partners, Jo was not surprised to see some familiar faces. Data fusion went through her mind as Jo panned the table, the host of characters, an unpredictable concoction of people, or so it seemed, a motley blend of scientists, doctors, investigators, lawyers and spooks. Like the nursery rhymes and counting games. "Tinker, tailor, soldier, spy" and "Rich man, poor man, beggar man, thief, ... doctor, lawyer, Indian chief." Jo smiled at the parallel metaphors they brought to mind.

Seated around the table was a veritable alphabet soup of agency acronyms: DHS, FBI, CDC, doctors and scientists. Jo, always panning, human scanner that she was, trusted no one. What do they want from me? Taking mind photos, like a camera shutter, Jo's eyes moved quickly, making eye contact for a millisecond, capturing the panoramic fusion of feds, agencies and think tanks gathered in that room. "Familiar." Jo thought. "I know who most of you are."

Across the table, Jo recognized Mike Oman, the genomics expert who testified in the trial against the bioterrorist Allbio Corporation. The case was forever under appeal. Mike collaborated with the FBI during the Operation Razors Edge investigation. His testimony was pivotal in getting a conviction. He slammed Allbio with DNA evidence of crimes against public health.

Referred to as a bioterrorism warrior, Mike rose through the ranks from lab bench scientist to world-renowned expert in the new field. He now sat in an unused conference room surrounded by photos of long-dead leaders from the Ancient Arabic Order of the Nobles of the Mystic Shrine. Incongruous, Jo thought it absurd that the guys in their red fez hats adorned with a sword, half-moon and star had no connection to anything Arabic or religious.

Jo first noticed Mike at a Providence university. He looked a typical professor with his blond pretty wife by his side. Local authors introduced their new books in a small lecture room. Jo rushed through a reading of her book's final chapter, a bioterror scenario about two bio-hacking rogues bent on making airborne bird flu, H5N1. The biohackers wanted to create a highly contagious, lethal superbug that could potentially unleash a plague of mythical proportions.

Jo, petite and curvy, looked a typical writer of mystery or romance, not the author of sinister stories and plots designed to release deadly bioweapons on all of humanity. Jo apologized for not looking the part. "I guess I don't look like the kind of person who would write this stuff."

"Oh, no." The professor mouthed, slowly shaking his head side-to-side.

After the reading, Mike brushed by the book-signing table. "Why do you write this kind of stuff?" Caught off-guard, Jo waffled an evasive reply, reiterating what she said before, "I guess I don't look the part." Jo later wished she said it was a warning, a cautionary note on the risks of releasing potential pandemic pathogens. She was afraid that her story of bio-hacking rogues who created deadly diseases was just a guess at what the future might bring.

Jo's scenarios intrigued the Partners. Always thinking the unthinkable, she constructed stories that at first alarmed the biosecurity community. But now, her stories seemed to be playing themselves out. So instead of viewing Jo as a pariah, the Partners brought her into the fold as a source of imagination. And more than imagination, Jo backed up her speculative scenarios with solid research.

Jo thought the tattered conference table unworthy of such a renowned assemblage known collectively to one another as "Partners". To Mike's right was another familiar face, Rich Valens, not-the-deceased rock star but the book author of a Venezuelan political allegory.

Jo first met Rich at a meeting of authors. When she asked him, "Have you been to Venezuela?" Rich, caught off-guard, hesitated and answered, "No". He didn't expect to be called on his ruse. Rich had a shy smile that Jo perceived as deceptive, as though he had something to hide. The red flag raised, Jo wondered why he would write a fictional allegory on a now defunct Venezuelan regime. Surely he must have lived there or at least visited the country?

Jo wanted to know where Rich's interest in Venezuelan regime change came from. It was only when she saw him at this Partners meeting that she realized his connection. It was not just an obscure interest but an assignment he carried out for years. With the FBI.

Rich's allegory was more than a search for truth. It was what he lamented, his government's failed attempt at changing the political leanings of a country that was destined to become a socialist dictatorship.

Jo suspected all along that Rich was a federal agent. Rich Valens always turned up when least expected. Travelling far to a tiny rural library to hear Jo talk about her newest book, Rich got what he wanted. His objective was to find out why. Why did Jo write this stuff, what motivated her. Was Jo searching for the truth too?

It was at that rural library that Jo revealed her fears, that the dangerous consequences of creating the deadliest microbes and releasing new diseases on humankind, was not just a threat, it was a disaster waiting to happen. The escape of a lethal man-made flu or superbug would make an outbreak like Ebola or MERS pale in comparison.

Rich sat under the gaze of the long-gone nobles, the Secret Order of the Mystic Shrine. Jo thought the Partners a parallel, a secret covenant, she fancifully dubbed the Mystical Order of the Partners. With Jo, her fantasies often superseded reality. She thought Rich Valens a mystery, or "a riddle wrapped in an enigma inside a mystery." She knew that behind his kind smile and gentle demeanor, Rich hid his true nature. A clever disguise, it was the cloak he used to quell suspicions of his covert life as a secret government service agent. His real objective, his passionate obsession, was to subvert terrorism and overthrow unfriendly governments.

But Jo wondered what else Rich was after. She mused to herself. "What else does he hide beneath his pale pallor and ocean green eyes?" What Jo *didn't* know was that Rich was the guy who buried the cryptic messages in plain sight on obscure websites where he assigned the agents their meeting places. What Jo *did* know was that Rich was her watcher, she was pretty sure of that.

Jo did not recognize the others. Not until Max burst into the room.

15 MAX

Jo knew Max. Nicknamed "Mad Max" he collected pieces to the puzzle. A founding member of the Department of Homeland Security, he put together teams. An aggregator, he assembled the people. Not conventional sorts of people, but disparate sorts, those slightly off kilter. People with ideas thought to be uncanny. Max lived by his own eccentric convictions, political and religious, two topics you wanted to avoid in any conversation, especially with Max.

Max wasted no time getting to the point. "We are here for one reason - to carry out the mission of Homeland Security. To stop terrorism before it can happen. And it *may be* that an attack has already begun."

Max paused and pointed with a hand wave to a middle-aged Chinese woman sitting across the table. "Doctor Zhu Ting will brief us on the first human fatality from bird flu on U.S. soil. Doctor Ting is a biosecurity advisor to DHS. She is an infectious disease doctor and an expert on pandemic flu."

Doctor Ting, a gray-haired matriarch and recognized guardian of public health, spoke to the group. "The first case of human bird flu, H5N1, entered the United States last year. She was a US citizen arriving on a flight from Hong Kong to Seattle."

She paused and looked directly at Mike Omen, deferring to the expert. "This virus is a mutant strain, similar but not identical to a bird flu strain that infected Bengal tigers in a zoo in China."

Reflective, Doctor Ting mused aloud. "It brings to mind the poem, *Tiger, tiger burning bright.*" Jo recognized the poem of William Blake.

An eloquent speaker, Doctor Ting went on. "It seems both poetic and prophetic, but we believe there may be a message, a clue hidden in the genetic code of this unusual flu. As Doctor Oman will explain later, it has an odd, bizarre mix of DNA."

Doctor Ting looked around the table for signs of confusion or lack of understanding. "During the woman's flight from Hong Kong to Seattle, the patient experienced malaise, chest pain and fever. Two days later her symptoms worsened and the woman went to the emergency room. Diagnosed with pneumonia, she was prescribed an antibiotic and sent home. Another two days passed and she returned to the ER with a very high fever. Her symptoms had worsened. Nausea. Vomiting. Headache. " Doctor Ting looked at her notes. "The patient complained of bright lights."

Jo whispered aloud. "*Tiger, tiger burning bright.*"

Doctor Ting went on. "The next day, our patient's heart beat out of control, her pupils dilated, she had no response to pain. These were not symptoms typical of bird flu. Diarrhea and coughing are common bird flu symptoms, but she had *neither*. This was uncommon. Even *more* unusual, her CT scans showed encephalitis. And *brain death*."

Pausing, Doctor Ting recited another line from William Blake's poem. "*In what furnace was thy brain?*"

With a solemn frown on her face, Doctor Ting spoke softly. "The woman was taken off life support."

For a moment, all were silent. Jo contemplated the outcome. Brain death. As if the brain had assumed a life of its own.

Max asked. "Doctor Ting, how did this woman pick up a bizarre strain of bird flu?"

Doctor Ting explained. "We questioned *where* she came in contact with bird flu. There were no other human cases where she visited. There had been no recent bird flu outbreaks in chicken. Not in Hong Kong, nor on mainland China. This patient had no contact with live chicken or other fowl. She visited no farms. She was educated and well aware of good hygiene."

Max interrupted. "The Chinese health authority suggested an illegal 'wet market' stall where live birds are sold. Is it possible she walked past one?"

Doctor Ting's skepticism showed on her face. "Yes they *did* make that suggestion. But no *trace* of the H5N1 virus was found *anywhere* the woman visited. She had no exposure. No reason to lie. Her husband swore by it. They were almost always together, but he was not infected with the bird flu." Doctor Ting answered. By the Partners expressions, she could tell they were flummoxed.

"Would you please give us your opinion, Doctor Oman?" Max met Mike Oman's gaze.

Mike took a moment to gather his thoughts. "Another thing to consider, this particular H5N1 virus is an undescribed strain. It has never been seen *anywhere in the world* before. It has a mix of highly unusual traits. The DNA is most similar to the strain that killed a Bengal tiger last year. It also has DNA from a H9N2 strain found in ducks. And, stranger still, it has DNA from common seasonal flus. These flus are easily passed between us humans."

"What an odd mix? A Tiger-Duck-Human flu. Does this happen often?" Max thought the weird combination fanciful.

"We call these strange concoctions 're-assorts'. This

one has a mix of the *worst* possible traits from the tiger and duck and human flu viruses." Mike had the Partners really confused. "Bizarre creations like this seem like the stuff of science fiction. Pretty hard to comprehend." Mike explained.

Jo starred at an empty spot on the wall. She said aloud "A chimera." She was thinking of ones she had seen in Tuscany created by artists. But a bizarre chimera with the head of a tiger, body of a human, and the tail of a duck? Very strange indeed. And this one was a bizarre microbial creation. She could see where the conversation was going. Theses chimeras were created in test tubes.

Max wanted it clear. No confusion. No mystical creatures. "So, it is a mix. Can a mix like that occur in nature?"

"Probably not. It has already been done in laboratories in what scientists call a gain-of-function experiment." Doctor Oman brought up a controversial topic. Genes had been added to flu viruses that increased virulence, lethality, transmissibility.

"The deadly bird flus have been changed to make them spread easily among us humans." He paused for effect. "Just a cough or a sneeze away."

Grimaces of partial understanding spread around the table. Eyebrows arched and wrinkled, the Partners reflected on what a lab escape or an intentional release of a new "Tiger" flu would mean. The recent revelations of lab insecurity, even in the world's best and most renowned, were a concern for all.

Max, attack dog that he was, barked at Doctor Ting. "But this woman must have been exposed somewhere? Correct, Doctor?"

Doctor Zhu Ting, taken aback by the badgering, relinquished. "But of course. But we don't know *where* or *how*. But we do have some idea as to when. The typical incubation time is three to five days. From her timeline, our Seattle patient visited Hong Kong and Shenzhen,

China. We know everywhere she and her husband traveled, the places and people they met with. We focused on their itinerary one week prior to their return flight to the US."

Mike Oman piled on. "But this Tiger Flu virus must have come from *somewhere* in the environment!"

Doctor Ting braced herself. "Everywhere, the hotels, restaurants, functions they attended have been swabbed and tested. Nothing was found. No trace of the virus was on their clothing, suitcases. And the patient's husband remains symptom free. He tested negative for H5N1."

Mike Oman pressed ahead. "Could this be an act of terrorism? If so, where did the strain come from? Was it stolen? Maybe a concoction created in a lab?" No one replied. How would they know?

Max jumped in. "And you, Jo." All eyes descended on Jo. Jo squirmed uncomfortably, her face flushed, her heart accelerated. She was not expecting an interrogation. "This is why you are here. You are the one who writes the scenarios, fictional they may be, but we need you to think about ways that this might have happened."

Jo could feel Max tapping his shoe against the frame of her chair. Not pausing for a reply he continued. "What if this Tiger Flu was a bioweapon? Was the woman targeted? Infected in China? Could it be intentional terrorism? Was the Seattle woman a living time bomb planted on a plane?"

Zhu Ting mused aloud. "Nothing is impossible. But it could be an isolated incident. Just an unusual infection with unusual symptoms. Currently we have Ebola and MERS to contend with."

Mike Oman shot back. "But this Tiger Flu strain is *not* like bird flu. It has new genes. It looks suspiciously like something created in a lab. And we know that type of thing is happening in labs all over the world, whether legitimate or labs in rogues nation where safety standards can be grossly inadequate. Even the world's best, our own labs have had accidents. And incidents."

All nodded remembering the much publicized mishaps

in the CDC and Pentagon labs.

Mike, intense and animated, challenged everyone. "Just use your imagination. Think about what an enemy rogue nation might conjure up in their under-the-radar labs. We don't even know *where* those labs might be? And what if a highly contagious Tiger Flu gets loose? We risk a potential pandemic. It's unfathomable! The smell of death would be everywhere."

Jo mumbled loud enough to be heard. "And if the US is the target…?"

Mike Oman paused, all eyes shifted towards Jo.

Max thumped his foot hard on Jo's wooden chair frame, as if to punctuate what he was asking. "What is your take, Jo? You are here because you see things differently."

Rich nodded to confirm. The Partners had obviously gone through boot camp together.

There is nothing like a good hanging to concentrate the mind, Jo thought as her pulse rate shot up. She tried to get hold of herself, pausing to give herself time to think. She then began with her interpretation of the incident.

"It might have started as a test, this untraceable, mysterious, isolated case. It's not impossible. The woman became symptomatic in flight, she was exposed somehow just days before. She was an American woman, educated in health and hygiene, well aware of the dangers lurking in the wet markets, an unlikely explanation." Jo paused only briefly.

"Was the woman inadvertently contaminated? Or was she willfully transporting the virus? Was there motive or intent? She didn't fit the profile of a terrorist, nor did her husband, an academic. Tiger Flu has unusual traits, and even stranger symptoms. It might have gone misdiagnosed had they not just flown in from Hong Kong." Jo stopped talking and looked around the table.

"OK, you told us what we already know." Max sarcastically berated Jo.

Jo felt composed and surprisingly calm. She had nothing to lose, so she speculated. "Deceptive. The symptoms are confusing, not typical of the common strain of bird flu. The altered symptoms make it easier to hide. I wonder, could it be a stealth weapon?"

"Yes, the altered symptoms are deceptive." Doctor Ting confirmed. "No cough or sore throat, but fever, malaise, chest pain. Eventual brain death."

Max agreed. "There are too many anomalies."

Mike Oman veered on a tangent. "One last thing, your tweets, Jo. Why do you send out tweets with genetic information? Like the DNA sequences of Tiger H5N1 H9N2. Why? Who the hell would be interested, let alone understand?" Only genomics experts like Mike had a handle on this esoteric field of science.

"Mike, I test my hypotheses. On social networks, communication can be as cryptic as genetic sequences. How many people on Twitter have any inkling of what DNA sequences mean? It's easy to narrow down the pool of people who understand."

Jo wondered if she made sense with her convoluted rationale. "There is also a high level of terrorist communication on social networks such as Twitter. And sometimes what seems like the most obvious message can be the most cryptic in meaning. I look for clues."

"Jo may be on to something." Mike affirmed.

~ PART 2 ~

Copenhagen, Denmark
&
Rhode Island, USA

16 MEI IN LOVE

It was in Copenhagen that Mei fell in love. After a long series of flights from Shenzhen to Kastrup Airport, she was too excited to be tired. Mei maneuvered her way through passport control with her student visa for spring semester and her fellowship grant both in order. The Danish authorities were kind enough as she spoke to them using her best English.

No suspicions arose over her luggage and laptop carry-on. Mei thought it comical, the questions they asked: Was she carrying any live birds in her luggage? Did she have any recent contact with live poultry, chickens or ducks? She knew from first-hand the fears about transporting Bird Flu viruses between countries. But she was unaware of the illegal trade in exotic live birds where smugglers transported the most beautiful avian species in their suitcases.

Mei's biggest worry did not materialize. Despite having a cursory look inside her overstuffed suitcase, the customs agent found nothing of interest, not even her ornamental hair pieces, including her decorative hair-sticks and metal lined bamboo chopsticks. She wondered if they would be picked up on x-ray as something weapon-like. But luckily, they were not flagged. Nor were the extra dollars she had stuffed into socks and zipped into the pockets of two down-filled winter jackets, all $50,000 dollars, a bonus she would use later for certain indulgences. The rest of her earnings from Kahliy had gone to Mother and her elderly grandparents, her obligations and duties were more than fulfilled.

Most importantly, Mei's special honey sweets had survived the journey along with her Shenzhen lab crafted pastilles, still secreted away in their protective spike container. The Tigers were safely caged, ready to spring into action, once freed from their DNA cages, for which Kahliy would pay a hefty sum. But for now the Tiger Flu viruses remained captive, lying in wait for their prey.

Mei's first indulgence was a necessity in Copenhagen. A bicycle. She bought a good one, second hand. She paid cash in dollars so there was no recorded transaction, which Mei did not think odd. Mei was not in the habit of buying anything new. Kahliy bought all her best clothes and jewelry in Hong Kong at the Festival Walk mall. But Kahliy warned her not to do anything in Copenhagen that would draw attention.

Her second indulgence, again paid with cash in a second-hand shop, was a very good camera, a Canon EOS Digital. It was quite a splurge; she would keep it hidden in her backpack for the most part. But knew she must have a good camera to capture the beauty and color and opulence of the palaces and the grandeur of the Danish Royalty. Mei would celebrate the beginnings of her new life by recording it in photos as it unfolded.

Copenhagen was a city of fairy tale fantasy: the castles the spires, the towers. Mei dreamed that one day she would be a princess, living in a fairytale palace, wearing the impressive crown with the two massive jewels, the blue sapphires she once saw in a photo. It would be a tribute to her Father who first brought home those red and purple microscopic beads and jewels.

The royal palaces were a far cry from the Urban Village she grew up in, the rotting decay, the stench in the hallways. Mei knew she lost her childhood in the ugliness that Mother imposed. Mei saw nothing like the Urban Village in Copenhagen. Only once did she come upon a strange village that she found unsettling. With her camera in hand she strolled through a colorful painted gate, which she photographed. Christiania, it was called. Mei thought it a pretty name.

When she entered the village, what she saw reminded her of a fly with black filigreed wings, only human-sized. At first, Mei thought it a thing of beauty, her black spider-web attire, with a lacework of silver and black. But as she came closer she was struck by a rat's nest of hair sprayed with silver-gray paint, a small sad face powdered with ghoulish white make up and darkened smoky eyes that dripped black tears.

As Mei approached, she thought to take a photograph, but she hesitated as she realized that inhabiting that crippled, disfigured body was a human being, altered in both body and mind from the hard drugs of the street mixed with the opioids of big pharma. It made Mei's stomach queasy as she watched the broken beast inching along, almost immobile, creeping just centimeters at a time. The young woman hunched over her aluminum walker resembled the walking dead. Mei thought it profound that from a broken childhood one could become a black fly or a beautiful butterfly. And that she had chosen the latter.

Mei was now walking down Pusher Street and the signs were everywhere, many hand-drawn with cameras inside crossed circles, which Mei clearly understood. No photography. Two disheveled, long-haired men walked towards her. Mei stopped dead in her tracks, she turned around and sprinted, whizzing past the human spider-fly, fleeing an abhorrent world she wanted no part of.

~

It was a sunny Sunday in April that Mei set off on her bicycle. The weather report for the day had been dry and warm, a balmy 13 degrees Centigrade or just over 55 degrees Fahrenheit. Mei adeptly calculated the mental math. Converting temperatures was not a skill ordinary people had. She bundle up with layers she could remove as the day and her muscles warmed up. She was proud of the shapeliness that the pedaling sculpted on her legs, quite visible through her tight fitting spandex riding pants.

The sky lighting was always best after early morning sunrise or late afternoon before sunset. Mei had become quite an expert photographer, good at framing the images, capturing the sun at angles as it slipped in and out from behind the clouds. Some photographs were record shots for her collection on the lives of the Danish Royals. This morning she stopped at their winter residence, Amalienborg, she snapped photos of the four identical Rococo palaces. She then rode past the prime area of up-scale art galleries, expensive restaurants, and high-end shops. She would shop there later when she wanted grand, fashionable attire, but this was not something she needed now. At least, not yet.

Mei rode her bike along the Inner Harbour and stopped at the iconic tourist attraction, The Little Mermaid. Smaller than she expected, the tiny four foot statue, perched upon a boulder in the harbor, peered forlornly out to sea. Mei wondered if the diminutive maiden's blank expression was the look of doomed love for her dream prince. Her tour book suggested that. But Mei thought, more likely, that if reflected the suffering of abuse, not unlike that often experienced by Mei in her childhood, when at four feet tall she was the target of Mother's whippings, beatings, berating and battering of her legs and her arms, but thankfully not the beheadings inflicted on the young Danish mermaid!

Mei looked at The Little Mermaid's perfect body, there were no signs of her nearly three decapitations, her severed arm, artfully mended by skilled metal artisans. There was no sign of her blast injuries, the holes in her wrist and knee, when explosives knocked her sky high off her pedestal. How often the young mermaid was drenched in white paint as was Mei when once assaulted by her classmates. But, unlike the young mermaid, Mei was not covered in green slime and left holding a dildo in her right hand. At least Mei was no longer a child when that happened. Mei briefly chuckled as she mused over one sexual encounter in particular.

Mei reflected on the fairy tale mermaid's beauty that hid the mutilations and scars of a turbulent past. Just as Mother hid the beatings she inflicted on Mei's young body, so did Mother hide the scars exacted on her own body from her cruel and sadistic clients.

But Mei thrived. She knew she wasn't merely a survivor. She evolved into a creature of her own making. Always "The Spider", she could not escape the curse of knobby knees, the gangly legs and the elf-like feet she was born with. But her transformation into a beautiful woman, one with unique talents, was something she worked hard on. She was the passion of her very existence.

Mei rode her bike north along the waterfront where she confronted the older mermaid. Here, also sitting atop her own boulder was the Madonna, the little mermaid had transmutated to an altered state. It was as if her genes, her very DNA, were forcibly ripped apart and shuffled anew, a conversion from a fairy tale princess into a monster in Norgaard's sculpture garden, The Genetically Modified Paradise. Mei gaped wide-mouthed at the Madonna, her arms and legs elongated grotesquely, her features twisted. Mei thought of her own limbs, stretched into impossible contortions as she was prodded and physically manipulated by men. The men who only thought they were in control. She knew who truly was the manipulator. It was not the men.

Mei inspected the Madonna's odd features, her notched

hips, her elongated wind-swept head, the limbs, the knobbed knees, her long, upturned feet. She thought, how like her, both the manipulator and the manipulated, when she coaxed and toyed with her DNA nanobots, forming her tiger-cages. Mei Wong, the artist and also the work of art. She felt, not only a fascination but a kindred spirit for this monstrous, yet humorous, post-modern genetically engineered woman.

"I, too, am one of a kind. Uniquely different, like the Tigers I create." Mei stated aloud to no one but herself.

She was busily planning her next iteration. Queen Mei, a stately Royal surrounded by opulence and indulgent men; she was every bit as worthy of the high price they would pay, set up in the palatial hotels frequented by the super-rich in the wealthiest cities of Europe. That would be her next adventure. But for now she must stay focused on the task at hand. With Kahliy's upcoming arrival and the genomics conference in May, she had planning and preparations ahead.

~

The next weekend was cooler. It rained on and off, but she strolled along Stroget, Copenhagen's main shopping district with its five interconnected shopping streets. A pedestrian only area, she left her bicycle tethered to a gigantic rack while she explored the narrow streets and cobble-stoned squares, stopping only for coffee and a Danish pastry in one of the many cafes.

So many trendy shops to explore, she found one with outlandishly short skirts and silky tops that would certainly draw attention. They would come in handy, but only when she needed them. It was not the finery she would someday adorn herself in, but it was a necessary fashion statement along the way. And she must lure her next victim at the upcoming conference.

Mei chose three skirts, one simple, a silky black synthetic that draped in a wrap around her narrow hips. The next an animal print, a leopard, not a tiger, she did not want to be so obvious. And a third skirt, only because she wanted it, was an iridescent shimmering blue-green. It reminded her of the sea on an island she would go to someday. Perhaps an Italian or Greek island or better yet a private island owned by the richest man she could find. But these skirts were only tools of the trade; she had no doubt that they would help her trap her next prey.

An exotic shoe store caught her eye, especially the gold stiletto heels. There were many variations to choose from, but Mei picked two. One pair, a perfect match to her favorite iridescent skirt, she pulled it from her backpack to check the color for a precise match. The gold heels would be her signature, the iridescent green of the faux snake skin with gold stilettos were best for special occasions. More conservative, the gold stilettos struck an elegant contrast with the black velvet pointy-toed shoe, a solid match with the black wrap skirt. She hadn't yet decided which of the two pairs she would wear with the leopard print skirt.

A few tight, scanty tops, black and gold, other lacey blouses, and a short dress for the summer weather to come. Mei felt equipped for anything that might come her way. And she did not forget the lingerie, very sexy indeed.

That evening, she modelled her findings in front of the full length mirror in her single dorm room. She found herself irresistible as she rubbed her mons with stimulatory lubricant gel, then plunged deep with an oversized sex toy she bought at the most intriguing shop of all. Mei felt truly in love with the one perfect person. Herself.

17 BELLA BELLA

Mei disappeared into the nearly 50,000 students at the Copenhagen university, several thousand of which were foreign students. Mei had the luxury of a single room typical of the Danish private dormitory. All compliments of her employer, World Genomics. The modern university campus, the vibrant city, were all in stark contrast to the thick waves of homogeneous humanity of Shenzhen and its boring sameness. Even the more cosmopolitan Hong Kong stifled her very existence with its crowded, high-density living. Relative to both, Copenhagen was a haven of wide-open spaces and parks, and pockets of serenity and quiet where she could study and plan her future.

Mei made no real friends, only acquaintances. Friends were not part of the plan. She didn't want to stand out but to blend in with the other international students, there were a fair number from Southeast Asia. Mei could easily discern where other Asian students came from, but in Europe their identities were not easily guessed. They all seemed to be lumped into one pot, like a noodle soup full of mystery meats and exotic vegetables.

Best of all, as an extra benefit, Mei was free to roam. There were no long hours in the laboratory. She whiled away her hours collecting information and data, researching PubMed, finding articles, putting together publications, setting up bibliographies. All those tedious constructs for publishing academic papers. Mei was more than happy to be a research assistant and no longer a lab rat. It was an academic fellowship windfall beyond her expectations.

She could eat on her own, no shared meals in corporate cafeterias. She rode her bicycle around the spread out campus. Her muscles became stronger, her breathing deepened, her stamina increased, she felt robust and eager to conquer the world.

Mei avoided romantic entanglements, not dressing to attract, turning down any men that expressed an interest. Yet she found Copenhagen an intoxicating experience, the freedom, the fresh air, it invigorated her. She redefined herself as "creative", not just an academic nerd, but a visionary, her future morphing and evolving before her eyes.

Mei swooned at the medieval stateliness surrounding her. "Just suck it all in, Mei," she told herself. "Once Kahliy comes to visit with my one million euros, I will have it all."

Mei's biggest mission was still ahead of her. The chosen spot for its execution, the Bella Hotel. The venue for the next annual International Genomics Conference, where test specimen number two would be selected. And the dead drop spike would be delivered.

~

On the hotel's website, Mei clicked through photos of the unusual architecture, its eccentric towers, the sky bar, the lobby, and the greenery designed to instill a calm, serene ambience. Mei thought it certainly had interesting possibilities. She should be able to find a safe and inconspicuous place to deliver the "spike". The plant wall caught her immediate attention. She stared at it, enlarging the photos down to the individual fronds of ferns and leaves of bamboo.

"How opportune." Mei mumbled as she inspected everything in great detail. As if she were taking a virtual tour, she imagined herself floating like a ghost, unseen by all, exploring the possibilities.

Orchestrating her second attack, finding an unsuspecting victim, shouldn't be too difficult. After all, Mei considered, "My first infected 'test case' went off as planned." It was seamlessly accomplished. Mei rationalized, her "sacrificed" human specimen was all part of a greater experiment. The proof of concept was confirmed, the execution flawless. No suspicions arose that could possibly connect her to the Seattle woman's demise. "Unfortunate", she replied when health officials interviewed her. The authorities questioned all who came in contact with the ill-fated woman.

At the upcoming genomics conference, there would be plenty of choices for "number two". Mei calculated the approximate number of scientists attending the conference from North America. Finding a willing case subject would be easy.

Mei repeated another mantra to herself. "Life does not come without death." She didn't consider her human experiments intrinsically evil. She mused, looking for just the right word and decided. "Utility, that is it. People have their uses." The word "ethics" was not in her vocabulary. She took no interest in the Nuremberg Code or the Declaration of Helsinki. The ethical concerns of experimenting on humans totally eluded her.

Mei didn't see the need for constraints or rules that would limit the boundaries of science. She felt unbridled whenever it came to science or to sex. "If it gives you an advantage, then you should just do it!" Another adage Mei added to her list of mantras.

The next morning Mei dressed and equipped herself for her next mission. Mei knew she must appear to be a typical Asian student. She intentionally wore generic clothing, her long hair piled up, hidden under a grey Chinese silk flat cap. She would not stand out in her common attire. She wore no make-up and carried nothing to distinguish her.

Mei now needed to find just the right place where she could bury a spike. She panned the lobby and the bar as she walked through the hotel entry. To her left, a few steps down, was an open business lounge where about a dozen people, mostly men, plucked away on their laptops. Mei quickly assessed the area as too busy to locate her special "dead drop".

Mei turned her head to look towards the reception desk. She panned the massive plant wall that wrapped around the front desk and lead to the bar lounge. Mei thought it a fitting place when she first noticed the photos of the plant wall on the website. It surpassed any open atrium area with potted shrubs and plants. The two floors of wall greenery stated a message of eco-friendliness and perhaps even more user-friendly for Mei's purpose. Mei imagined that curious tourists and hotel patrons might ogle and paw over the thick vegetation. It would not be out of the ordinary for her, if observed, to gawk and finger the bamboo leaves and fronds, a natural reaction from any plant admirer. And it would be easy to hide the spike, out in the open, where it could be retrieved. Mei felt confident she would not arouse suspicions.

Mei browsed as if shopping, looking for somewhere inconspicuous that she would describe to Kahliy in a "tweet". Mei thought the plant wall so lush, more so than she had imagined. She ran her fingers over the tropical leaves. The densely planted ferns, airplane plants and bamboo stood in odd contrast to the barren hotel exterior that was mostly devoid of vegetation. The road outside approaching the hotel was only sparsely planted with occasional trees.

Mei wondered about her specially designed bamboo chopsticks, her spikes. Would the soil be deep enough?

Today she carried test spikes, plain wooden chopsticks to gauge the depth of the plant wall. She needed to make sure her plan would work by first conducting an experiment.

Mei walked past the bar lounge, around the curved plant wall into a second lounge area where she was surprised to find no one drinking. She surmised it must have been too early for happy hour with the after-work, before-dinner crowd. As she strolled past, she knew she had found the perfect "dead-drop".

"Ah, the perfect place," Mei thought. She casually inspected a lime green sofa. It was a one-of-a-kind. All other sofas and chairs in the bar lounge were a soft grey-blue of simple, modern Scandinavian design. Mei looked behind her and saw that everyone was now out of sight, hidden beyond the curvature of the plant wall.

Mei lingered a while, standing to the right of the lime settee, fingering the bamboo leaves gently, lightly touching the ferns and other vegetation. "I must take care that no one notices," Mei warned herself as she slid the wooden chopstick out from where it was concealed, under the long linen Juliette sleeve of her tunic top. Adept with her fingers, Mei grasped hold of the chopstick and drove it in at a forty-five degree angle, deep into the soil. Mei calculated about eighteen centimeters.

"Ah, seven inches." Mei was quick to compute the conversion. She thought through every detail, every nuance, every angle. "It must go very far in. And firm. It must stay in tight." Mei instructed herself as she pushed the stick in until it almost disappeared. Her index finger dampened as she touched the moss and soil.

Mei then retracted the chopstick just two or three centimeters. "Don't hide it," she told herself, "Or the real spike will not be found." The spike must be noticeable to someone who has reason to look, but not to a casual observer.

Her very special dead drop spike would be filled with tiny pastilles and their captive "tigers". Next week when

Kahliy arrived, she would execute the plan, the special dead drop with its cross-hatched design, would be planted. She would then tweet Kahliy a cryptic message on where he would find the drop. It was all part of an exciting game. And Kahliy would show his appreciation with the euros he promised. Mei tingled at the thought. Money excited her, more than sex or her scientific achievements, which were both really just means to that end.

Mei then turned around, trying to look nonchalant. She could see the hotel elevators in the distance. Next, she would survey the sky lounge where she would eventually meet with Kahliy. Once in the elevator, she saw that access to the sky bar did not need a room key card. She pressed the button labelled "Sky Bar". The quick accent to the 23rd floor made her slightly dizzy. Stepping out of the elevator, Mei walked towards the bar and passed the ladies room that was sign posted *damen toiletten.*

On entering the top floor sky bar lounge, Mei was struck by its fashionable furnishings. She walked the lounge perimeter, reminding herself to be casual, to just look the typical student tourist, her flat cap helped with her anonymity. Mei smiled her most disarming grin.

As she walked, Mei gazed out at the panoramic view, a common calling card for visitors. She strolled along passing a few wicker hanging chair baskets, Mei thought a perfect place for her to meet Kahliy. A 'kitten in a basket' will await him soon. She mentally composed her next tweet to Kahliy.

Mei didn't linger long and descended back down the elevator to the lobby. Once out of the hotel, she focused her attention on her next mission. She paused only once to turn around and look back from a distance. The hotel's unusual architecture, an eccentric leaning double tower, seemed to mushroom up from out of nowhere. Pleased that her plans were progressing, Mei sprinted to the Bella Center train station to head back to Copenhagen Central.

On the train back to Copenhagen, Mei watched as the

Bella Hotel disappeared into the distance. Satisfied she had found the perfect spot to bury the dead drop spike, Mei fine-tuned her next two messages. Limited by the confines imposed by the twitter-sphere, she found words that would describe the location in less than 140 characters. "A tweet to my sweet." Mei mumbled aloud amusing herself with frivolous humor. She posted her next two cryptic tweets.

@XOXOXMay You make me want you. In May on Tuesday, my bella. Your kitten will hang in a basket in the sky.

@XOXOXMay My Spike in bella bamboo. Right of the green settee. Our tigers will await you. Next week after 16:00, we meet again in the sky.

Spike knew exactly what she was talking about. At 4 pm next Tuesday, he would find Mei.

18 DEAD DROP

During the week she waited for Kahliy to arrive, Mei focused on her studies at the university. Her professors and other graduate students thought Mei shy, or perhaps aloof, she spent hours in the lab and seldom socialized. Mei heeded Kahliy's advice to keep a low profile. "Don't let anyone know what you are capable of."

Ultimately, Mei worked at a fierce pace to achieve her goal. For love or for money, Mei only wanted the latter. Her planning was meticulous. Nothing would go wrong. Not now. But how could they? Mei knew she was in total control.

When the time came, Mei mulled over her plan. Ruminating, chewing over every minute detail, she reminded herself, "Don't be obvious". She dressed herself with that idea in mind, donning her baggie beige cargo pants paired with a dark green tee-shirt. Wrapping her long dark hair into a bun, she secured her hair with the two brown ornamental chopsticks with ivory colored cross-hatch designs on their ends.

Mei applied no makeup. To complete her casual look, she wore simple rubber sandals on her long feet. Wanting to appear a typical student, she draped her small black knapsack over her shoulder. Inside her bag, she packed a transformation kit with the slinky black skirt and black velvet stilettos with golden heels that she bought on Stroget Street. At the last minute, she tossed in her gray silk flat cap. Just in case she needed it.

Mei, now familiar with the layout and amenities of the Bella Hotel, felt comfortable. At ease, she ambled past the lobby bar to the adjacent lounge. Neither the lobby nor the bar were busy at mid-afternoon. Mei flung her knapsack off her shoulder as she plunked down on the lime green sofa.

Mei made every effort to look as though she were relaxing, enjoying the surroundings, the earth-friendly designs. She pulled her tourist guide booklet from out of her knapsack and buried her head in it, thinking "Do not be obvious." Two hotel guests with rolling cabin luggage passed by en route to their rooms. Mei thought they might be businessmen arriving early for the International Genomics Conference. Mei knew the type. Vendors most likely. They didn't look like researchers or academic types. Academic guys never dressed in business suits.

Still seated on the lime-green settee, Mei waited until she was alone. She then bent her left arm upward, wrapping her hand behind her neck. In one quick move, Mei grasped the left chopstick embedded in her hair. She slowly pulled the stick out, lowered her arm and impaled it at an angle, burying it in the plant wall. Seven of nine inches plunged deep into the loose moss and soil amidst the fern and bamboo. The protruding couple inches displayed the geometric designs, prominent, but still hidden amongst the lush vegetation.

As Mei pushed in the spike, just the thought of deep penetration excited her. The dead drop spike was so exquisite in its design and so diabolical in it use. She knew she would be with Kahliy soon. It had been months since she gazed into his sea green eyes as he rode her like a wave crashing onto the shore. Mei's libido often got the best of her.

Mei's second chopstick remained undisturbed, holding solid her coil of hair wound in a tightly knotted bun. Mei stared straight ahead of her. Across the lobby, opposite the elevators, a large golden ceramic frog with open arms seemed to greet her. Or maybe he cheered her on? She smiled at his affirmative gesture. It was as if he congratulated her on executing an important mission.

Another casual stroll to the elevator, she climbed nonstop to the sky bar on the 23rd floor. Mei felt dizzy as she arrived to the top, in addition to the excitement of an adrenaline rush. Just a few steps down a hallway, Mei opened the door marked *damen toiletten*. She slipped into the farthest enclosed toilet stall. Wasting no time, she dropped her baggy trousers to the floor and with a wiggle, up came her clinging black skirt. Her negligible underwear showed not even a thin line. Peeling off her olive green tee-shirt, she revealed a tiny black tank-top. Mei seldom wore a bra, her small but firm breasts did not need supporting.

Releasing her black coil, her rope of hair untwined and slid down her back. A thick-toothed comb aligned her long stands in parallel. She tucked her second chopstick into a side-pocket of her black knapsack. Carefully, she applied two smoky black pencils to her eyelids and scarlet red to her lips. No longer was she the plain-faced Asian student who sat in the lime-green sofa.

The two barmen noticed Mei when she slinked in, how could they not. But it was not uncommon for beautiful women that offered high-end "companionship" to frequent the bar. She stopped at the bar and asked only for a glass of water before disappearing to where the panoramic glass windows overlooked the Copenhagen skyline.

No one yet sat in the hanging chair baskets, Mei rotated the basket in the far corner to face out towards the city and eased herself into it. She nearly vanished from anyone's view. It was four in the afternoon and the sky bar had just opened. Mei wasn't looking for any unwanted attention.

Mei felt calmer now. Pensive. Pleased with herself. Especially with what she accomplished. She delivered the dead drop spike with its 19 tiny "candies" as promised. Kahliy's hefty payment was imminent. But she had one more thing to deliver, her honey-filled "sweetie" candy embedded with the Tiger Flu virus. Mei thought about the upcoming International Genomics Conference. She only needed to select the "chosen one". And there would soon be plenty of "specimens" to choose from.

Anticipating Kahliy's rewards, her money and her means of escape - a handful of European passports, Mei daydreamed. Kahliy promised her the keys to living a life of comfort: multiple identities, great riches, an opulent lifestyle. She would have the power to disappear into the European Community and never return to China.

All the hard work was done, especially getting hold of those designer strains of Tiger Flu. Mei reflected on "Little Brother", how useful he was in the execution of the grand plan. He gave her enough strains, a variety like no other. Not only did they vary in their lethalness but also in their ability to infect humans and spread easily. And the bonus was the way they could defy detection. Stealth weapons. Some had no typical symptoms of flu, like coughing or sneezing. Those viruses could fester in silence, limiting themselves in contagion. Where others, even more deadly beasts, were only a cough or a sneeze or a kiss away.

"Thank you, Little Brother." He was the most useful of men. "You are such a sweet yet silly man." She thought how foolish and trusting someone "in love" could be. She opened his door to erotic pleasures beyond anything he would ever experience again. But, in turn he gave Mei the deadliest bioweapons known to exist. All in exchange for the *Gong Fu* fucking that she dispassionately gave him in return.

Mei mused and smiled for a while. Then her smile turned to a frown as she gazed over the horizon at the city's silhouette to the north. The image of Yi Lo in his office rushed into her mind.

Yi Lo, another tool, she found disgusting, the way he poked at her like a bowl of fruit jelly. Revolting, yes, but he *did* give her the skills, the time, and the access she needed to manipulate the DNA nanobots. Mei knew how much more she got from him in return for her favors: the Hong Kong courses, her privileges, her fellowship, and an incredible escape to Copenhagen. Mei's beaming smile returned.

Without Yi Lo's free access to the lab, she could never have trapped the Tiger viruses in their nano-cages. Deeply embedded, these tiny ferocious tigers, once warmed and released, would escape from their cages into the wild, wild west.

From here on out, things would be easier. Compared to all she achieved, manipulating men was "a breeze", as the Americans might say. Mei fantasized about how she would stay in only the best hotels, like the Bella. No more tacky housing in student dorms. Kahliy would pay her today, a whopping one million euros. With the promise of much more to come in private bank accounts.

Mei's thoughts shifted yet again. To Mother. Mei didn't know whether to smile or to frown or to weep. All the pain, yet Mother's promises eventually came true. Mother somehow prophesied Mei's brilliant future, even if she had to beat it into her. Mother's bashings were a blur in the past. And yes, it was true what Mother showed Mei her values, especially the importance of carrying a well-equipped backpack.

Mother's men paid her money to get what she needed, to feed and clothe and send Mei to school. But for Mei, it was not just the money to buy what she needed, but the opportunity to become someone new, to fulfill a life's dream. "Someday, I will be what I truly want to be." Mei promised herself.

And being a dutiful daughter, Mei made sure Mother had plenty of cash before she left Shenzhen. She did not tell her she would never see her again. It was all a matter of fate. Mei knew she could never return to China. But Mother had taught her a lot of life's lessons, through example.

With Mother's beauty fading, she could not continue to sell herself at a high price. Her value diminishing, Mei provided her with a life of relative comfort. And Mother in turn made sure her parents in the countryside could idle out their days without struggling for survival. In China, there was an explicit code that parents must be kept safe and comfortable. Mei congratulated herself, holding herself in high esteem for fulfilling the moral duty of a devoted daughter, that Chinese filial obligation for care of aged parents to honor their sacrifices.

Mei basked in the glow of a self-satisfied grin, but then a hovering shadow pulled her out from her daydreams.

19 KITTEN IN A BASKET

Before Kahliy arrived at the sky lounge, a few other people had settled in. A small group of animated older men and women sat in a central area with boldly patterned red and white designer chairs. They laughed and bantered while gulping down Danish Amager beer. Adjacent to Mei, a casually-dressed young couple were suspended in the two other hanging baskets. Only a tiny table separated them. They stared out at the city on the distant horizon, the young man pointing out various landmarks trying to impress his date.

Kahliy could see a glint of Mei's brushed gold high heels in the distance as he entered the sky bar lounge. Her shapely legs hung below the egg-shaped woven basket.

"Ah, my kitten in a basket." Kahliy muttered to himself.

Mei, her eyes glazed and transfixed by her fantasies, did not notice Kahliy as he approached until a shadow cast over her. She startled in surprise when she noticed Kahliy peering at her from the side of her hanging basket. Mei barely recognized him at first. His hair longer, his amber-flecked green eyes shielded by large dark-rimmed glasses, he wore black dress trousers with a pin-striped shirt.

Nothing too daring or distinctive but Mei thought him more handsome than ever.

Careful not to draw attention, Kahliy mumbled a brief message. "Meet me at the elevator." Kahliy moved away, taking a few steps at a time, he then paused to gaze out from the lounge perimeter. Walking slowly to the far corner, Mei could see him admiring an elegant piano adorned with leather, wrought iron and glass. Classical piano music soothed Kahliy, he abhorred rock and roll.

Mei waited until Kahliy disappeared from view. When she stood up, she saw him loitering by the elevator. Kahliy watched Mei as she approached him, silhouetted against the blue grey sky, so ethereal in her beauty, like a delicate butterfly. But looks could be so deceiving, he thought. Mei Wong, a venomous reptile, was a capable murderer. She had so easily poisoned her first prey.

Kahliy stepped inside the elevator and held the door until Mei was safely inside. Kahliy inserted his card pass and pressed the 19th floor. Mei half-smiled at the irony of the number, thinking it somehow auspicious of the #tigerblake19 attack yet to come. Finding it humorous, Mei began to laugh but Kahliy frowned at her in return. He never knew what was really going through her mind.

As Kahliy pushed open the hotel room door, Mei smelled a sickly sweet odor. She knew the strong fragrance came from a bouquet of pink and white lilies gracing the desk. Beautiful, Mei thought, but horribly pungent. To the right of the flowers was Kahliy's computer and cell phone. To the left, a decent but inexpensive bottle of champagne, but Mei wouldn't know the difference. The hotel room was too small for Mei's liking. She didn't expect the penthouse suite but hoped for something grander to celebrate the occasion. But Kahliy was wary of drawing attention with exorbitant room charges.

An array of small food plates on a low coffee table tempted Mei. Picking up a plastic toothpick, she popped a small cube of smoked salmon into her mouth. She wanted to sample everything, the Danish windy sausage, a basket of assorted breads. But most of all the tray of miniature deserts.

"Ah, very delectable Kahliy." She devoured two pieces, both flaky, one with chocolate, the other with berries. Mei loved her Danish pastries.

Kahliy glanced at a text message that pinged on his phone. "It has been retrieved." Kahliy said with a grin. It was the first time Kahliy broke a smile since being together again.

Mei nodded; she assumed a courier of some sort had picked up the hidden drop spike. Where the spike went next, she had no idea.

Little more was said between them as Kahliy popped the cork and poured two glasses of champagne. Kahliy handed Mei a fluted glass. "You still have your second experiment to complete. It must go as planned." There were no special words to commend Mei's success.

That was the extent of a toast to Mei's success. Kahliy poured his champagne down and gulped a second glass. Mei sipped slowly. Much too slowly for Kahliy.

Mei strolled around the room, curiously inspecting the floral arrangement, stroking the long tongue-like petals of pink and white. "What kind of flowers are these?" Mei asked.

"Lilies. There are so many varieties of lily, these are called Stargazers, and like you they are stunning." Kahliy knew she was fishing for a compliment.

Mei loved the flattery. She found the lilies attractive, yet too gaudy, and their odor was overwhelming.

"Mei, you must always remember these lilies." Kahliy instructed.

"How could I forget? These lilies are very beautiful but their odor is so strong." To Mei the flowers smelled of decay, as if something had died. "They smell more sickly sweet than the honey candy that delivers the Tiger Flu. It is the smell of death when the Tiger devours its prey." Mei grinned her most devious yet seductive smile.

Kahliy said nothing. Mei intrigued him. Her total lack of caring for her victims, she seemed to have no qualms. No conscience. It went beyond not feeling, Mei seemed to derive pleasure in the death she would bring. Her aura of temptress, enticing, and ensnaring her victims seem tied to her perverted sense of sexual indulgence.

Thinking of Mei, Kahliy became aroused. He had little control over his carnal desires. He wanted to take her, to please her, to reward her for her cunning and expertise.

"Tomorrow night you will kill your next victim, infect him with the Tiger Flu, Mei." He said.

"I do not kill, Kahliy, I conduct experiments. The execution of my second experiment will be flawless." Mei spoke as a commander, not a soldier. Tonight, she would be in control.

Kahliy saw that Mei could not be compromised by her own emotions. She seemed to have no guilt, no regrets, no emotional entanglements. Strangely odd, unlike the other women he had known.

"Mei, I have the money I promised you. There will be more money in accounts set up for you. You will have them when I finish my journey. Our third and final experiment is elaborate, the details are intricate. It will take time to set up and for me to meet with my soldiers." Kahliy explained. Mei nodded as he spoke.

"You and I will meet again. You must remember the lilies." Kahliy reminded her again.

"I will never forget." Mei confirmed.

Kahliy then flipped open a small suitcase. Inside, over a dozen packets of euro notes, some 500 and mostly 200 EU were neatly stacked. Kahliy waved a single bundle of Danish Kroner. "For your local expenses." Kahliy had thought of everything.

Mei picked up a stack of euros, she stroked and fanned through them. Her eyes widened in amazement, her jaw dropped, and with a look of sheer ecstasy she tossed back her head. She let out a groan unlike any Kahliy had heard before. "Ahh!! My daydreams come true."

Impatient now, Kahliy poured Mei another glass of champagne and ordered. "Drink up quickly."

Mei did not need coaxing. She ran her tongue along the rim of the glass and matched him by downing the glass in one go. "Now, my Spiko, it is your turn to deliver."

"Yes, my little tiger. You are my pussycat now." Kahliy lifted her short black skirt for one last encounter. He pulled off her thong panties and massaged the inside of her thighs. "But first, give me your mouth." Kahliy pushed Mei down, seating her on the edge of the bed. He unzipped his black trousers and let them drop to the floor, revealing his rock hard intent and lack of underwear. Premeditated, he wanted extra favors for the bundle of bills. Grabbing Mei's long strands of hair with both of his hands, he lined up her lush lips and thrust himself into her mouth. Mei sucked him like a piece of hard candy.

Mei stopped short, holding him off. She chortled with Kahliy's favorite taunt. "Mei is a greedy girl!' She would not let Kahliy finish until he delivered. Pushing him away from her mouth, she lay back on the bed, lifted her skirt and spread her legs to the ceiling. Grabbing hold of what she wanted, she directed him to where she liked it best. Mei now gave the orders. "Go slow…now deeper… more, now harder… now faster… more, more, more." Mei wanted it her way. And Kahliy obediently let her have it.

20 SACRIFICIAL FERRETS

As Kahliy promised, the one million euros would not be too heavy to carry. Kahliy calculated the weight of a mix of 200 and 500 euro notes, 2 kilograms (5 pounds). If they were US $100 bills, they would have weighed about 25 pounds. "Much too heavy and bulky to carry in your backpack, Mei."

Another advantage, Kahliy explained to Mei, is that euro notes are preferred by money launderers. They are the underworld's currency of choice. Kahliy told Mei that she could easily get the 500 euro notes broken down into smaller denominations. Many of the euros in circulation are 500 EU notes. And they are perfect for smugglers too.

And her new passports the colors of gemstones. Mei flipped through a stack of names and nationalities, some stolen, other beautifully forged. Mei saw her tickets to anonymity. At least in the meantime, Mei had what she wanted.

Kahliy knew he would no longer need Mei. He promised her a healthy bank account and more opportunities for them to be together again. But Kahliy was playing her on. His next mission did not include Mei. He thought it would be best to "quiet" her in the off chance that someone tied her to those infected victims. If Mei were discovered, he knew full well that she would expose him. But soon enough, she would no longer be a problem.

As Mei dressed back into her student garb, Kahliy wondered aloud. "How will you seduce your next victim? Your 'test specimen', Mei?"

Mei paused to gather her thoughts. "Tomorrow is the opening night for the International Genomics conference. There will be an informal get-together, what they call a 'meet and greet'. It was announced in the on-line syllabus. The scientists meet with other researchers in the lobby bar and lounge. I will drift through the crowd to find an opportunity. I can always spot the American men by their unstylish dress. And I have my honey sweetie filled with nano-cages." Mei was ready to forge ahead with her next challenge, she was invincible.

"Is this Tiger Flu like the last strain, Mei?" Kahliy found it exciting, the way Mei could so nonchalantly move from one task to the next. As if there was no difference between fucking and murdering. She never seemed to have any qualms about anything. No worries. No misgivings. And she never seemed coerced. It was as if everything she did was her idea.

Mei took her time to answer. "Yes Kahliy, this Copenhagen Tiger Flu is the same strain as the Seattle Tiger flu. It does not spread easily in people, not too contagious, but it will create more fear in America when this second mysterious, unexplained case arrives. It is the dreaded fire to the brain that scares people most." Mei kept Kahliy's attention fully engaged; he was riveted by what poured out from Mei's devious mind.

"I will find a nice friendly American man. My second time will be just like routine. I am worth every euro you've paid me and more. Sometimes you even get more that what you pay for, Kahliy." Mei crooned.

"And there are 19 pills in the spike as you promised.

Correct? I must soon deliver them on my journey as planned." In Kahliy's mind he would bring about the apocalypse. "Are you sure these are the ones that will create a pandemic, Mei?"

"In a veterinary lab in the north of China, scientists created 127 different varieties of bird flu virus. They infected small animals, ferrets, and passed the bird flu viruses from one generation to the next. And in doing so, the best "killers" like the Tiger Flus, were selected."

"Are there many Tiger Flus, Mei?"

"Five are the hyper-virulent, lethal Tiger Flu viruses. They are the ones that are the most infectious and highly contagious in humans. Very deadly. Your pills are filled with baby tigers with voracious appetites!" Mei laughed almost hysterically.

"How many people will be killed once they get out, Mei?"

"Easily a million, Kahliy." Mei smiled a half-twisted grin.

"Only a million people will die?" Kahliy thought it a paltry number for a global pandemic.

"A million in every city your soldiers attack. And from those cities, the Tiger Flu outbreak will spread." Mei assured Kahliy. "Perhaps eventually billions!" Mei gloated with glee.

"The Tiger Flu strains are packed into small pills, the size of a baby aspirin. There are 19 in the drop spike. But it is up to you to execute our greatest plan." Mei taunted Kahliy.

"I find that very exciting, Mei." Kahliy's eye glitter sparkled, so absorbed he was by her ruthless execution. He believed there was no limit to what Mei would do for money.

Mei warned, "These Tiger Flu viruses are very infectious, it is best if your soldiers arrive with no symptoms, especially with no detectable fever. They must take the pill, absorb it slowly on their tongue the day of their flight. They will become highly contagious in three to five days. Then they should travel on planes or buses or trains. Keep traveling until they are so sick that they must go to a hospital emergency room. Sit among the other sick and injured people in waiting rooms. Expose as many contacts as they can." Kahliy envisioned the horrific outcome. He would watch from afar the news reports, the panic, the chaos, the destruction, the demise of the West.

"We must bear witness to the event. Our vaccines will protect us, Mei. Before my chosen soldiers depart on their planes bound for America, I will tweet you under the hashtag #tigerblake19. Then we will meet on an island off the coast of Italy. You will understand the name of the island. You must figure out the clue, translate it to Italian. It is easy for you. You are clever in that way." Kahliy looked at Mei the schoolgirl. Her bookish attire did not change the strong desire he had for her. He would have her one last time on the island. Before she too would be sacrificed.

"Yes, you will tweet me before your soldiers land on American soil." Mei knew colloquial American expressions, having taught Kahliy a few.

Mei kissed Kahliy softly. "I will understand your clue. I will find you." Mei promised. "I will find the island."

~

21 CANDY GIRL

Albert tried to act nonchalant as a long legged beauty glided towards him. Struck by her long black hair that shined like obsidian and her garnet colored lips; leave it to Albert to describe a woman in geologic terms. During adolescence, Albert was an avid rock and mineral collector. Always the scientist, Albert's unrequited lust for women seldom progressed beyond his sexual fantasies.

It was the opening night reception of the International Genomics Conference at the Bella Hotel. Tonight's reception preceded the next three days of symposiums, presentations and seminars. But now an unexpected treat was fast approaching and came to a standstill smack in front of Albert.

From her accented English and Asian eyes, he wondered if she was part of the Chinese research contingency. But from the way she was dressed, he was not sure if her expertise lied in decoding DNA. Well, thought Albert, this was one Chinese babe he would really like to give his DNA to. As she slithered slowly towards him, it was all he could do to keep his jaw from hitting the floor.

Mei knew she had her pick of men, but she chose one who was alone. He looked a good choice to Mei, a fine specimen. Mei thought his baggy khaki trousers a dead giveaway, his boxy shirt and unstructured jacket were typical attire of American scientists. At least the European scientists had some sense of style with their tight jeans, snug-fitted shirts and tapered jackets. Mei could always tell the difference.

"So what do you think of this place? Isn't the architecture amazing?" Mei coyly sidled up to Albert with her sweetest of smiles. She knew her approach had already thrown him off balance.

Dumbfounded, Albert had to process not just one question but two from this distractingly sexy young woman. He was excited about meeting up with his colleagues from around the world, but he hadn't expected a hot chick like this to initiate a conversation.

Albert momentarily froze but he recovered with a half witty reply. "Incredible how they incorporate the natural settings in the lobby, the plant wall is unique." Albert had admired the lush green foliage when checking into the hotel earlier that day.

"Ah yes. It is like a tropical forest inside the lobby." Mei sucked on a hard candy as she spoke.

"And outside, wow, the two hotel towers, so eccentric, they are really eye-popping!" Albert thought her two long legs even more eye-popping. He hoped he wasn't too obvious but he found the sight of Mei's shapely legs rising up her short animal-print skirt a real turn on. His face blushed along with a synchronized surge that welled up in his trousers. Albert took a deep breath, trying to calm himself. He hoped no one could see his erection poking a tent in his olive green khakis.

Albert knew that guys like him were not chick magnets. An academic, congenial nerd, but he liked to think of himself as gregarious and not incapable of attracting women. But, wow, he could not believe his luck. He must regain his cool. Don't blow it Albert, he admonished himself.

"My name is Mei." Mei seductively smiled her Cheshire-cat grin. She knew the art of animal allure. Mei sucked a hard sweet as she spoke. "Yes, eye-popping, as you say." She knew she was an eye-popping piece of eye candy. And Albert was not thinking of architecture.

"Mine is Albert. But you can call me Al." Albert always used the Simon and Garfunkel song in his introduction. He could smell Mei's sugary sweet breath as she inched in closer.

"Al, how long will you be staying in Denmark?" Asked Mei, still sucking her sweet, she licked her lips as the candy dissolved slowly in her mouth.

"Unfortunately, I must fly back to Boston right after the conference." Albert tilted his head and frowned in disappointment. He fidgeted slightly, rocking back and forth, but he managed to regain his composure.

Mei did the math. She thrust out her hand and offered a wrapped candy. "Here, these are so good. Have a 'Honey Sweetie'." Mei calculated it would be about four days before Al would board his flight home to the US.

Albert could only wish that that Mei would be his honey sweetie. A familiar song came to his mind. "Oh sugar, honey, honey…"

Before Albert could answer, Mei tempted him again, "Honey Sweetie?" as she invited him again to try a tasty pleasure. Like the witch-goddess Circe, she would turn him into her next guinea pig.

Albert tried to convince himself that she was smitten with him. So sensuous the way she spoke to him. Was she being suggestive? His fingers grazed her palm as he picked up the wrapped candy, peeled off the plastic paper and popped the hard candy into his mouth.

"You must not be too much in a hurry. Suck it slowly. Let it warm up in your mouth. You will enjoy it so much more." Mei murmured. She knew she had him. Ah, the power of suggestion.

Albert felt himself flushing again, he wondered if she was flirting with him. "So I shouldn't just bite into it?" Albert gave an allusive smile, he could be suggestive too. Perhaps she might pick up on his innuendo.

"Take your time. Suck it. Go slow." Mei purred. "The honey is so sweet."

Almost in sync with Mei's instructions, the flavor burst in his month, exuding a thick, granular honey flavored ooze. Albert's eyes inflated like balloons as Mei watched the orgasmic look on his face. He was now playing a dangerous game beyond mere flirtation.

Before Albert could speak, Mei waved at someone in the distance. Albert couldn't see who it was. "Al, I will see you again. I must go talk to someone." Before he could say goodbye, Mei disappeared into the crowd.

As Albert panned over the lounge, he noticed two of his research buddies standing at the bar queueing for a drink. They had been watching him in amazement, but they kept their eyes mostly focused on the striking beauty, her long black hair, and endless legs. The two researchers ordered up three beers in a rush to rag on Albert.

Beers in hand, Albert's two colleagues, one British, the other Australian, disappointed at having missed an introduction, hand slapped Albert. Robert the Brit shoved a beer in his face. "Al, where did you find her, you dog!"

"Woof! Woof!" Albert barked a reply. Leave it to Albert to always come up with something corny.

Robert yelped back. "Not until Friday night at the Barking Dog Bar! You will join us, won't you? We are going on a pub crawl." They all laughed in synchrony. Albert nearly choked on his beer.

Mel from Melbourne answered for Albert. "Hey, but of course he will. And will you bring your new girlfriend with you, mate?"

"Oh, my China doll, quite a sweet young thing, don't

you think?" Albert knew that was an understatement.

Robert threw his head back, snorting a guffaw. "Ha! More *hot* than *sweet*, I'd say."

"You mean like an Italian sausage?" Mel nearly pissed himself, laughing even harder. He thought himself funny beyond his own words.

In a hushed tone, Robert could not resist a retort. "Don't you mean what Al would like to *do* with his sausage?" The adolescent humor of naughty schoolboys got the best of them as they broke out in paroxysms of laughter.

Albert now turned redder than ever, he did not do well at concealing his embarrassment. To avoid getting further baked by his two companions, Albert tried to bring the conversation around to shop talk and the new genomics seminars lined up at the conference.

"Well, I don't know if she is part of the Chinese delegation, I'm hoping so, but you don't find many Chinese scientists that look like that!" There were indeed plenty of researchers from China at the International Genomics Conference. Having captured the global market in deciphering human DNA, they possess the largest computational power of any other "Genomic" nation.

"Well, you know what they say. The Chinese own the world's DNA." Mel then seized the moment. "And I bet you'd like to share yours with her!" They just couldn't stop searing Albert to a crisp.

Albert stayed on track. "We really need to talk to the Chinese researchers about their "Genius Genome" study. They've sequenced the DNA from high IQ geniuses, thousands of them from all over the world. None of us are *even* close to finding all the myriad of genes that control intelligence." Albert and his buddies focused their research on cognitive intelligence genes.

"Yeah but it's not going to be easy. Not like height or hair or eye color. They're simple stuff, a handful of genes. But finding all the myriad of genes for 'smarts' is going to be one hell of a lot harder. There are *thousands* of them." Mel was right; it would be no easy feat.

"Hey, but the Chinese have got a huge lead on us. And they don't have to find *all* the "smart" genes, just *some* of them." Albert suggested.

"What do you mean? What good would it do if you only found a handful of the intelligence genes?" Robert shrugged.

"Gene editing for your babies. You know that, Robert." Albert thought it obvious.

"Yeah, duh! There is plenty of interest in the inheritance of intelligence." Robert added. "Like creating baby Einsteins or even smarter. Apparently Einstein had only an IQ of 145 but some of these Genius Genome project guys are up in the 165 range."

"Apparently it's not that difficult to edit the genes of embryos to create designer babies." Mel added. "It's quite controversial. Isn't it?"

"Yes, and its already been done in China, although they haven't let the embryos grow and develop. Well, at least not yet."

Robert carried on. "A lot of countries already do embryo selection: India, China and many other places. In some countries the girl fetuses are aborted. They want boys for obvious financial and linage reasons. Also when they are limited by one-child policies like China."

"And in the States and in Europe, *in vitro* fertilization of eggs with sperm donors has been going along for ages. Some people will do anything for an advantage over others. Even hand crafting their children." Mel directed the jibe at Albert and Robert.

"Yep, plenty of people are not adverse to selecting the traits they would want in their children. And with the new CRISPR gene editing, they can easily snip out the genes they don't want in their babies and insert new and improved ones." Albert was up on this new technology. "And just imagine, say a country like China decides to enhance even 5% of their population by genetically enhancing embryos. My what an advantage they would have over the rest of us!"

Mel chimed in. "And what about the wealthy in the US and Europe? They can choose their designer kids too."

The conversation went late into the night. After a few too many beers, the banter deteriorated from selecting genes for intelligence to selecting genes for penile enhancement. And genes for long legged women, like Al's new hot chick. From there, it came back around to sausages, hot or sweet. Robert and Mel teased Al relentlessly. But boys will be boys.

Having exhausted the repartee, their blather finally came to an end and Albert went back to his room. His thoughts drifted back to the honey sweet flavor of Mei. He hummed a hit song of the 60's that was popular long before he was born. "Oh sugar, honey, honey, You are my candy girl, And you got me wanting you." Albert pulled up the old hit on i-tunes and plugged in his headphones. He slid his hand down his pajama bottoms and dreamed on and on and on.

~

Albert didn't see Mei again. Perhaps he just didn't recognize her without her short leopard-skin skirt? Or was it a tiger? But he remembered her as if she were a passionate but fleeting affair. She would always be his China Doll fantasy. Albert's "Honey Sweetie".

22 POOR ALBERT

Albert was not himself. He closed his eyes as he rode the hotel shuttle to Copenhagen's Kastrup Airport. Woozy or boozy? He wondered if he was halfway between drunk and a hangover. Perhaps too much partying with his buddies at the Barking Dog Bar. Albert knew he was feeling rough. Maybe he needed some hair of the dog that bit him? He smiled at his own humor. Or maybe he was punch drunk in love with that knockout woman he could never have? One thing he knew for sure, he just wasn't himself.

After boarding SAS Flight 221 to Boston Logan, Albert collapsed into his seat. Overwhelmed with fatigue, he dozed off for a while before waking with a headache. He touched his face; his forehead seemed warm, a bit sweaty. He hoped he wasn't flushed an embarrassing color of zombie green. His head began pulsating to the rhythm of his heart.

He reprimanded himself. "OK, Albert, looks like you've gone and done it again." He figured, this was his punishment for a wild night out. He beat himself up, as Robert would have said, given himself a good "flogging". He had no one else to blame for the self-inflicted malaise that now clouded his head.

"A slight fever, I think." Albert self-diagnosed. Most likely from the mix of those fine brews?" He questioned. Albert consumed plenty at The Barking Dog, but he dismissed the idea that it was the beer, his tolerance for hops and grain alcohol was well-tested over time. And he didn't have any specialty drinks, those crazy-named cocktails. Only Mel from Melbourne was mad enough to "test" a few, as if it were one of his scientific experiments.

At the bar, Robert egged Mel on. "So, is this all part of your research on your 'stupidity genes'?" Mel took the brunt of the roasting that evening. He brought it on himself as he knocked back a series of cocktails. Starting with a spicy Caribbean pineapple express, graduating to "Hemingway's Mistress", the name alone set the three of them off. But when Mel ordered the "Candy Floss", the boy's night out descended into a tailspin. That was when Albert chimed in with his Candy Girl singing rendition that nearly had the three ejected from their pilot seats.

"This is not a Karaoke bar", the bartender Diego warned. Albert had embarrassed himself enough for one evening. He just could not get his honey-honey, sugar-sugar, out of his head. But now on the plane a fierce fever was forcing her out.

Luckily for Albert he fell asleep, his head propped up against the airplane window, the air flow directed full blast at his face. And lucky again, the middle seat was unoccupied. He snored lightly and drooled per his usual. For the time being, sleep was a welcome reprieve.

On arrival at Logan, Albert's head continued to throb, his chest ached. He barely made it through passport control and customs. He found the bright white light of the arrival hall intolerable, as if someone shined a high lumen flashlight in his face. He walked only a short distance before nausea overwhelmed him. Staggering as if drunk, he dropped his hand luggage. His stomach churning, he wretched and spewed vomit on the scuffed linoleum floor before passing out.

When Albert came to, he found himself in isolation at Boston General hospital. The young attending doctor diagnosed him with pneumonia, but thought Albert's symptoms were suspicious.

Albert complained. "I feel dizzy, everything is wavy, something is going on with my vision. And my head is pounding."

"Did you drink on your flight?" The attending doctor asked.

"No, nothing to drink since the night before my flight." Albert never had a hangover that lasted this long nor felt like this.

Albert seemed to be gasping for air. The doctor thought it odd that Albert had no runny, stuffy nose. Albert did not sneeze, nor did he cough as the doctor would expect in cases of pneumonia.

"Albert, would you stand up and take a few steps for me please?" The doctor asked. But Albert stumbled and swayed before being ordered back into his bed.

Albert's staggering gait, his confusion, and high fever alarmed the young doctor. Bearing in mind warnings from the CDC on patients arriving on international flights, the doctor ordered tests that included Ebola, MERS and unusual bird flu strains.

The quarantine stations at US airports remained vigilant on arrivals from West Africa, still fearing the spread of Ebola. And flights from the Arabian Peninsula also aroused suspicion. MERS had already been found in passengers in South Korea and other countries. But Denmark was not subjected to the same scrutiny.

An array of tests and assays were run on Albert. MERS was a possibility but he had no symptoms consistent with Ebola. Flu looked like a possible culprit, but so little time passed before Albert's condition rapidly deteriorated. The medical staffed were alarmed and cautious. The doctor had already ordered intravenous antibiotics and antivirals, although he thought there was a slim chance they might help Albert.

Within 24 hours, Albert no longer complained of the bright lights as he lapsed in and out of consciousness. He was isolated, intubated and ventilated.

Two days later Albert's heartbeat quickened, his blood pressure spiked and then took a nose dive. Albert's eyes dilated, he was no longer in pain. Despite efforts to revive him, Albert's CT brain scan showed encephalitis and brain death. Albert no longer needed life-support.

Performing a spinal tap, the doctor inserted a needle into Albert's lower back to collect cerebrospinal fluid. Just what kind of superbug did Albert pick up? Maybe the CDC could find the answer.

~

Doctor Ting of the Centers for Disease Control and Prevention, the CDC, called her counterpart at the World Health Organization, WHO. As global health partners, this was standard protocol. Along with the CDC and Danish health and security authorities, the FBI and Interpol were also alerted. The investigatory wheels had been set in motion.

"I am confirming that a second case of H5N1, bird flu, has arrived in the US on an international flight from Copenhagen to Boston."

The WHO director was at first incredulous. "This is alarming to say the least!" The first case of bird flu arriving from Hong Kong to Seattle wasn't totally unexpected. But Denmark?

Doctor Ting asked. "Have there been any outbreaks of bird flu in chicken and poultry in Denmark or other Scandinavian countries?"

The WHO director did a quick search of their database. "About ten years ago, highly pathogenic H5N1 was found in wild birds in Denmark. And one case was reported in a backyard poultry flock. But there have been no reports of humans infected with bird flu."

Doctor Ting had a report on her desk showing that

there had been just over 700 cases in people worldwide since 2003. The most severe infections were in Asia, Egypt, Indonesia and Vietnam. Most had close contact with poultry.

The WHO director added. "For the most part, bird flu doesn't transmit between people. Only very rarely in close family members."

Doctor Ting wondered aloud. "Could this young man's infection with H5N1 be the same Tiger Flu strain that infected that unfortunate woman last year who flew to Seattle from Hong Kong?"

Neither one knew the answer. Only the DNA could tell for sure. This was something the Partners would have to think about.

23 BACK IN RHODE ISLAND

Lost in a daydream, Jo barely heard Jeremy bellowing as she stood under the water raining down from the showerhead. She could only faintly detected Jeremy's garbled voice.

"Wait, I cannot understand a thing you are saying!" Jo shrieked back, wondering what it was that couldn't wait. The whirring of the overhead fan didn't help much.

Jo toweled down and draped a towel like a shawl over her shoulders. She emerged from the bathroom finding Jeremy outside the door, wearing only a pair of boxer shorts, flashing a lusty grin.

"So what are you in such a hurry to tell me?" Jo smiled at the obvious hankering in his facial expression.

"It can wait." Jeremy grabbed the ends of the towel, pulling Jo as he stepped backwards down the hall towards the adjoining bedroom. "Ah-ha! Now I have you captive."

Trapped, Jo playfully resists while Jeremy pulls her on to her bed, proclaiming it all her fault. "You are a wanton woman!"

Jo smirked at his wry accusatory British humor, a common routine in his art of seduction. Each knows what the other wants, playing to each other's rhythm, the pace, the known dance, the steps practiced many times over the years. Almost to perfection.

~

It was mid-afternoon on a Sunday. Jo woke first from their brief nap, still glowing from an encounter with the man she had come to know so intimately. Jo loved the coziness they shared, cuddling up to Jeremy under the quilted cover.

It was springtime but the weather was still decidedly winter. Jeremy stirred, peaking at Jo through his half-shut eyes. Jo hovered over him, ready to pounce.

"What was it you were going to tell me before we got distracted?' Jo laughed, referring to their romp.

"Oh, the news alert. There's been a second case of bird flu. It looks like it might be the same Tiger Flu strain you've been so intrigued with." Jeremy knew Jo was more than interested.

"Another case?" Jo pinched hold of her bottom lip. The news surprised Jo but it didn't strike her as unexpected. "Did it come in from China?"

"No, Copenhagen!" Jeremy screwed up his face, it struck him as odd. Both of them found it perplexing. "Now that is a bizarre occurrence, isn't it?" Jeremy had tuned into what would certainly be high up on the Partner's agenda.

"But Jeremy, that doesn't make any sense. How could that happen?" Jo knew deep down this was not a coincidence.

"Would you call it a black swan?" Jeremy asked.

"Or a zebra among horses?" Jo added. "Whatever you call the metaphor, it is definitely an unusual event."

"Read this." Jeremy brought up a News aggregate. He thrust his tablet in Jo's face.

Jo read aloud. "Last week, a US researcher fell ill at Boston Logan airport after returning from the International Genomics Conference in Copenhagen. Following his death from what was initially diagnosed as

123

---

pneumonia, a vigilant physician sent blood specimen for analysis. An H5N1 variant of bird flu was detected."

Jo paused, her mouth agape. "What the fuck! Why didn't you tell me sooner, Jeremy?" She knew the answer. He would never have gotten what he wanted.

"Just keep reading." Jeremy answered with a grin.

"Upon further analysis of the culture, the genome, the avian virus DNA that infected the man is identical to the bird flu virus that infected a woman returning to Seattle from Hong Kong last year. Both the man and woman died from this extremely virulent strain of H5N1. Its closest relative is the virus that infected and killed a tiger at a zoo in Jiangsu, China."

"So it probably is the same Tiger Flu that infected the woman who flew from Hong Kong to Seattle. Her Tiger Flu was not an isolated case after all." Jo suggested.

"Well you know the saying, 'Once is an incident. Twice is coincidence.' There isn't yet a pattern." Jeremy reminded Jo.

"But Jeremy, how could the same bird flu strain pop up in two different parts of the world? Copenhagen and Hong Kong are over 6000 miles apart!"

"Good question, grasshopper. It sounds like something you need to think hard about." Jeremy poked his finger on the end of Jo's nose.

~

The next morning, Jo's encrypted cell phone pinged. Wondering if the Partners would reconnect again, she was not surprised with her instructions to go to another obscure location, this time in southern Rhode Island.

The address took Jo to a roadside motel on Route 1. It was a throwback in time, an old 1950's style of single-storied rooms from the days when people traveled on routes rather than interstates. Jo saw it as a substandard but convenient motel room you might stay in for a cheap night's sleep.

Jeremy would have described it as a "knocking shop".

Jo chuckled to herself.

But Jo did not have the right of refusal. She agreed on the Partner's mission and the unusual meeting places were part of the commitment.

"Sometimes we will meet." Those were the instructions from Max. The time and the place were not negotiable. Jo knew that much. One doesn't question tactics in the war against terror. Obligations, duties and directives are understood and executed without question. Her handler, Rich Valens, told her that after their first meeting in the Shriner's Hall, the ancient order had closed the building, another relic of the past.

Jo wondered if "ancient" was a theme with the Partners? Or perhaps they just operated on a shoe-string budget. Jo answered her own question. They did not want to draw any attention to their activities. And they remained anonymous with cash only transactions that could not be traced.

Route 1 had a string of tawdry motels, but Jo thought this one looked a cut above the rest. She parked in the back lot as she was told. Six doors lead to the rooms but only three parked cars abutted them. Given no room number, Jo sat in her Hyundai for a minute or two before one of the doors opened, just wide enough for a large hand to emerge, pointing in her direction. It was a signal Jo obediently followed.

Approaching the cracked door, the hand opened just enough to let her in the room. Max stood wearing a plain but well-fitted pin-striped blue suite, his white shirt unbuttoned, a solid dark blue tie draped over a metal desk chair.

Max sensed which women found him attractive, his intimidating manner, demanding impatience and aggressive nature. His hands were large but his fingers quite thin. His peppered gray hair and piercing coal dark eyes defied you to look away.

Jo, uncomfortable, afraid to lock eyes, looked around at

the room at the 1950's décor. Beige and pale yellow striped wallpaper and a floral quilted bedspread. Clashing, Jo thought, but probably a cheery invitation for the weary traveler. Ancient dual shaded wall lamps above the headboard were lit for late night reading. Or perhaps romance, Jo couldn't help thinking.

"This won't take long, so stay focused." Max demanded. Always standing too close, Jo could detect the smell of mint. "Your assignment is Copenhagen." He pointed with a wave to tickets and a folder that lay atop the nightstand. Jo nodded. She wondered if there was more going on with his gesture than the obvious.

"Here are tickets for you and your husband. And hotel reservations." He lifted the tickets.

"Yes, yes." Jo could only muster a simple reply as she took the envelope in her hands.

Max stood solid as a statue. As if waiting for Jo to make the first move. His breathing became shallow as he leaned in closer. Wintergreen, Jo thought. She breathed it in, nearly tasting it.

Jo looked down at his polished wing tip shoes, the folds in his dress trousers.

"Do you have any questions?" Max finally broke the silence.

Jo searched for questions in her mind. She had so many that she didn't know where to begin. She was afraid that whatever she would ask would be met with a reprimand. Jo looked up at his eyes which revealed nothing. She thought he must contain unimaginable secrets buried within. Jo underestimated just how much power and influence Max really had. She would find that out much later.

"What are the next steps?" Jo asked for lack of anything better.

Max broke with a crooked half smile and almost in a whisper replied. "Report back with everything you and Jeremy find out."

He could have blown Jo over with his wintergreen breath.

~

Jo was already packing when Jeremy arrived home. He thumbed through the briefing packet and itinerary as he disappeared into his computer den. Printing up his research, collating, copying, and loading up his flash drives. There wasn't much time before their flight departed tomorrow evening from Boston Logan.

The list of places Albert visited intrigued them both. Jo searched late into the night, reviewing all the available images, reading the promotional material describing the Bella Hotel and The Barking Dog Bar.

Most importantly, Jo arranged and reviewed the tweets she and Jeremy collected on the chance that they would lead them to something. Jo often saw connections where no one else would even look. Lucky for Jo, Jeremy no longer dismissed her intuitive sense.

People too often ignored her when she constructed reasons why such and such happened. She was "looking for connections that don't exist." One psychiatrist labelled her obsession as "apophenia".

Apophenia: the human tendency of perceiving patterns or connections in random or meaningless information.

The accusations and diagnoses didn't end there.

"Randomania" some called it. Or paranoid narration. Or fuzzy plotting. Others thought her schizophrenic or just plain mad.

But Jo believed in her insights into the nature of reality. The interconnectedness. So long as she could back it up with research. Jo did not believe in unexplained mysteries nor did she dwell on conspiracy theories. But Jo was intuitive none-the-less.

And Jeremy supported and encouraged her by collecting the pieces she needed. She knew Jeremy may joke that she was "fucking nuts", but he believed she was fucking smart.

He emerged from the computer den. "So let's get packing, Jo."

24 BARKING DOG

Jo and Jeremy had their assignments. There wouldn't be much time left for their own explorations, their schedule was tight. However, it was not the first time either of them had been to Copenhagen. Only recently they toured Scandinavia, seeing the sights of Oslo, Stockholm, Gothenburg, Malmo and of course Copenhagen. They were old hands when it came to world travel and also lived in quite a few exotic places on four continents.

Still trying to deal with the unavoidable jet lag, Jo and Jeremy took a stroll down Stroget in the morning and in the afternoon headed to the first location on their list, "The Barking Dog", a bar in the quiet suburb where Albert and his friends spent their last evening of the Genomics Conference together. It wasn't the possible source of Albert's infection on the list of places they would visit. By that time Albert's body was already brewing the Tiger Flu virus like a human bioreactor. Most probably, he was on day two or three of his flu infection. He would not yet have shown any symptoms to himself or to his colleagues that final night in Copenhagen at The Barking Dog. Nevertheless, Jo and Jeremy hoped it might give them some clues.

Albert, Robert, and Mel must have been tired after the final conference day full of presentations and seminars. Despite this they were in party mode, but luckily for Jo and Jeremy the three researchers decided to forgo the hordes of humanity that descended on the Nyhavn bars. Each had flights the next day and there was really only so much drinking they could do. They all preferred some new surroundings after being closeted in the conference hotel. They had long flights out the next morning. Looking for something off the beaten tourist track, the Bella concierge had given them the Barking Dog recommendation and ordered them a taxi.

Luckily for Jo and Jeremy, the group only visited this one bar in the city according to the information Max supplied. The other bars they drank in were those inside the Bella hotel. Tomorrow, Jo and Jeremy would take a train out to the Bella. But today they wanted to glean first-hand anything the bar staff might remember about that evening when Albert celebrated with his colleagues on their final night together.

Following a printed out internet map, it was a long trek out over the canals. When Jo and Jeremy found The Barking Dog bar, Jo wished they hadn't walked so much earlier that day. Along with the fatigue of time-shifts from continental travel, they were dragging their feet.

Outside the door, they stopped to read a sidewalk chalkboard. "Candy is dandy but Liquor is quicker." Jo took a record shot of the sign with her camera. "Well this might just be a bit of fun after all." Jo enjoyed mixing business with pleasure, and Jeremy wouldn't mind sampling the brews. Both were ready to take a rest after their overly ambitious walkathon.

Jeremy ducked his head as they stepped down into a red alcove, following in poor Albert's footsteps. When they entered the cave-like bar, a straw-hatted barman nodded a greeting while he prepared for the evening onslaught. An array of spirits spawned from around the world lined the ledge behind the barman.

Jo pointed out a colorful chalkboard that read, "Pop-up Circus Menu that Comes and Goes". She remarked to Jeremy that the names of exotic cocktails like "Candy Floss" and "Lolly Hopps" sounded more like the sweeties sold in a candy stop.

The bartender, Diego, introduced himself. Jo and Jeremy did the same in turn. Diego showed them to the adjoining lounge. They were the first and only patrons of the day, the bar had just opened at four in the afternoon.

Jeremy perused a bottled beer lineup on the menu of unusual craft brews. He was already starting to enjoy this assignment. Diego told Jo and Jeremy that the bar sold none of the typical commercial Scandinavian brews. Jeremy ordered the "Red Hot Double Brew" allured by the label sporting a vampire caricature drinking a glass of bright red blood and noting the alcohol content.

Jo, less adventurous, ordered the milder Barking Dog Pilsner. With so many things to take in around her, Jo's eyes panned the assortment of colorful mugs, some ceramic, others were glass and metal, they came in all different shapes and sizes. There were mugs with faces; others had logos and fancy scripts.

While they waited for their drinks, Jo nosed along the walls of the lounge, inspecting every framed photo and piece of artwork, reading through humorous clips, chuckling at a few. The sombrero lampshade in the far corner made her laugh out loud. The lamp base was roundly shaped like a dough boy with its head a light globe. A tiny red nob protruded from its crotch. "Jeremy, this is the Sexican." She turned around and rolled her eyes grinning.

"Trust you to find the local cultural highlights, Jo." Jeremy replied drolly. In return, Jo flipped him the British two finger salute to which Jeremy replied with a fine one-finger American gesture.

When Diego returned with their drinks, Jeremy wasted

no time asking. "Would you be willing to answer a few questions about the American who died from the exotic bird flu?" The expression on Diego's face turned sour.

"You aren't more reporters are you? Not health inspectors? Or police investigators?" Diego was leery of their motive.

"No, not any of those." Jeremy insisted. "We certainly don't work for any agencies; we just read about the incident and we were curious."

"Well you can see that we have no live birds or chicken in this bar." Diego laughed, injecting a bit of humor. "The Health inspectors asked if any of us had been to a chicken farm." Diego shrugged his shoulders and raised his eyebrows at the absurdity of their question.

"Cluck, cluck." Jo made a joke trying to convince Diego to bring down his guard. "Did anyone ask if you kept tigers here? The American man had a new flu strain called Tiger Flu." Jo used more humor to disarm him.

"We only serve Tiger Tails, perhaps you would like one? It is a mix of coffee and orange liqueurs and peppermint schnapps." Diego grinned, joining into conversation.

"Oh, that sounds right up your alley, Jo." Jeremy teased Jo for her love of syrupy sweet liqueurs.

"It will not mix well with the vampire's blood." Jo jabbed back as Jeremy drained the last of his Red Hot Double Brew.

Jeremy smiled at Diego. "The American who died had two friends with him the night he was here. A British friend and a friend from Australia."

"Those accents both sound the same to me. I'm Spanish, working my way across Europe. I've bartended here for almost one year. But I think the Australians have more of a twang. But not compared to the twanging of Americans." Diego caught himself and spoke directly to Jo. "Please take no offense."

Jo grimaced unconvincingly, shaking her head. "Damn

twang, I can't stop it however I try!" She and Diego laughed. Jo smiled as she remembered her colleagues at work often complained about the British phrases she had unwittingly picked up from her marriage to Jeremy. Jeremy had often said that their marriage was based on "what and pardon". He would ask *pardon?* at some American idiom while Jo asked *what?* to some of his British slang. Their long marriage was always infused with humor.

"So, Diego, did the boys behave themselves that evening?" Jeremy probed and glanced at Jo who smiled back. Jo needed the narrative to construct the story of Albert's last days in Copenhagen.

"A bit loud, but I've seen much worse. Someone was singing. Oh yes, it was the American. He sang off-key in a high voice, something about honey sweetie. Maybe he was inspired by our candy themes?"

"Yes, perhaps. Well this place does remind one of a Sweet Shop with the candy names for many of the drinks." Jeremy encouraged him.

Diego tilted his head thinking. "You are my candy girl. Oh yes, now I remember. It's an old song I have heard before." Diego hummed a few bars.

"And you got me wanting you." Jo mumbled but neither Jeremy nor Diego took any notice. Upping the volume, she said. "It must be all your signs, the "Candy is Dandy" sign out on the sidewalk. And your sweet Candy Floss and Lollipop drinks."

Diego and Jeremy both nodded, yes. They considered that the probable explanation for the spontaneous sugary gum-drop song. Jeremy was thinking. "It just seems like an odd golden oldie choice for a young researcher. Why not something more contemporary?"

"But there could very well be more to it than that." Jo said under her breath. She wasn't sure, but something was starting to play a familiar tune. Jeremy made a mental note of what Jo was intrigued by. Jo was filing this odd information away for questions later with Albert's researcher friends.

25 SKYPE

Copenhagen – Melbourne – London

"Jo, I've set up a three way call." Jeremy fiddled with the computer and the signature Skype ringtone pings melodically.

Copenhagen Jeremy: "Jeremy here. And Jo. Thanks for agreeing to this interview. We want to know what happened to your friend, as you clearly do as well."

Jo nods as Jeremy adjusts the camera so that he and Jo are framed and in focus. Three screens populate the computer monitor with Albert's friends and colleagues, Mel from Melbourne and Robert from London.

Melbourne: Hey Jeremy and Jo, Mel here with my morning cuppa. (Mel looks unshaven, he is still in his pajamas.)

London: Hello Jo, Jeremy. Robert, here. Just having a beer after work. (Robert toasts with his beer mug.) Hey Mel, what's in that coffee you're drinking?

Melbourne: Wouldn't you like to know. (Mel toasts with his coffee mug). So Jeremy, Jo, what questions do you have for us?

Copenhagen Jeremy: We won't reiterate the questions you've already answered. We know you've been given the third degree by health authorities.

London: Not to mention the interrogations by the Danish Police, Europol and the FBI. Jeremy, do I detect an un-American twang? Are you another limey?

Copenhagen Jeremy: Got me. Born in South London. Now before Jo gets into the specifics, I'd like to start with Mel in Melbourne. My, how alliterative! So Mel, we're interested in your timeline, specifically, places, dates and people. From the first time you met up with Albert to the last. Anytime you were together, whether socializing or at meetings during the conference. But let's start with generalities. How well did you know Albert?

Melbourne: Look, Albert was a great guy. Very funny, bright, quick as a whip. His work on cognitive genomics was groundbreaking. Right, Robert?

London: Yes, significant. We all collaborated on research publications. We've been looking at the genes that are associated with intelligence. And Albert had plenty of those.

Melbourne: Right mate. He will be sorely missed not just as a good scientist, but as a friend. We both loved his deprecating sense of humor, such a smart guy, yet always so self-effacing. No ego and easy to get along with. And vulnerable, especially with women. We would give him grief about women and he just took it all in his stride.

Copenhagen Jo: Hi Robert, Mel. I'm just wondering, did any of you have any connection to the research on exotic flus, the bird flu in particular?

London: The H5N1 strains? No, but I have to admit I've been doing some homework. Albert's infection is just so bizarre. And I admit to being somewhat afraid of catching it from Albert. We wondered if we had all been exposed. But I suppose we would have had the flu by now. We did have one hell of a send-off on our last night together at the Barking Dog Bar.

Copenhagen Jo: Did Albert seem his usual self that evening? Was he symptomatic with fever at the bar?

Melbourne: Al, we called him Al. He didn't seem ill, no coughing, he didn't complain of anything. He was in high spirits, but he was pie-eyed.

London: Honestly, we were all a bit under the weather. Hey, it was our last night together, just partying before flying back to our respective homes.

Melbourne: We teased him about his China doll fantasy.

London: We watched Al chat her up while we were queuing for drinks at the Bella bar. She ran off before we could make our way over to them. She scurried off somewhere. She was so fucking hot! Long legs. Leopard skin, short, short skirt...oh, sorry Jo. Excuse my French.

Melbourne: Cool down, horn dog. Although I agree she did have legs right up to her neck. We were surprised that he pulled this gorgeous bird. He didn't seem to scare her off with his corny humor.

London: And Albert had no sense of style. Always in baggy khakis and checked shirts. Like most American scientists. It must be the uniform of academics.

Melbourne: Anyway, none of us ever saw her again. How could you miss a hot chick like that? There were plenty of Chinese scientists, researchers, genomics geeks roaming around. Some of them were in our symposiums. They have bigtime genetic sequencers.

London: They're sequencing the world's DNA. They are the so-called "Genomic Nation". But I didn't see any Chinese researchers that looked like her before.

Melbourne: Most of them were men, you dolt. You drooled at the sight of her. One other thing, Al said she gave him a hard candy that oozed honey in his mouth. You can't get bird flu from a sweet can you?

London: Hardly. He called her his "honey sweetie".

Melbourne: Al was such a hoot when he started singing about his honey, his sugar. His candy girl.

Copenhagen Jo: That's funny, when we visited The Barking Dog bar, the bartender told us that Albert was singing in a falsetto, a rendition of the old pop song. Was it "Sugar, Sugar, Honey, Honey?" You must know that teeny bopper gum drop song."

London: Barely. But Albert only referred to her as his Candy Girl, we never did hear her name. Just who was this woman? No one seems to know. And they've got to have her on the hotel security cameras. Has anybody looked in to her identity?

Copenhagen Jeremy: Maybe Albert was trying to tell us

something. The investigation is ongoing, so who knows what they will turn up.

Melbourne: He was our buddy, we want to know how this bird flu could have happened to him.

London: After all, there are no live chicken markets in Copenhagen. Are there?

The Skype call continued. There were more questions. More speculating. Without giving too much away, Jo and Jeremy were piecing together the clues. Like assembling the sequences of DNA to find out what it all means.

Jeremy said to Jo. "Just who is this Candy Girl? Tomorrow, we're going to the Bella Hotel. Let's put together those twitter feeds I've been collecting."

26 TWIN TOWERS

Walking from the Bella Center train station, Jo was struck by the eccentric architecture of the Bella Hotel's double towers, twisting and turning as if an explosion had frozen them in time.

"It looks eerily like the Twin Towers, doesn't it Jeremy?" Jo remembered gazing upward in August of 2001 on their trip in to New York City. That morning they greeted Jeremy's parents as they disembarked from the Queen Elizabeth the Second, the QE2 ocean liner. The reunited family drove from the harbor into the city for lunch in Little Italy. After lunch at an infamous Italian restaurant known for its well hung sausage, they ascended Tower Two for the view over Manhattan. Jo's linguine with meatballs dropped like lead in her belly on the elevator rise to the top.

Driving away that afternoon, Jo sat in the back seat of the car, her neck twisted around, gazing upward out the rear window, trying to see the top of the towers as they drove away. In one month only a ghostly twisted frame would remain.

Today Jo gazed up at the twisting towers of the Bella Hotel. As they walked toward the hotel entrance, Jo refocused on their assignment. "So we are going to follow the clues. Jeremy, please indulge me on this."

"Ok Jo, this might or might not pan out. It could lead us down a blind alley. But we'll follow your lead, one tweet at a time." Jeremy chuckled as he tweaked Jo's nose. "Let's not be obvious." Jeremy took Jo's hand as they entered the lobby to keep her from wandering off on her own, making them look more like ordinary tourists.

Jo's eyes darted around the lobby. She thought the reception area sterile, metallic feeling, but then she spotted the earthen walls winding up the first and second floors. As they ambled past, Jo inspected the ferns and bamboo. She noticed there were occasional airplane plants in the mix.

Jo carried her three by five cards listing the "tweets" that went back and forth between @XOXOXMay and @YOYOYSpiko. She flashed the first card at Jeremy and pointed out a tweet. He barely glanced at it, he had read them over more than once before and hadn't seen any obvious connections. It seemed like a longing, a "we will meet again", between two lovers with a good sprinkling of sexual innuendo.

Jo had a constantly changing narrative going on her head. When she didn't know something she would invariably concoct a story. Her overactive imagination could be the source of the outlandish or the inspired, she fluctuated between madness and brilliance.

But Jeremy indulged Jo on more than one occasion; her intuitive connections pieced together some sinister associations that few others could see. And Jeremy helped eliminate the clutter of her mind. Jeremy read again the first Tweet on Jo's list.

@XOXOXMay See you in May at the conference. Tiger candy is ready.

"So they were coming to a conference in May and her name is also May. And you think it was the Genomics Conference here. Hmmm." Jeremy paused to think. "And the tiger candy? Could that be a euphemism."

"For sex, most likely." Jo whispered, giving Jeremy a nudge with her elbow. "Just look at the next tweet."

@YOYOYSpiko Tiger candy is what I want. Your spike.

Jo spoke softly but still loud enough for Jeremy to hear. "She must be his Tiger Candy. Don't you know what his *spike* is?" Jo chuckled childishly.

"So what the hell does this next one mean?" Jeremy screwed up his face. "This is corny stuff."

@XOXOXMay Our love burns bright in the night sky. Tigers in cages in the spike. My chopstick.

"Our love burns bright in the night. The first bit sounds like poetry." Jo shrugged. "But the rest?"

Jeremy rolled his eyes. "Tigers in cages in spikes and chopsticks. This make no sense at all." Jeremy didn't have even a glimmer of an idea. He shook his head, flummoxed.

"Well, I don't know but I am sure we can figure this one out. It's those cages. I'll think about them." Jo vaguely recalled an article she had read about nanocages and DNA. New technology intrigued her. She made a mental note to do some research when she had the time.

Then Jeremy prompted her. "Jo, look at this next one."

@YOYOYSpiko Where will you find the right spot to unleash the tiger spike?

Jo wondered if there was a hidden meaning. "Unleashing the tiger spike. I think it has something to do with the Tiger flu."

Jeremy smirked. "But Jo, maybe he just wants to unleash his tiger spike on May?" Jeremy beamed a lusty grin. "I would like to do that to you, Jo."

"Oh, you are so naughty!" Jo widened her eyes and reddened like an embarrassed girl. "Don't get distracted. Look at the next tweet on the list."

@XOXOXMay Spike in bella bamboo. Right of the green settee. Our love is for tigers.

"Now that could have a number of interpretations, couldn't it?" Jeremy fingered his lip as he thought about it. "Maybe sex on a green settee? It could be sex or could it be something else?" Jeremy raised his eyebrows suggestively. Jeremy perused the lush vegetation. "The bella bamboo refers to the plant wall here. Don't you think?"

"Bamboo and ferns mostly." Jo confirmed and moved down on the tweet list. "Now this next one sounds like sex to me."

@YOYOYSpiko I will eat you with your chopsticks. Drive the spike deep. It will be found.

Jo continued. "Except for the part about 'it will be found', I don't know what that means."

"Oh my, he certainly is very randy indeed, our Mr Spiko." Jeremy commented in his best British vernacular.

"Yeah, like you, always horny." Jo elbowed Jeremy in the ribs. "Eating May with his chopsticks?" Jo made a face as if disgusted. "I don't think so."

"Jo, look at this next one." Jeremy pointed at the next in the list.

@XOXOXMay You make me want you. In May on Tuesday, my bella. Your kitten will hang in a basket in the sky.

"Let's take a ride up the elevator and check out the Sky Bar." Jeremy suggested. "We can have a beer and a snack if you like?"

"Sounds good to me. We can muse over the others tweets while we refresh ourselves." Jo nodded and sprinted after Jeremy who was already headed towards the elevator. He stopped abruptly when he reached a huge golden frog with outstretched arms. "Now he is different, isn't he?"

"Froggie wants to give you a hug." Jo quipped, outstretching her arms, giving Jeremy a quick loose hug around his waist. With her camera in hand, she backed up to take a photo of the golden frog. Jo often took record shots with her small pocket camera, documenting whatever seemed interesting. Jo could see more in retrospect when she could tie her thoughts together with the visual images. Sometimes something hidden would reveal itself in a photograph. Perhaps something relevant would be shown in the photos. Jo always found more inspiration in images than in words, whereas Jeremy revealed the hidden meanings in words. Together they could construct the words and images to best tell a story. The clues could tell a story that would unfold over time.

Jeremy brought Jo around to his side and wrapped his arm around her shoulder. "Now how about that Danish beer?"

After the dizzying ascent to the top of the elevator, the stylish Sky bar offered a quiet retreat. It looked nothing like The Barking Dog. Fashionably appointed, a clustered foursome of red and white patterned lounge chairs were centered on a red circular rug. A striking piano in the corner seemed filigreed with its glass and wrought iron lid that made it look like a bug.

Jo gasped when they veered over to the bar's perimeter, but it wasn't the view from the 23rd floor. Jo loved being high up in the sky. Her childhood dreams of gliding birdlike, seeing the world in its smallness, peering down from great heights, excited and amused her. But now Jo was looking elsewhere. She pointed with her hand towards the chairs hanging near the windows. "Let's sit there, Jeremy."

"Oh, my! Curiouser and curiouser said Alice." Jeremy alluded to Alice in Wonderland. "Golden frogs, an insectivorous piano, and hanging baskets!"

Jeremy and Jo stood still as they contemplated the mystery of the hanging basket. "Where are the kittens?" Jeremy asked.

"And Spiko's kitten, May, was hanging in the basket in the sky lounge. She was telling Spiko where to meet her!" Jo savored the revelation. Her bugged-eyed expression matched Jeremy's. "What a great find!" They both said.

"Shall we climb into the baskets, my kitten?" Jeremy endeared. They curled themselves into the tan rattan baskets with dark blue cushions and gazed at the cumulus clouds studding the pale blue sky. Off in the distance, they could see the city of Copenhagen on the horizon.

"There are only three baskets here. Quite possibly May sat purring in one of these when Spike found her." Jeremy's eyes were alight, intrigued that the clues had begun to make a narrative in his head.

For a while they sat in silence, clearing their thoughts, gazing into the perfect baby blue with white cottony puffs. Panning the horizon, they tried to get their bearings, while absorbing the images and connecting the related words in the tweets.

Jeremy ordered two Danish beers. Jo added. "Some smoked salmon, please. And your assortment of breads."

Jeremy added to the order. "And the windy sausage and Danish cheese plate." They waited for the waiter to leave before Jeremy asked. "May I have another look at the tweets on your list Jo?"

Jo handed them across the cocktail table separating them. Jeremy mused over them again. He read to himself one in particular.

@YOYOYSpiko You have sweetie for a chosen friend. He will be surprised with your treat.

Jeremy commented. "May's chosen friend was surprised with a treat, and I'm beginning to think it isn't necessarily Spiko getting the sweetie treat." He handed the list back to Jo.

And the next one, Jeremy, is from William Blake's *Tyger Tyger* poem. We flagged that clue from the start but I still don't know why May referenced it here." Jo mused. "I'm still thinking it was a reference to the Tiger flu."

@XOXOXMay Yes a surprise treat. Tiger, tiger burning bright, in the forest of the night.

"Maybe you should read the entire poem. Perhaps something else is alluded to." Jeremy suggested.

"Could it be a metaphor?" Jo asked. She could see what was coming.

Jeremy attacked with his usual dig. "We know how good you are at mixing up your metaphors, Jo." She stuck out her tongue like a child being teased. With the note cards on the cocktail table, she turned it towards Jeremy and pointed to the last tweet on the list.

@YOYOYSpiko The world will belong to us. The tiger will be uncaged. Forever.

"Are you thinking what I'm thinking, Jo?" Jeremy's big brown eyes looked wise like a barn owl. Jo nodded, her gaze unfocused, a clamoring cacophony of mind chatter assailed her head.

Playing mind association games they bantered and ruminated about those 'tigers in cages', 'sweeties', 'bamboo' 'the green settee', 'the kitten in the baskets'.

They questioned, "Was 'driving the spike deep' and 'spike in by bella' as obvious as it seemed?" Words cannot always be taken literally. But figuratively, what does it all mean these allusions to "spikes"?

"It's Blake's poem, Jo. The Tiger. *What dread grasp, Dare its deadly terrors grasp?* And by uncaging the tiger, releasing the terror, the dreaded grasp…"

"Jeremy, now here's a scary thought. And if the tiger flu is the deadly weapon of mass terror…and if the tiger flu is uncaged forever…"

"…it will be free to roam the world." Jeremy punctuated the unthinkable horror.

On that thought, Jeremy settled up with the waiter and they made the 23 floor decent. As they stepped out the elevator walking back through the lounge, Jo spied one lonely lime green sofa set among awash of pale blue-grey sofas and lounge chairs. Stopping to photograph, Jo did not need to explain to Jeremy.

Jeremy uttered as he exhaled. "The green settee by the bamboo wall."

27 GREEN SETTEE

So, there it was. Not the dark racing green of British sports cars, but a light hue of lemon-lime, the sofa had been wedged up closed to the bamboo plant wall. Perhaps that is why neither Jo nor Jeremy noticed it. It seemed to blend in rather that stand apart from all the blue-grey sofas and lounge chairs in the lobby, but it was indeed the settee that matched the description in the tweets. Jo and Jeremy didn't see it before, having been distracted earlier by the Golden Frog as they went toward the elevator for the Sky bar.

Jo couldn't resist the temptation. The "green settee" was unoccupied, although a few visitors were wandering through the area looking for places to seat themselves. The lobby bar was hidden just beyond the curve of the plant wall greenery. Jo plonked herself on the left end of the small loveseat, gesturing to Jeremy, patting the cushion, for him to come join her.

Pulling out her notecards, Jo again found the tweet:

@XOXOXMay Spike in bella bamboo. Right of the green settee. Our love is for tigers.

"What was our right side is now on your left, Jo. Now don't be too obvious." Jeremy turned his head to look at Jo. "I want you to explore the bamboo wall for me on the left of you." Jo had a similar idea but she willingly followed his instructions.

"I'll caress the leaves and gently feel them." Jo's left arm extended and her fingers fluttered lightly over the fern, the bamboo leaves and the mossy earth they were planted in. "Like a butterfly, Jeremy." She didn't find anything unusual, at least not at first. She brought her hand back around and glanced at Jeremy frowning slightly in disappointment.

"We won't have this opportunity again. Try a wider area." As Jeremy spoke, Jo stretched her arm back as if in a yawn. She brushed a broad stroke and happened upon on what felt like a stiff plant stem. Or was it? Jo thought.

Probing with her fingers between the plants, feeling the soil, she discovered a hole about the size of her finger. Pushing her finger in deep, she did not find the bottom of the orifice; it was damp and earthy, the walls seemed compacted. "There is a deep hole in the soil. About the width of my finger."

"Oh, interesting, keep feeling around." Jeremy pursed his lip inquisitively. "Curious and curiouser in best Lewis Carroll fashion." He mumbled under his breath.

"Is this a hard branch of wood, or is it a stick?" Jo said aloud. With her thumb and index finger, Jo pulled slowly, smoothly, warning herself to be careful, no jerky motions. A dirt covered piece of wood about seven inches long emerged. Jo placed it on her thigh, soiling her designer jeans but that would not matter. Both she and Jeremy stared at the wooden stick for a while.

"I hope we haven't disturbed a piece of evidence." Said Jeremy, concerned about potential complications. He wrapped what appeared to be a wooden chopstick in his white cotton handkerchief. Jo often teased him that only Englishmen carry around archaic cloth hankies, but she was pleased he had it with him. Jeremy slipped the neatly packaged chopstick into his jacket pocket.

Jo looked over at Jeremy again. Incredulous, she just couldn't believe what secrets they had uncovered. "I'm even more concerned about what was in that empty deep hole in the soil. It was only a couple of inches away from the chopstick we just found."

Jeremy pointed again to the list. "And then there is this tweet, it seems to have taken on a whole other meaning."

@YOYOYSpiko I will eat you with your chopsticks. Drive the spike deep. It will be found.

"Well, that is certainly true!" Jo exclaimed in astonishment.

"Let's go now. We'll talk about this later." Jeremy hushed Jo, tapping his index finger up against his lips.

As they walked back to the Bella Center train station, Jeremy asked Jo. "Do you know what a dead drop marker is?"

"Is it something used by spies? Tell me, please." Jo knew Jeremy could fill in the gaps.

"OK, listen. A dead drop "spike" is a concealment device. Spies use them to pass messages. More in the past but they still have their uses, only now they pass digital rather than paper messages."

"So a spike is a tool for spy games. Hmm." Jo began to catch on.

"Yes, and if we were to play secret spy games, we would agree upon a place, a "dead drop" to leave our communications. It would maybe be in a potted plant or a hollow in a tree or maybe a metal box." Jeremy explained. "The spies would often use a chalk marker to show when the dead drop had been left or picked up. So the wooden chopstick would tell the person sending the "message" that the spike in this case was picked up."

"So the dead drop chopstick we found is a spy gadget,

like using chalk to say something is to be picked up. This reminds me of spy movies and John le Carré novels. So the hole I found next to the chopstick had a message spike in it. And it was clearly picked up?"

"Correcto mundo." Jeremy confirmed.

"And can the message spike be made impermeable to water?" Jo asked.

"Yes, they usually are. They are often metal tubes that are water and mildew proof."

"And can they preserve small items not just paper messages?" Jo asked.

"That they can do." Jeremy kept nodding yes.

"Oh my, oh my, oh my. How very, very interesting."

~

The Bella Hotel security cameras had spotted Mei Wong a couple of times. Ever since the 2009 Climate Change Summit at the Bella in Copenhagen with all the dignitaries and heads of state, the hotel security video system had been upgraded.

During the Climate Summit, the United States listened in on the cell phones conversations of their allies, as they did with their adversaries, and back at home with their own citizens. Every country wanted an edge on what people talked about as they prepared for the big Climate pow-wow. There is nothing quite like real time revelations. Some called it unfair advantage, but since when has advantage ever been fair? Advantage was there for the taking and only if you maintain an advantage do you maintain your edge. In diplomatic terms, it was called "Negotiating from a position of strength".

But now in the aftermath of the United State bugging fiasco, the hotel security upgraded their radio wave detection and video surveillance. Albert had been spotted many times during his stay at the Bella at the recent Genomics Conference seminars, informal meetings, and socializing with his colleagues and friends. But one "colleague" in particular stood out. How could she not?

Danish Intelligence, the American secret service, Interpol and hotel security more that noticed the leggy, Asian sex goddess, her leopard print skirt, her long black hair trailing down her back. No one recognized her; she was not a conference attendee but Chinese most likely. Quite a stunner, they all agreed. But she hadn't register for the Genomics Conference, nor was she a hotel guest. She was spotted entering the lobby and the ladies restroom, the European WC, the Danish *damen toiletten.*

The mystery woman entered the hotel hidden under a cap, simply dressed, and then emerged from a ladies room in attire appropriate for a high-end hooker. Did she shake hands with Albert? They analyzed her every move and gesture but in the crowd some of the detail got lost. Could she have been the source of his flu infection? She and Albert talked only briefly. Was she soliciting him? Prostitutes were not unknown in the hotel especially during conferences. Those that became frequent visitors were recognized and ushered out promptly. This woman was not a known prostitute but by the way she had acted coming into the hotel, changing her clothes suggested she was a high-class freelance escort.

Questions arose, but the right questions were asked to the wrong people. Prior to Albert's arrival, security cameras had not been screened. There didn't seem to be any reason to do so, the woman's brief meeting with Albert didn't seem to be important. She probably was there to meet someone else who had hired her services that evening.

And it was now that Jo and Jeremy were first to connect the mystery woman, Mei, to her twitter handle @XOXOXMay. Mei certainly could be the kitten self-referenced in the tweets. Although Jeremy thought maybe this kitty had claws, like the tiger her and Spiko kept talking about!

Jo and Jeremy would meet with the Partners after they returned to Rhode Island tomorrow.

~ PART 3 ~

Italy
&
European Rail Journey
&
Rhode Island, USA

28 NONNO

Just one day passed since Kahliy found his grandfather not breathing. He feared the worst. "Did Nonno have a heart attack?" He didn't know what it was that took away Nonno's last breath.

This was the second time Kahliy was orphaned, the first time in an Apennine village. Born to a mother he never knew, his grandfather in Naples took him in. No other family was left in the little mountain village. Kahliy had no father that he knew of, nor any siblings, just distant cousins who left years ago for jobs in Caserta.

Grandfather's small pension paid for a one roomed apartment in Naples. Nonno worked odd jobs as a handyman and asked neighbors to watch over his little grandson. In Italian, Kahliy's real name, Carlino, meant "manly". Being a man was important to Nonno, he knew Carlino would have to fend for himself at an early age as grandfather was advanced in age.

There was always enough money to eat and Nonno made sure Carlino attended good schools, encouraging him in his studies. Nonno always told him, "Latin is the key to all understanding." He was emphatic, insisting that Carlino be schooled in the classics.

By eleven years old, Carlino grew to be independent and spirited. He knew the neighborhood and how to get around on his own. He could think on his feet and argued a good case, much to Nonno's amusement. His knowledge of Latin opened the door to his interest in the biological sciences where Carlino (Kahliy) began to see the value of being well versed in Latin derivations. He studied the Latin-based binomial system that named all living things, devised by the naturalist Carolus Linnaeus. Carlino felt a kindred attachment to the Swedish scientist. Perhaps it was in his name, Carolus, or perhaps it was the Latin names Linnaeus used to create a sense of order. Or perhaps it was both.

One Saturday morning, Carlino awoke to find Nonno not sitting at his wood table drinking his morning coffee. It was unusual for Nonno to still be in bed sleeping. When Carlino tried to wake him, Nonno could not be roused, his body was still, his deep heavy breathing had ceased. Carlino sat next to him until the shock dissipated along with the heat from Nonno's body.

Carlino reflected for a while, remembering their recent holiday together on a small island off the coast of Rome. They traveled by train then took a ferry, the Maregiglio, the "sea lily". For a week they stayed in a tiny *albergo*, swimming daily in the warm waters of the Mediterranean.

Carlino was fascinated by the small island. The people were more like himself with clear blue-green eyes, unlike the brown-eyed Neopolitans. He remembered when he and Nonno walked in the sand dunes they could smell the sweet yet delicate fragrance of the snow white sea lily, the Giglio di mare, or *Pancratium maritimum*. He learned its Latin genus and specie name. *Pancratium*, borrowed from the Greek athletic event, was a brutal type of fighting that combined boxing, wrestling, and kicking. Perhaps it was a symbol of his life to come. But now, sitting next to

Nonno's motionless body, Carlino realized he must focus on what that life to come might be. What would be his future? He must decide for himself his own fate.

Nonno spent most of his meager earnings on Carlino's education, little was ever saved. Carlino found lira in Nonno's brown leather wallet, he slipped the bundle of assorted bills in his pocket. Even at eleven years old, Carlino knew enough to assume his fate would otherwise be an orphanage. "I'd rather take my chances in the world."

Carlino thought through his options and devised a plan. He could take a bus to the eastern outskirts of Naples, where he would join up with the Roma and travel with the gypsies. If he stayed in Naples, he feared he would be found. The neighbors would report him missing, which was of course what they did once they became suspicious of no one coming and going from the apartment.

Carlino heard there were Roma camps, you could see them if you took a bus and traveled east. He heard stories of the gypsy life, the allure of some romantic fantasy. Roaming with the nomadic group he could travel the world in search of adventure. He reckoned this his best possibility of escape, find a roving band of gypsies and convince them into to take him with them. He would invent an incredible story, he was quite clever at that. He embarked on his journey.

~

When the two men found Carlino, he was hidden under a pile of blankets in the back cabin of their white van. Shocked at the sight of the small boy, expletives in an unfamiliar language fell from their lips.

Just the night before, Carlino heard similar foreign words and songs being sung at a Romani camp in Naples. Carlino watched from nearby bushes, looking for an opportunity when he could steal his way into the open van. Only for a moment did the two men step away before locking the van's rear door for the night. Carlino found the perfect opportunity to steal away in the van.

Early the next morning, the men drove the nearly 600 kilometer distance from Naples to Pisa, stopping only once in the small town of Montaldo di Castro where they lunched on pasta and *vongole* in a typical *osteria*. The two men, one elderly with a long scraggly beard, the other younger and clean-shaven, had been handing out supplies and blankets to Romani families in two campsites on the outskirts of Naples. That second stop was a camp under a Naples' motorway that was populated mostly by gypsies from Bosnia-Herzegovinia.

When the two men arrived near Pisa, the men were both surprised and annoyed at discovering their stowaway. They fired questions that Carlino neither understood nor wanted to answer. He curled himself into a ball, refusing to talk. The younger man punched numbers into his cell phone and yelled loudly in animated tones. The older man stroked his beard as he sat on the edge of the van's cabin, staring curiously at the young boy.

"But he must be from one of the encampments, is anyone missing a child, a boy of about ten years old?" the younger man asked in an Eastern tongue. Carlino understood some words common to Italian, but he acted ignorant and afraid, using a ploy to stall them. He knew that the longer it took for them to find out his identity, the better were his chances of not being turned in to the police. He did not want his true identity found out. Life in a Neapolitan orphanage was something he wanted to avoid at all costs.

But now the younger man interrogated him in Italian. He pulled Carlino out of the truck by his arms and forced him to stand upright on the ground.

"You must answer me or I will call the *carabiniere*!"

Carlino did not want the police, not at all. He complied. "*Si, si.*"

"*Come ti chiami?*" The young man asked.

"*Si, si.*" Carlino, buying his time, did not want to give his real name.

"What are you called, do you have a name?" The young man angrily demanded, pulling on Carlino's left ear.

A muffled "Kahliy" came out. An attempt at disguising, morphing into a name that would be hard to identify.

"Kaa-lee? What kind of name is that?" The younger man interrogated. "*Scritto per me.*" He produced a ball point pen and a newspaper, handing both to the boy.

That is where the name "Kahliy" was first scribbled onto the front page of *L'Unita*, the now defunct Italian Communist Party newspaper.

"Kahliy? What kind of name is this?" Perplexed by the odd sounding name, the younger man's skepticism showed on his expressive face.

The two men talked among themselves. The older man combed his fingers through his long thin beard, intrigued with the unusual name. "There are similar names in Hindi and Sanskrit. But he has not written Kahlil, he is too light to be Eastern, although his looks could come from many places."

"Where are you from?" *Dove?*" The elderly man asked in Italian. "If Kahliy really *is* your name."

"I am from the Roma camp in Naples." Kahliy lied.

"How can that be?" Both men, irritated, spoke in synchrony.

"I am Roma." Kahliy answered.

"But you can't be!" The young man snapped, reddening with angry. "No child is missing from the camps I just checked the Naples Roma camps on my cell phone. You don't even understand the language. And both camps say no child is missing!"

"Where did you steal your way into the van? Where did you come from?" The older man was more amused than mad.

"*Nell'Ombra.*" Kahliy answered.

The young man harrumphed. "So you came from the

dark? From the shadows?" He angrily laughed, spitting out. "That is absurd!" Kahliy cowered, looking down at the ground.

The old man, still stroking his long beard, said to his younger friend in the language Kahliy did not understand. "He is like you, my friend, he operates in the shadows." He gave a wry smile, his old grey eyes glimmered.

"*Nell'Ombra.*" The younger repeated. He realized Kahliy was purposely obscuring, obfuscating, so as not to reveal his true identity. "Clever boy." The younger man said as he nodded in agreement with the older man. But he would not let a child try to outsmart him.

Exasperated, he grasped Kahliy by the shoulders, moved in closer and peered inquisitively into Kahliy's flecked green eyes. "You must tell us the truth! What is your name?"

"It is whatever you want it to be." Kahliy brashly answered. He had nothing to lose.

"But how can that be?" The young man questioned why this boy was leading him in circles, never directly answering anything he asked.

Kahliy knew he was testing the limits of his inquisitor's patience and in one last desperate effort he pleaded. "I will be whoever you want. Your servant. Your soldier. Your slave. I can be a mercenary soldier. I will work for food. I can clean and I can cook. I will live in a tent. But please do not call the *carabinieri!*" Nearly breathless from his strident elocution, Kahliy paused and inhaled. Long, deep but silent heaves followed.

No longer annoyed, both men grew interested in this small boy who it appeared would do anything to keep his identity secret.

"Where are you from?" The elder asked.

"*Napoli.*" Kahliy replied.

"Yes, we know that. But where in Naples? The old man repeated.

"I do not know."

"Why do you lie to us?" More aggravated than frustrated, the young man grasped hold of Kahliy, shaking him hard to get the answers out.

Kahliy understood the rough gesture. "I will lie for you." He promised the same in return.

"What do you mean?" The older man asked.

"I have secrets." Kahliy said flatly.

The old man tilted his head. "What secrets do you have?"

"Secrets I will never tell." Kahliy's point was well taken. The two men considered without comment what Kahliy had implied by holding tight to his secrets. The boy had promise!

Not understanding their silence, Kahliy pleaded. "I will be your slave, and I will keep your secrets." And pausing, in a moment of weakness, he begged them. "Please, I do not want to end up in an orphanage!"

"He is in despair." The old man told the younger in their private language. But Kahliy understood one word, he was, indeed, desperate.

Kahliy made more promises. "I will stay in the dark. In a closet. In a hiding place. I will never tell any secrets."

"You promise to live in the shadow?" The old man asked

"*Si!*" Pledging he would live in the shadows of darkness. *Nell'Ombra.*

.

161

29 UNCLE

Later that evening, the white van stopped at another Roma camp, seven miles outside of Pisa. The men fed Kahliy some tasty food, differently spiced than the Neapolitan food he ate while living with Nonno. The young man watched that Kahliy did not try to escape. He gave him a chance to relieve himself, before locking him back in the van. The two men then decided Kahliy's fate.

Wrapped tightly up in a blanket, Kahliy now thought of Nonno. How much he missed him, his warmth, his kindness. How Kahliy would recite his Latin to Nonno, who assured him it would be invaluable later in life. But it was here with his new life that Kahliy's interest in different languages and ideas began. It would kindle a fire, bringing a flame that would ignite and begin to burn with such ferocity that it would encompass his very existence.

That evening, the two men drank hot chai with others from the camp, all sitting around a wooden fire. They knew each other well, drawn together by ideology their philosophical discussions went late into the night. But tonight, the two men shared the small dilemma sleeping in the back of their van with their camp friends.

"He has the ability to change like a chameleon." The

old man told them. "And he can easily hide, as he said, 'Nell'Ombra.' As if he understands his fate is to live in the shadows, to hide in the dark, as he has promised."

"He seems wise beyond his years." The younger man explained. "Very quick to think. And he will not let anyone know his secrets. We still don't know who he is or where he comes from. He would not divulge anything, fearful of being apprehended by the police. Not a street urchin from Naples, although Naples is his origin, his clothes are clean and he has money in his pocket. Otherwise, he has no identity. If he is a runaway, no one would expect him to show up in Pisa".

The older man added. "But most impressive is his ability to change, to morph, to become whoever you want him to be, and to do so convincingly. Our young boy may have talents that can be invaluable to us. He can certainly keep secrets."

The group of men bantered back and forth on the fate of young Kahliy. To become a soldier, he could be groomed. They would train him, indoctrinate him. He would absorb the languages, the teachings, the philosophy.

The next day, the Roma Elder remained at the Roma encampment while the younger man drove the seven kilometers to his apartment near the University of Pisa with Kahliy.

Once in Pisa, the young man told Kahliy he must from now on address him as "Uncle". The story evolved over time, Uncle told anyone who asked that Kahliy was his sister's orphaned child. Uncle also bought forged birth certificates and an Italian passport from one of his collaborators who had access to illegal documents. Kahliy's impeccable Italian, his lighter skin and green eyes blended in well with the Italian northerners. No one ever suspected any differently.

Kahliy gratefully accepted his new role as nephew to his uncle, the professor, and seized his new life as fortunate and enlightening. Fully engaged, being surrounded by academics and university students was stimulating, especially the beliefs and ideas of Uncle, who taught courses in philosophy at the University.

~

Over the years, Kahliy proved he could live "Nell'Ombra". He would not be discovered, nor did he have any inclination to return to his past life. Quick to learn, he showed himself to be more intelligent than his peers. He picked up languages quickly and continued to study Latin and other languages under his Uncle's tutelage. Always the chameleon, he adapted many roles and assumed different personalities. Kahliy would be whoever Uncle wanted him to be. He was the perfect soldier who would execute whatever Uncle commanded.

Student followers often gathered at Uncle's apartment, small groups, usually four or five at most, enough for dialogue. They spoke in hushed tones and whispers. Uncle would sometimes play classical music to drown out the discussions. Secrecy was foremost. Always curious, Kahliy wanted to know what secrets they held, the meeting's ritual so appealed to him, but Uncle did not include him with these small chosen groups.

Uncle chose his disciples carefully. Loosely linked, he formed autonomous cells. They operated under the radar, in the dark, hidden in the shadows. Uncle knew it was prophetic when he found Kahliy at such an early age. Uncle adopted the name "Nell'Ombra" for his most disciplined student followers, the concept that Kahliy brought with him to Pisa as a young stowaway.

When Kahliy was fifteen, Uncle invited him to sit and listen with a new group of younger students. There were perhaps a dozen students that Uncle invited from his seminar course, a basic review of works of selected philosophers. Meeting regularly, usually in the evening, they congregated in Uncle's spacious front room, curling up and sprawling out on an oval hand-braided rug that covered most of the room. A strewn mix of young men and women littered the rug. Four early arrivals snared the four dining-table chairs along the walls. Uncle sat on a distressed leather easy chair when he wasn't pacing among his students, badgering them with questions, challenging them to think beyond the parameters of their ever present electronic boxes.

Uncle insisted his students read actual paper books, no matter how worn. "You can often find new insights in the notes scribbled on the margins."

Kahliy joined the rug perimeter along the frayed braided edge. He was no longer a child and nearly as tall as Uncle, his shoulders not yet broad, but his thighs and calves, muscular and strong, gave him the beginnings of a good-looking manly stature. On daily bicycle rides, he rode the streets and outskirts of Pisa, often covering great distances.

Quiet and reticent, Kahliy was far from outgoing like some of the students in the groups. As he sat down, he cast a diffident glance at the young woman next to him lying supine with her legs bent like a cricket. Kahliy's brown hair, windblown from his ride, was left uncombed but his translucent green eyes revealed a glitter of gold that captivated the interest of Bianca. She blatantly stared at him during that evening's study session, an introduction to the works of Friedrich Nietzsche.

Kahliy was mesmerized by the array of bodies, their sensual nature, some loosely spread out, others tightly compressed, while others snuggled together indicating way beyond casual friendship. Uncle chose this adjunct group of novice thinkers based on a variety of their attributes. It was from this group of minds and bodies that Uncle would select the best, but not necessarily the brightest. The best, by Uncle's definition, were committed and passionate with minds open to unusual ideas. Malleable in many ways to his own brand of ideology and dogma. The elevated status of *Nell'Ombra* was reserved for only those who passed muster.

Tonight the group discussed the three stages of man, Nietzsche's animal, human, and god. They were assigned readings from his *Thus Spoke Zarathrusta* to contemplate.

Uncle told them that some think of "God" as a supreme being, but not Nietzche the atheist who declared that God was dead.

Uncle quoted the German text and its Italian translations, suggesting that the interpretations could be misleading and sometimes misinterpreted. But they should tease and dissect the meanings.

Quoting Nietzche, Uncle began with the basic quote. "Man is a rope stretched between animal and the superman – a rope over an abyss" The students nodded, they had read the verse. "A different translation is 'Man is a rope tied between beast and overman – a rope over a bridge'.

"Well, at least they agree on something about animal and man." Bianca mumbled sarcastically, tapping the back of her hand against Kahliy's thigh.

Uncle explained the warning. "It is a dangerous crossing when man emerges from out of the animal…" He went on and on, explaining the nuances, reading more aphorisms. It was all too much for Kahliy's uninformed mind to take in. Bianca watched the confusion on his face.

As the group dispersed, Bianca suggested to Kahliy that she could help him better understand the three stages of man. "We could start with the animal, the beast." They planned to meet up later that evening. "I will read you the important passages. We will discuss the subtle and varied interpretations." Bianca had eyes the size and color of chestnuts, her high octave voice, small stature, and a face framed with ears that protruded, reminded him more of a cartoon character than a beastly animal. Perhaps, Minnie Mouse. They agreed to have coffee together in a nearby square. He thought it could be an enlightening experience. Little did he know how illuminating it would be.

At 10 o'clock that night, Kahliy walked to *Borga Stretto*

and waited outside an historic coffee bar and ice cream parlor. It was famous as a crossroads for Pisa's literary men and university students. When Bianca arrived, they decided that gelato was a better choice than coffee and then settled down in seats in the open-air hall.

It was early Fall, both dressed in their jeans and pullover sweaters like so many other students once the weather began to change. The evening temperatures had dropped despite the days being still quite warm and sunny. Bianca gazed at Kahliy as he licked his sugary cone full of *Zabaglione*, an egg custard, while she licked suggestively on her Sour Cherry. Once they had finished their expensive treats bought by Bianca, she opened her dog-eared copy of Nietzche and began reading quotes she had carefully chosen and annotated.

"Man is a bridge and not an end." Kahliy nodded saying nothing in reply. Bianca continued. "What is love? What is creation? What is longing?" She paused and looked inquisitively at Kahliy to gauge his reaction. "What is a star? Thus asks the last man, and blinks."

Kahliy felt an urge, a longing for something that sent a tingling and warmth through his lower half.

Bianca pressed on with more of Nietzche's provocative quotations. "One has ones little pleasure for the day. And one has ones little pleasure for the night."

Kahliy's thoughts dwelled on tonight's pleasure, he felt a flush to his face that he hoped Bianca wouldn't notice. Bianca, four years his senior, of course could tell exactly what he was feeling. She then embellished her quotations with some thoughts of her own. "Tonight, I can be one's little pleasure, Kahliy." Kahliy began to imagine what that pleasure might be.

"Now a man – you are the rope over the abyss, Kahliy. You must make the dangerous crossing from animal to superman." Bianca paused and leaned in close to look into his eyes. He did not avert her piercing look.

"Kahliy, you are like the sprint of the lion." Said

Joann Mead

Bianca, paraphrasing Nietchze. "Your eyes sparkle like gold." She focused on the glimmering golden highlights in his green eyes.

As they walked back towards campus, Bianca brought him to a dark alcove that abutted a draped window belonging to a church rectory. Removing her jeans, she spread them out on the dried grass, pulling Kahliy's hand, urging him to lie upon them. Unzipping and exposing, tugging his jeans below his narrow hips, Bianca roamed through his loose fitting jeans, pawing and licking, her appetite voracious. Tonight, Bianca found not just "one's little pleasure of the night," but an extra helping of *Zabaglione*, a treat of the largest portion and proportion. Mounting her lion, she rode him like any hungry lioness in heat.

The private "tutorials" continued for a few months to come, finding any convenient time and place, the nooks and crannies, in a courtyard or amid the thickest trees and bushes, anywhere they could find before the weather got to cold. But not at Bianca's shared dormitory apartment, she insisted that other students not know.

Kahliy began to sneak Bianca into the apartment, either when Uncle went out or when he was asleep. But tonight Uncle caught them on the braided rug when they disturbed his dreams with sounds of clapping thunder and heaving sighs. He found an unbridled Bianca riding hard, galloping full throttle on her submissive stallion. When she saw Uncle watching, she leapt up and slipped on her clothes. She ran off in haste without saying as much as two words.

Uncle turned on the brightest of lights and sat down a now fully clothed Kahliy in a dining room chair. He lectured.

"Do not be controlled by your urges or emotions. No woman must ever control you. Use them for their sex, their hormones, and their excessive emotions to control them. Use their vulnerabilities to maintain power over them. Use that control wisely and they will do anything for you."

Kahliy nodded in agreement, what else could he say.

"Kahliy, you will be a leader, not a follower. Do you understand?"

"Yes, Uncle."

"From now on, your education and instruction begins."

After that night, Kahliy avoided Bianca. He would have other women, but from then on, he would be the one in control.

30 NELL'OMBRA

From now on Uncle included Kahliy during discussions between Uncle and his Roma mentor. The bearded Elder was an old world theorist whereas Uncle constructed his own odd philosophical mix incorporating the beliefs of his Roma mentor with the teachings of Nietzche. It was those beliefs he ingrained in Kahliy.

Uncle drilled Kahliy with aphorisms he considered "Truths". But, unfortunately, his truths were founded on a contradictory premise in the nihilistic fashion.

Uncle lectured him. "There is no truth inherent to life. Truth is a subjective creation applied to life to give it meaning. And if there is no meaning, then what?" Uncle asked.

"Then it must be destroyed if we are to become the supermen Nietzche wrote about." Kahliy answered.

Uncle also critiqued with Kahliy the modern age, the age of the "Moderns". "The West has rapidly lost its values, its decline has led to a creeping emptiness. You must feel nothing but fear and contempt for them. You must become hardened to resist this new age of decline. We must not lose the will to fight back!" Uncle was adamant. He perfected the skills and the art of indoctrination.

Kahliy listened hard, remembering the one most important piece of advice that Uncle gave him. "You must use the Modern's technology to turn it against them. Use any dangerous new tool." Uncle advised him. And Kahliy became determined to find the most dangerous tool in the new technology. And he would study science to find it.

Uncle preached. "Nietzsche declared war against an entire modern world. War must be waged against aristocratic values. They think themselves "good", so happy with their wealth, their strength, their power. They think of the poor as weak and disgusting."

"Yes, I can see that there is no empathy or compassion for the poor, Uncle." Kahliy often felt pity for those who had less than him.

"But you are missing the point, Kahliy. Remember neither the aristocrats *nor* the poor have any value. It is both that we must destroy."

Kahliy appeared confused at Uncle's statement.

"Listen to me, Kahliy. Humanity must be destroyed because existence has no meaning. Read this Kahliy." He shoved a text under his nose, pointing to a verse.

Kahliy read aloud. "Man is something that shall be overcome. What have you done to overcome him? But first you must overcome yourself."

"The world must descend into chaos, Kahliy." Uncle concluded. He gave a stack of reading on nihilist philosophy for Kahliy to absorb.

It was not the first time Kahliy had heard the term "nihilism". Uncle's students sprinkled it liberally in all their chatter, their discussions, their hushed debates.

But it was the first time Kahliy thought the word through, his study of languages enriching his understanding. From the Latin *nihil*, it means "nothing", but Kahliy took it a step further in meaning "not anything". He became more intrigued and romantically drawn towards nihilist and anarchist tendencies.

Kahily studied similar words and their derivations, like "annihilate", to bring to nothing, to destroy completely. These words were the seeds of accepting the creed of total annihilation. To Kahliy, it meant the destruction of those "Moderns" who felt they had value. His creed of annihilation became a passion that would lead to an ethos of subversion and anarchy.

Uncle and the Elder laid out their strategy for the coming apocalypse and Kahliy's role. He would not be just another foot soldier, he would be a leader.

Uncle demanded that Kahliy take up the calling. "What have you done to surpass man?"

He gave Kahliy his directive. "You are the Kahlil, the compass. You will lead others to follow your ways, to do as you command. The world must be purified by striking the head of the snake, the Moderns. You will be our navigator of the modern world. Your mission is to strike the final blow of the coming apocalypse."

"Will you pledge your allegiance to strike at the world of the Moderns?" Uncle asked Kahliy.

"Uncle, I will always be you servant, your slave, your soldier." Kahliy told Uncle and meant it.

"And as a servant, what do you pledge?" Uncle asked.

"As your servant. I will obey your orders." The young Kahliy served his masters well.

"And as a soldier, what do you pledge?"

"As your soldier, I will fight for you. I will kill for you." Kahliy meant what he said, he would do anything to serve them, to accomplish the objectives of Uncle and his mentor, the Elder.

"You truly are the chosen one." The bearded Elder proclaimed. "You are pre-ordained. But you must first develop the mental integrity. You must become hard, Kahliy, before you have the authority to lead. For now, you are a soldier."

~

How rooted Kahliy became. With his life of stealth and

secrecy, he could remain in the shadows. But Uncle was confident that Kahliy would one day bring down those who seek only to control, to own, to dominate, to suck up the world riches. Their just demise would be complete annihilation.

Kahliy thought perhaps "Nihil" would have been his better name.

But Kahliy was never a simple idealist, he was a pragmatist, looking towards science and practical applications. Always, what is the most logical way of getting to the end. The apocalyptic end. With the least amount of fire-power. Something subliminal. With his own students. He would someday carry out an audacious attack outside of the usual armamentarium of the common terrorists.

He would mimic Uncle, the way he preached to his students of the coming apocalypse, but he must acquire a way, a means, of getting to the ultimate goal.

As Uncle one day instructed Kahliy, "You can crack a black egg with a pinprick. You don't need a sledgehammer. No nuclear weapons, or bombs, or the massive fire power of armies. Just a small targeted wound that will fester and spread like a disease. Like the bubonic plague, the Black Death, or an exotic disease that can wipe out armies. And governments."

"I know Uncle. I know what I need. The tiniest of weapons. The germs. Microbes."

Kahliy knew it would be hard to achieve his ultimate goal, but one day he would find just the right tiny weapon to inflict that pinprick in the black egg.

And one day he would have his own students, his soldiers he would lead to carry out his plan.

31 ZITA

Ultimately, Kahliy received advanced degrees in both philosophy and microbiology. Philosophy grounded Kahliy. It gave him the explanations he needed to justify his ultimate goal, the reasons for his existence as Uncle's "soldier", and the language he needed to influence others. Microbiology, however, would give him the weapons of war, the microbes. They were the practical means of achieving his goals. The destruction of life would be facilitated by the study of life itself.

"You must understand what you want to destroy." Kahliy told himself. "And to destroy humanity you must first understand the basic ways it functions." He would instruct his followers that life is nothing more than the product of biological functions. It formed the basis of his teaching and defined the relationships he would have with his student conscripts.

Kahliy cultivated his group of dedicated disciples as he had seen Uncle do. Altogether there were nineteen students, all drawn to him for various reasons. But most were lured by a combination of Kahliy's charisma, his charm, his mystery, his ideology, and his sexuality.

When Kahliy enlisted new followers, he chose them

carefully. Most were loners, alienated by their peers, some by their own choice. Others were inherently unstable, suspicious of others and marginalized. None operated in cliques or social groups.

Kahliy chose his select students by testing them. Were they open to new ideas and ideologies? Kahliy's philosophy seminars, a general introductory course, drew this disparate lot. Most were interested in the great metaphysical questions: Why am I here? What shall I do with my life? What happens to me at death? Kahliy also selected students based on their belief in a god or other supreme being.

Kahliy would ask his seminar students. "Do you believe in a god, a supreme creator? Yes, no, or I don't know, must be your answer." Kahliy culled from this group those who answered, "yes" or "no". They would be too ridged in their beliefs.

He considered those who answered "I do not know" as good possibilities, perhaps the right subset for his purposes." Kahliy reasoned that they were the ones who were open and willing to explore. They were not committed to a definitive answer. They were flexible and could be forged into whatever Kahliy wanted. Willing to experiment, take on new ideas. This was the group he invited to his private sessions and further filtered by probing at their individual psyches. It was all part of his recruiting process.

In one such private meeting in his office on campus, he asked, "What is the truth of your existence?" Five students in their late teens and early twenties, three women and two men, pondered the question. Kahliy found this group particularly intriguing.

The first to speak up was the golden-haired Flavia. She answered his question with another question "It makes no sense to me. Why do I exist?" Somewhat outgoing, Flavia desired the attention of others.

Khaliy prompted her. "Are you saying that life makes

no sense?"

"Yes. Yes, it makes no sense at all." Flavia nodded, gesturing with waving hands.

"Then what about death?" Kahliy probed.

"Then death makes no sense." Flavia deduced. "It follows."

Gregor, a lanky blue-eyed German student, nodded his head in agreement. "Yes, neither life nor death make any sense."

Sabine, a coffee-colored French anomaly, mumbled something inaudible.

"Sabine, what have you to say?" Kahliy looked into her sunken hollow eyes. He thought her so thin she appeared malnourished.

"They are both absurd." Sabine mumbled louder. "There is no purpose."

Gregor wondered aloud. "Do life and death exist for any purpose?"

Sabine answered bluntly. "There is no purpose in life or death."

Khaliy probed. "But if neither exists for any purpose, then what is the truth of existence?"

"But it is an absurdity!" Sabine blurted. "How can there be any truth?" Her darkness pervaded the small room. Like drinking a double expresso, Sabine made him nervous.

"Yes, it is the horrible truth." Kahliy need say no more. The students nodded in agreement. All except for Zita, so small she looked like a child. Tight curly hair, pear-shaped bottom. Silent, she had not uttered a word. Nor did she make eye contact with anyone, always looking somewhere beyond, as if there was something she saw in the distance.

"Zita, please comment." Kahliy would not let her sit in silence.

"Sometimes, it is all very confusing." Zita looked at the floor, shaking her head as if she had nothing more to offer. Kahliy didn't push her any further.

Kahliy wrapped up the session with "We are *Nell'Ombra*."

"*Nell'Ombra!*" The students chanted. It was a salute to their ultimate goals.

Kahliy groomed his followers telling them to always stay under the radar, just as he had been taught he infused them with the philosophy he learned in his youth and at university. He taught them to stay in the shadow of darkness, "*Nell'Ombra*", just as he had done growing up from boy to manhood.

Zita lingered as the other students filed out of Kahliy's office.

Kahliy inspected her small stature, her plump bottom. He wondered if she would be a good soldier. Perhaps she was weak mentally. She was too introverted to tell from her closed persona.

"Perhaps you need to open up more, my Zita. Explore more with the group. I must know you better to be able to trust you. Would you like to talk more tonight?"

Zita nodded. "*Sí*". She peered into the distance.

"Please follow me, but not too close. I will walk to my car, but it is best if we are not seen together." Kahliy instructed her. He felt this was a good time to test the malleability of Zita to his will.

When Zita arrived at his mid-sized Fiat, Kahliy had left open the rear door. She climbed in. He then drove to a remote spot with thick overhanging trees and no streetlights. It was a moonless night.

Opening the back door, he climbed in next to Zita who had rolled herself into a ball. His hips pressed in against her head matted with thick brown curls.

Kahliy spoke softly, commanding her to talk. "Zita, you must answer my questions to truly belong to our special group. To accomplish our goals, I must be able to trust you. Obedience is required."

"I will obey." Zita answered to his demand.

"Zita, you must be my subordinate, my soldier."

"I am your willing obedient soldier." Zita complied.

"You must prove yourself." Kahliy insisted.

"I will do anything." On Zita's reply, Kahliy smiled and remembered the same words he used as a child. Thinking Zita just a child, her size, her mannerisms, her simple statements, Kahliy felt almost paternal. All his students were his obedient children.

Kahliy cupped his left hand behind her head, lifting it slightly. Zita knew what was required, it was not the first time she was asked to perform this for a man.

"I am *Nell'Ombra*. I will do anything in the dark." Zita promised, still wrapped up like a small bundle in her quilted jacket.

Kahliy stroked her face lightly, feeling her cheeks, her broad nose. Running his fingers against her lips he inserted his index finger into her mouth. Zita sucked it like a baby bottle.

Zita then rolled over on to her knees, her back arched like a cat, she hung her head above Kahliy's lap. As she unzipped his jeans, pushing his undergarments down, Kahliy lifted himself. Zita found what she was looking for, her hand pulling him erect, squeezing him like a toy, pawing, stroking. With open lips, she dragged her teeth, lightly, rhythmically, over him. With her tongue she licked, a swirling motion, repetitive, round and around, over and over. Kahliy, nearing a crescendo, gripped hold of Zita's tightly wound curls as she sucked his bottle until he exploded. She swallowed.

"I obey you, Kahliy." It was the first and only time she would address him by name.

Afterwards, Kahliy dropped Zita close to campus not far from her shared run-down apartment, one that was designated for low-income students. He felt the evening was successful in his campaign.

Driving home though, he could only think of Sabine, fantasizing that it had been Sabine's head buried in his lap. It was Sabine Kahliy obsessed about ever since he first noticed her in his philosophy course lectures. She stood out, so different than the others, her unusually tall thin columnar stature, and her very dark skin. Ethiopian extraction, he came to find out, but French by birth.

Sabine was tall like the Italian Cypress trees that juxtaposed the leaning tower of Pisa. Kahliy thought of her as a *Cupressus sempirvirens*, the ubiquitous evergreen cypress that dotted the Tuscan countryside. Like a cypress and its connection with Artemis, the goddess of magic, he thought of Sabine as a sorceress. And Ovid, the poet, connected the cypress to grief and mourning. The ancient Romans linked cypress trees to ancient funerary rites and the underworld. Certainly, Sabine had connections with all three.

He anticipated the next private group session, hoping to find stimulation from Sabine, thinking to himself, "I want the dark French roast with triple the caffeine."

When Sabine did not show up for their next evening discussion, he hoped she wouldn't stay away. Her thinness worried him. Was she too frail to be a good soldier? She seemed so fragile she might shatter. He would have to find out.

32 FLAVIA

Kahliy modeled his groups after what he learned from Uncle where he, the leader, educated the younger students. He molded, manipulated, disciplined and indoctrinated his students.

Disaffected in some way, some rose from poverty, Zita of Romany decent. Others came from families from whom they rebelled. All had European passports from Italy, France, Germany, The Netherlands, Spain. One lived in Vienna. Many had mixed ancestry but, most importantly, they had passports that would allow them to travel freely. None had drawn too much attention to themselves; they were not the student leaders of political movements. Like Kahliy, they kept their core beliefs private, buried deep within, except in discussions with their special groups.

Kahliy's conscripts varied but his message to them was consistent. One of his lessons that his groups found most liberating was his conception of life as the product of biological functions. At first they wondered how this concept could have any truth or relevance.

"Since life and death have no purpose, we can only find comfort in our bodily functions." Kahliy suggested.

"Bodily functions like digestion? Do you mean eating?"

Flavia, robust and full-bodied, hid her curves under baggy sweatpants and oversized-tee shirts. Flavia loved Italian bread with cheese and the fresh fruits of Tuscany.

The gangling Gregor added. "And functions like excretion? It would only follow that other functions give comfort."

"Yes, even a good shit!" Kahliy exclaimed to jolt them, to awaken their understanding. "The satisfaction of our digestion and excretion give comfort to us."

"And breathing, deeply, in and out? Another bodily function." Flavia suggestively smiled at Gregor.

"Yes, breathing gives comfort." Gregor answered, not smiling back. He saved his smiles for René.

"Or sexual pleasures give comfort." Kahliy paused for effect. "We can pleasure ourselves. Pleasure others. Or comfort one another." Kahliy gave them what they wanted to hear.

Gregor gave a knowing look to René, the Frenchman, as Kahliy lectured on.

"Our bodies are merely products of biological events." Kahliy then reduced life to the activity of its cells.

"But we can comfort one another in the meantime." Flavia suggested with her eyes fixed on Kahliy.

Kahliy, a few years older than his students, had the advantage of experience. He could smell the hormonal secretions and juices flowing in his small office. His handsomely chiseled face, his clear green eyes and lithe body did not go unnoticed by his pupils. Not René, the Frenchman from Paris, nor Flavia from Pisa, the most reckless and sexually charged of the group.

"Flavia, if you were the last person on earth, you would have only the comfort of yourself." Kahliy said it for all to consider.

"But I am not." Flavia wasn't sure if he meant it to insult her.

Flavia looked over at Gregor but he was, as usual, stealing glances with René.

"René, your name means reborn. If you could be reborn again, would you want something different?" Kahliy probed his leanings.

"Something different? But how could different be anything truly different when it is 'nothing'?"

"Yes, a conundrum. And there is no difference in life or death." The room became silent as they reflected. Kahliy looked around and refocused on Flavia.

"Your name, Flavia, means 'bright light'. You will bring sunlight before the darkness. To truly free yourself, you must subordinate yourself." Kahliy instructed.

Flavia nodded "Yes, I must." She thought it a cue that she should act upon. Flavia was on a mission to comfort others before she would sacrifice herself.

~

Flavia returned to Kahliy's office not long after the group had left. Waiting in the shadows of the hallway, Kahliy found her when he opened the door to leave for home. Her golden hair glowed softly like a halo in the dim lighting. He gestured for her to come into his office.

"I will one day find comfort in my death, but I am ready to subordinate to truly free myself. I will follow your directives." She parted her lips and ran her tongue along the rim of her mouth.

Flavia did not need to be any more obvious. She made no attempt at being shy. Walking across the room where bodies had just littered the worn circular woven rug, she turned on a floor lamp that directed a beam over Kahliy's desk. She then reached into her pocket and placed a standard-sized condom sheath under the beam of light.

"I will bring sunlight before the darkness. Comfort me, Kahliy, my biological urges overwhelm me, but we mustn't bring new life into this nothingness."

"I can comfort you, Flavia, but you must prove you can be trusted. Promise me you do not want the fantasy of love." Kahliy warned her.

"Sex is only a bodily function, Kahliy." She said as she

untied her sweatpants, dropping them to the floor to reveal a thick mound of strawberry blonde hair and broad hips that curved to a thick waist. Leaning up against the desk, with both hands she pulled her tee-shirt over her golden locks. She wore no bra to hold the hanging breasts that Kahliy had noticed on more than one occasion. Flavia's face was freckled, pale and ordinary, her features uninteresting, but Kahliy could see that her entire body was creamy white and flecked with the smallest brown spots. Kahliy thought it likely that she was of Northern Italian decent.

At first Flavia was confused as Kahliy pulled his wallet from his jeans. He removed a small packet and laid it next to the condom she brought with her. "You will be getting more than what you anticipated, Flavia." Flavia picked it up and smiled as she read the XL label. She sat upright on the edge of the desk, her legs slightly spread.

"I can take what you give me." Flavia assured him, but Kahliy took it as a challenge. "Make me ready, make my juices flow." She demanded.

Kahliy knew she must be disciplined, he needed to control women with sex. "Reckless animals need to be tamed." Kahliy warned as he grasped a firm hold on both of her breasts, squeezing, nibbling and biting as Flavia gasped and stiffened with pain. She knew Kahliy must tame her, to make her ready and pain seemed to be part of the lesson. But she had come for sexual comfort and pleasure.

"Massage me, Kahliy." She requested. "Please be more gentle." She implored, she found his biting painful and too intense.

Kahliy shifted his focus to her strawberry colored mound, pulling a strand of hair to give a needle-like jolt before massaging her inner thighs with his thumbs. Flavia felt it a stimulating reprieve from the pain. Flavia was learning who was in charge in this encounter. She moistened as Kahliy penetrated her with his middle finger before inserting two more deep within. "This will prepare you for what is to come, you need to follow my lead." Stirring her like a pot of tomato sauce, she simmered slowly until he considered her ready.

"Do not be in a hurry, Kahliy." Flavia begged.

"I will prepare you to truly free you from yourself. Self-emancipation is necessary. Subordination begins with the human flesh. Prepare yourself for death. Subordinate as a soldier who sleeps until awakened. You must not bring life, only death."

Kahliy rolled his sheath over his baton-like club. "You are being punished for succumbing to your desires, Flavia." Grabbing her round fleshy hips with his strong hands, he pushed himself deep into her dampened abyss.

"I will split you in two." He threatened. Pulling her tight against him, Kahliy turned and slammed her up against the adjacent wall where he continued to punish her as she panted with shallow breaths. As she groaned, her eyes tearing, Kahliy heaved and thrust. Unrelenting.

"You must submit to pain, a biological function. The flesh is nothing and pain is only a function of the flesh." As he pounded he lectured. "This is part of the discipline you need to become a soldier. There is no love in sex. Remember this Flavia, your body is a vehicle for the ultimate destruction of the West."

Flavia, her body thrashed, abraded and raw, had learned Kahliy's lesson from his display of discipline. Kahliy, not Flavia, would be in control through sex. She would do what he said or she would know the pain of his discipline.

33 SABINE

The following week, Kahliy commended his students.
"You are good soldiers. You must be good sleepers. When
the time comes, you must spring into action."

He ordered them. "As soldiers you will someday
sacrifice yourself to eliminate the values of emptiness, to
destroy the western systems that perpetuate them and the
machinations that prop them up."

He reminded then. "Complete annihilation, we are
nihilists at our center. You must condemn even your own
existence. We are dedicated to the absolute destruction of
the superpower. Death to the superman!"

The students stared in silent, unified determination.
Even Zita made direct eye contact as Kahliy, a sophist like
the specialized teachers of ancient Greece, applied the
tools of rhetoric to persuade them. To motivate them. He
infused them with his beliefs. His rage was against the
prosperity of the West, especially America. He hated the
way Americans believed that their country had a perfect
purpose defined by God. They, the Americans, spawned
capitalism expecting the rest of the world to emulate their
soulless modernity.

In reality it was Kahliy's own customized nihilist brand

that dictated his desire for power and domination. He manipulated his followers individually as he had with Zita and Flavia so that they would become the tools to carry out the strategy, in the name of his boyhood mentors Uncle and the bearded Roma Elder. It was they who set up the financial networks to carry out the grand plan. And they would supply the funds for mobilizing the "sleepers" to fully execute the attack on America.

"The strategies, my soldiers, for our mission are not the conventional ways of warfare. We will not carry traditional weapons. Our strategy does not recognize borders. You are pre-ordained. We have the moral authority. We are obligated to scare the shit out of them!"

The student's laughed at Kahliy's Italian vernacular. Kahliy went on. "We will hit them with their greatest fears. Not MERS or the Ebola promise of a plague, but an outbreak beyond anyone's control!" Kahliy emoted his most passionate appeal to the group.

He asked his student to contemplate mass death. He spoke with academic and philosophical precision. "You must accept the premise." He convinced them without any doubts.

"We will go together to unleash an unstoppable plague that will bring the USA and other Moderns to their knees."

"I can offer you a good time, with some beer or wine, or I can offer you danger and death."

Kahliy pointed at Sabine. Which do you chose?!"

"I choose danger and death!" Sabine exuded with passion.

Kahliy took a step back. "But we are not open warriors, we are stealth operatives, remember what I tell you!"

The stillness in the room seemed supernatural.

"There will not be an orgy of bloodshed – that is not our *modus operandi*." Kahliy had them mesmerized.

"You can crack a black egg with a pinprick. You do not need a sledgehammer." He paused. "Think about this until the next time we meet."

They chanted in unison. "*Nell'Ombra.*"

On her way out, Sabine handed Kahliy a note. "I am a black egg. Please kill me with your sword." Kahliy read it quickly, it seemed like an auspicious promise in a Chinese fortune cookie. He looked up at Sabine with a knowing gaze. He understood what she wanted, it was time to reinforce her obedience. He nodded yes. Her cell phone number followed the message.

~

It was a late on a summer night, it had been unseasonably hot that day but the evening had cooled to comfortable. Sabine wore a light cotton tunic that cascaded to her ankles. Long bell sleeves hid her skeletal arms, an understated print of brown on beige, simple but she portrayed the royal elegance of a tall cypress.

They drove awhile into the forests of the night before they came to a small clearing where Kahliy parked his Fiat off the road. Isolated, it was not that far from the Romany camp that Kahliy visited as a boy. He had been there many times with Uncle to visit the bearded Elder, listening to them until late into the evenings.

He brought Sabine into the thick of the mixed woodlands, under the shadow of trees.

"You can crack a black egg with a pinprick. But I will kill you with my sword, Sabine."

They went farther into the woods against a large chestnut tree, *Castanea sativa*, where he propped her thin body. He encircled her upper arms with the palms of his hands, pinning her against the tree as he kissed her deeply with his tongue, something he never did with the others, and there were many, but he wanted a taste of her espresso.

Unlike Flavia she did not need the pain of his discipline to bend to his will. Kahliy took his time with Sabine, gently massaging her tiny peaked hills, she had no fleshy breasts. He hiked her dress up, gathering the cotton fabric up around her neck, exposing her silhouette in the filtered moonlight and her lack of underwear. He licked and nibbled while exploring her inner thighs with his hand. Unlike the ripe fruit offering of Flavia, she wasn't yet damp.

Her legs were so thin that her thighs did not touch, but more muscular than he had imagined. Carefully, inserting his middle finger he felt a pulsating rhythm inside her, her inner muscles rippled as she writhed with desire. She contracted, tightened and relaxed in waves, controlling muscles that did not exist in any women he had been with. Kahliy dipped two fingers into her narrow shaft, and as if testing a borehole for a well, she began to produce. Pausing, she pulled her dress over her head. Kahliy draped a blanket over her shoulders to protect her spine from the thick bark of the chestnut.

"Kill me! Kill me with your sword!" Sabine pleaded. Taller than Kahliy, she did not need lifting. Her stilt-like legs allowed him to push in perfectly aligned. Her muscles contracting, massaging Kahliy inch by inch, he pushed and thrust, higher, deeper, until penetrating her up the hilt of his sword. Cutting, stabbing, piercing, Kahliy killed Sabine until she was breathless, limp in his arms. He carried her back to his car before setting her blanketed body in the front seat of his car.

"You have accepted death, Sabine."

"I will die for you, Kahliy."

"Not for me. Remember, I am nothing. I can only comfort."

~

Later sated and alone, Kahliy cogitated, reiterated and churned over his strategic rationale that you can crack a black egg with a pinprick. You do not need a sledgehammer. No nuclear weapons, or bombs or the massive fire-power of armies. Just a small targeted wound that will fester and spread like ...a disease? Like the bubonic plague, the Black Death or a lethal flu that can wipe out armies, and governments, and eliminate the avarice and greed of capital and those who control it.

"I know what I need." He pragmatically thought, I can use the tiniest of weapons. The microbes. Kahliy knew it would not be easy to achieve his ultimate objective, but one day soon he would find the deadliest microbe of all and he would find the right opportunity to inflict the pinprick.

34 MOONLIGHT

Kahliy, meeting with his students for the last time, echoed his emotional final appeal. "I offer you a good time or I offer you death. Which do you chose?"

"We chose death!" They ejaculated in unison.

"Have you prepared yourself for death?"

Some proclaimed, "I am prepared!" Others, "I am ready!" They cheered their own near obliteration.

"I will return with newly created weapons, ones to poison America, destroy their crops, their cattle, their chicken, their eggs, and most important, the people. We will attack the "Moderns". He seemed more hateful and derisive than ever. "We will attack their human biologic functions. But we will use pinpricks."

"We will carry no ancient weapons!" Gregor pronounced.

"We don't need bullets or bombs!" Sabine cheered. "No bullets, no bombs!" They all chimed in as expected.

"Our weapons are designed by the very people we will bring down. Their designer bioweapons that not even *they* will be able to stop. Kahliy proclaimed.

"I will seek the most virulent, infectious disease with the highest rate of death. They will have no cure. No vaccines to protect themselves. And no time to make them. We will catch them unprepared. My mission now is to find the mortal microbe that you, my disciples, will deliver. Each of you will be silent human bombs."

A chilling silence settled over the room as the students contemplated their mission.

"What do you mean, please tell us more?" René asked.

"You will become 'super-spreaders'." It was the first time Kahliy used that term.

Flavia interrupted. "I think I've heard those words before. Ebola in Africa."

"Yes, but Ebola is not very contagious. You nineteen will carry a newly created flu that causes the plague of the millennium. "Why nineteen? Remember those fearless ones who made the terror of 9/11. The nineteen that produced death and fear. You will each fly to America next summer. At the end of spring semester, some of you will remain here in Pisa and others will return to your home countries. I will contact each of you. I will visit you, give you air tickets and weapons."

"We will wait *Nell'Ombra*." Zita added. Out of character, she seldom uttered a word.

"Yes, in the shadows. But remember to keep your passports current. For now, you will sleep. And when you are called upon, you will spring into action." Kahliy instructed. "For now, sleep in the shadows."

"We will sleep." A few mumbled.

"When I awaken you, you will travel to American cities, and keep traveling on trains, on buses, on the metros of big cities, like New York. When you are too ill to travel, visit the hospitals, sit in the emergency rooms, find the smallest, most confined of spaces. By sneezing and coughing, you will contaminate your surroundings with your phlegm. Ride in elevators; choke up what is deep in your lungs, the microbe laden mucous droplets will infect all within reach."

Gregor added. "We will infect the doctors, the nurses

and the other sick patients. We will spread the comfort that comes with death."

"Super-spreaders!" Sabine exclaimed then whispered aloud with passion. "We will kill them with our sword."

Sabine's passion stirred Kahliy's sexual desire, he reasoned it gave her strength for her task. He imagined he would have her one last time, in France, when he visited each of them next summer.

"You will each receive a message from me, instructing you where we will meet." Kahliy thought he must assure them that their preparation was not for nothing. He caught himself and reverberated his mantra. "Life is nothing. Death is nothing. We are in the shadow of darkness. *Nell'Ombra!*" He saluted with a hand fist of solidarity. He felt a little acting on his part would create the right tone of solidarity and purpose.

They rose to their feet and chanted for one last time. *"Nell'Ombra!"* Good soldiers that they were they marched in silence out the office door.

Kahliy thought about his tasks ahead in Hong Kong. He read about the lab created flus that were capable of spreading and easily transmitted between people. Variations of the Bird Flu with extremely high mortality rates. He had the money and the backing of Uncle and his cohorts. He could buy what he needed to carry out the plan - a super-hyper-lethal flu.

As Kahliy turned to switch off his floor lamp, he noticed that the keys to his Fiat were not on his wooden desk where he left them. Perhaps I left them in my car? He thought, as he grabbed his light jacket that hung behind his office door.

In the parking lot, he found his car unlocked, his keys in the ignition, and a small person curled up in the back seat. Without saying a word, he drove to a familiar location where there were no streetlights. When he parked his Fiat and turned off the engine, he heard a faint voice. *"Nell'Ombra."*

Kahliy reached into his glove compartment where he kept a stash of condoms and lubricant gels. He walked around the car and as he opened the rear door, the moon cast a glow, a pale blue-grey light shined on a round cleaved mound. Zita offered the darkness within her but instead, this time it was he who used his tongue to bring her to a climax. He felt that was what she wanted. Kahliy thought that there is always a first time for a student to seek him out. He wondered what it meant.

~

The following week, Kahliy flew from Pisa to Hong Kong. Three flights and twenty hours later he arrived. His university courses were carefully chosen. His travel, visa and passports, arranged and financed by Uncle's network.

In Hong Kong, he would learn more about the newest strains of bird flu, ones that had been manipulated to carry the most lethal, virulent and infectious genes known to man. With so much control over DNA, scientists could create designer biological superbugs by using a variety of different scientific methods. The DNA could be sliced and diced and edited with techniques easily mastered by novices. With the new DNA editing technology called CRISPR, even the do-it-yourself DIY labs had the capability to create hideous monsters of nature. Editing microbes had now become child's play.

Kahliy hoped to meet other science researchers in Hong Kong who would have similar interests. And maybe some would have the skills and resources to create designer flu strains. If not, they would at least have connections to scientists who could. Kahliy knew he had access to large pots of money to pay handsomely for their services.

Little did Kahliy know that in Hong Kong he would hit the honeypot, Mei Wong.

~

When Kahliy first arrived in Hong Kong, he planned to find criminals who would sell him bioweapons on the "dark market". The black market trade of conventional weapons now included nuclear devices and bioweapons. Rogue terrorist nations advertised on the dark web for mercenary scientists, especially microbiologists, who knew the technology to brew up special strains in basement labs.

But women were Kahliy's forte, easiest to manipulate using sex and his useful tool. A certain type of woman, one easy to lure, one drawn to the entrapments of extravagant lifestyles, one who wanted to escape, one who wanted riches and money. And his sexual prowess. He had plenty to offer.

That semester in Hong Kong was more fruitful than anything he could possibly imagine. It was in his Genomics 101 course that Kahliy first met Mei Wong and the rest became history.

Only Mei Wong possessed both the bioweapon and the ingenious way of delivering a fatal blow. It was a new type of tactic never used before, a destructive hit beyond recovery incomparable to any traditional military attack. It threatened America's very existence.

The new tactic redefined "shock and awe" as a subtle insidious surprise. Unsurpassed by any explosion, nuclear or IED, the stealth invader would be the ultimate weapon of mass annihilation. And deceptively hidden, it defied detection.

~

35 EUROPEAN TRAIN JOURNEY

Khaliy left the Bella Hotel in Copenhagen with his buried treasure: His metal cylinder spike filled with nineteen Tiger flu laden pills enclosed in an innocuous looking wooden chopstick.

Kahliy's multiple identities and array of foreign passports stumped even the most skilled agents. He eluded border controls with the ease of a pro. The lucrative trade in stolen or forged passports made it easy for Kahliy. Average in height, roughly 5'10", brown hair, green eyes, more handsome than most, he kept his appearance as generic as possible. Westernized, academic, he could easily pass as an engineer or a computer geek or a scientist. But his nihilist philosophy and convictions ran deep and true.

Kahliy emulated the life of those he wished to destroy and in turn he would banish the "moderns" to the bowels of the earth. As he so poignantly put, "Back to the shithole from where they arose". When the time would come for the ultimate, audacious attack, Kahliy knew he would no longer need Mei. In his mind, he knew she would become collateral damage. Damaged goods as she was.

From Copenhagen, Kahliy would embark on his train journey. His first stop would be Hamburg, Germany. His final resting place, the island of the lily, the Isola del Giglio, where he would savor the moment the outbreak begins, watching it pepper across America as disease clusters sprouted, growing exponentially out of control, overwhelming the hospitals and healthcare system.

There would be no quick way of ramping up production of new flu vaccines. Existing stockpiles would no longer be effective against the genetically altered Tiger Flu strain. And big biopharma would lock down and "shelter-in-place". Only the wealthy on their private islands might stand a chance of survival. But only if they had basement labs with scientists to make up small vaccine batches that targeted the Tiger flu." But, for the most part, their efforts would be too little, too late.

Kahliy told Mei before leaving Copenhagen, they would meet again on a beautiful Italian island. "I will let you know which island, just decipher my clue on Twitter." He told her that she would know. "Just read my tweets. It will be my first and only posting under the hashtag #tigerblake19. "Remember Mei, translate the message. It will be easy for you."

He constructed the tweet in his mind.

@YOYOYSpiko: Meet me on 8/16. Take the ferry, the sea lily. I will wait at the harbor. #tigerblake19

Kahliy knew it would be easy for Mei to translate the words Sea Lily into Italian. It was easy enough to figure out the translation. Take the ferry, the Mare Giglio. I will wait on the dock at the harbor.

Mei liked clues and mysteries and playing games of secret messages. She loved to be intrigued, excited, it stimulated her intellectually and sexually. In Copenhagen, while Kahliy took her "around the world" to the edge of erotic extremes, Mei complained of the scent from the white and pink Stargazer lilies. "Overpowering." She said. "They smell like rotting flesh."

Kahliy's lilies were a clue to help her uncover his cryptic tweets. "Remember these flowers, Mei." He told her when we were last together.

"How could I possibly forget them? They smell of death." She could never forget the Stargazer lilies pungent sickly sweet odor. She wondered if Kahliy had left her a message of what might become of her. She didn't trust him any more than he trusted her. But Mei put the thought of death to rest.

On the Isola del Giglio, the spiny white sea lilies wafted a delicate sweetness, very different from the *Lilium* specie that Mei's delicate senses found so offensive. Kahliy picked a small fragrant bouquet from the sandy beach ready for their last dalliance on the Island.

On the island, Mei would collect her final payment, the bank account, or so Kahliy promised her. He told her they would watch together as the infection spread and the fear and chaos ensued. Together they would realize the success of their grand experiment. Kahliy thought; if not a fatal blow for America it would at least bring them down, reduce them to third world status. They would take a devastating hit to their health, their economy, to their political system and their world domination. Kahliy savored the thought.

Kahliy's biggest weakness was the trappings of sex, especially with Mei. He justified his lustful interludes as a means to annihilate the west. Manipulating women provided him with the vital tools he needed. My caged tigers and the soldiers. You can control with violence, or you can control with sex. Kahliy controlled with both.

Mei understood Kahliy's vulnerabilities and to what extremes he would go to. Manipulating microbes may have been Mei's skill but she had a talented gift when it came to manipulating men; the same gift Kahliy had in manipulating his students.

~

Today, preparing for his train journey it was Kahliy

who manipulated each pastille with his small tweezers, placing them into their protective bags. So small, he handles them with micro-tweezers; thin, delicate, precision tools that will not dent or harm the tinniest gnat or fragile lepidopteran. Kahliy very carefully, gently slips the little pills into miniscule zip-lock bags. Nineteen pastilles the size of sunflower seeds, hard coated, they are flavorless, odorless, the color of cream. Buried within, the DNA nanobots cradle the virus, the Tiger flu, engineered, created to be the most lethal, contagious pathogen known to man. Kahliy knew he held in his hands the potential to destroy humanity.

Focusing on his task until all nineteen packets were meticulously lined up in his plastic container, Kahliy then sat back and mused. He imagined a chaotic scramble as US air travel, yet again would be shut down as it had been on that fated September day. He admired their goal and audacious plan but he was contemptuous of the medieval philosophy that drove jihadists. There is no god so how could Allah approve what they did? To him it was childish as they strove for the non-existent paradise and all those women. The metaphysics were laughable.

The Tiger Flu would maim and devour, spreading exponentially. *Nell'Ombra* would overpower and devastate. Kahliy reveled at the thought. Controlling life itself was his sole prerogative. The time had finally come for his ultimate, most audacious attack. He would administer a mortal blow to the heart of America, deliver the fatal strike - a destructive hit beyond recovery. And in the end, Mei would be expendable having served her purpose. He could just as easily kill her as fuck her. He would do both again in due time.

But now, his rail journey was imminent. Kahliy embarked the next morning.

Sleeper cells awaken. This is your time.

From Copenhagen, Kahliy hopped a ferry then boarded an early morning train to Hamburg, Germany.

Four and a half hours later he met up with Gregor, who waited at the station. Together, they purchased flights to New York City. All the flight reservations he made on his train journey were timed to arrive at approximately the same time. The air ticket was a round trip so as not to arouse suspicion.

Kahliy trusted Gregor, he could handle anything given to him. In Manhattan he could frequent the gay bars, handsome enough he would make plenty of acquaintances, spread the flu on the Metro, and loiter in the ER of major hospitals. A pocket full of dollars would sustain him for his excursion on a grand tour of America's most densely populated city. Gregor loved Kahliy, as did most of his students. A hug at the station, he promised to fulfill the mission of *Nell'Ombra*.

As he departed, Kahliy told Gregor. "You will find your last pleasure in the orgy of destruction."

It was a long journey to Amsterdam, after six hours on the train, dozing on and off. Arriving late at night, Kahliy slept in a cheap hotel near the central station. There was no time to explore the thrills that Amsterdam had to offer.

The next morning Kahliy bought airlines tickets for two students, cash transactions from back street agents. He thought it best to hide the source of the money. More cash to his students, a pocket full of dollars, enough to sustain them for a couple of weeks, so long as they stayed in budget hotels. And of course each had their packets with a Tiger pastille. One student flying to Boston, the other to Chicago, all flights were synchronized within a sixteen hour window. All soldiers must arrive at their destinations within a tightly constructed time frame and strike as simultaneously as the vagaries of travel made possible.

From Amsterdam to Brussels in just over two hours, Kahliy met up with two more students, both women he fucked, but neither left him with any lasting desire. Again he killed two birds with one stone, a metaphor he now understood, Mei had explained the English meaning to him. Kahliy thought how apropos, since these two birds would fly to two different destinations carrying the Tiger stain of the bird flu. He instructed the women to have sex with as many men as possible, as soon as possible. They must act quickly using their art of seduction. They had only a short time before the symptoms would spring forth, maybe four or five days at most.

"Kill the birds that flock together." He joked and wished them their "last pleasure in the orgy of destruction." The phrase seemed to comfort the two young women.

Just three hours to Paris, and three more students to visit. The first, René, he met late afternoon, and arranged his air travel to Los Angeles. They drank wine, dined on steak and frites, a small extravagance. Another cheap hotel near the Gare du Nord, one star, where René insisted on sucking Kahliy dry. Kahliy did not deny him his final wish.

The next morning, he met up with two more students in the southern part of Paris. More air tickets purchased, pills given in packets, cash, encouragement, and a review of the grand plan. Chanting *"Nell'Ombra!"* as they parted, they were committed nihilists to the core.

On to Bordeaux from the Gare du Sud, a short stop, it was becoming routine. Different place, different train station, and one more soldier prepared for the mission of *Nell'Ombra!*

Kahliy was weary, the next trek took forever. He arrived in Barcelona, where two young men awaited. These two seemed too close. Kahliy wondered if one would try to convince the other to opt out. Diego would fly to the East coast, Arturo to the West. One was Basque, the other Catalan, they shared their separatist leanings. In the end, he felt reassured that they remained truly committed soldiers. Their fight to the death. *Morte* to America. They pledged their allegiance to *Nell'Ombra.*

Such a long distance to Marseille, but Sabine would

await him. He purchased her tickets to Chicago. From there she would travel onward through the Midwest by bus where she could stare out the dark windows and contemplate death.

Kahliy wanted to indulge himself just one last time, he could not resist. A two star hotel, cash only, she did not spend the night, but the tall Cyprus, *Cupressus sempirviren*, wrapped her long branches tightly around Kahliy as she begged to die. "Kill me! Kill me!"

Kahliy stabbed, plunging deep with his sword. "I will kill you before you die, Sabine." Such were the sweet nothings he whispered in her ear.

The next morning, Kahliy arrived in Nice before lunchtime. A quick stop at the train station, his soldier pre-arranged his travel plans, making it the shortest stop on Kahliy's journey. Kahliy thanked him for his efficiency, gave him his pill packet, and wished him comfort in death. It all seemed like an expedient business transaction.

Kahliy boarded for another long haul to Milan, arriving at dusk. He'd grown so accustomed to the clangs, the clinks, the clunks and the sameness of the stations. When he arrived, he found the weather unseasonably hot. He read the graffiti that filled the walls adjacent to Milan's central station.

The next morning, Kahliy met with two students, one at a time, to prepare, make reservations, deliver pills, instructions, logistics. Reiteration *ad nauseum* but he forced himself to project passion and fervor.

"You will find your last pleasure in the orgy of destruction." He stayed on script.

Kahliy hated Milan, the contrasting inequality, the aura of high fashion juxtaposed with the perils of poverty. Where the fashion lords of Dolce and Gabbana evaded taxes on their billion euros until strong-armed with the threat of prison. The company disgusted him.

Kahliy took a side trip that afternoon to the financial district to see the marble sculpture "The Finger", a hand with the middle finger extended, on front of the stock exchange, a gesture pointing outward from the 1% to the 99%. Kahliy gestured in kind with his long middle finger pointing outward, directed against the stock exchange, saying aloud to only himself, "You too will be fucked. You will succumb to the global disruption. Your wealth will disappear. Evaporate into the air." He knew he controlled their future with his bioweapon; it would bring the world's financial system to its knees.

36 SAINT ZITA

Once in Pisa, where four students remained, Kahliy had the luxury of time. But the time was short for making their travel reservations. Over the next two days, Kahliy planned the logistics, travel, cash for each remaining student, and he delivered, most importantly, the four final mini-zip-lock baggies with their precious Tiger Flu pastilles.

In just about six weeks time, the students would fly to their designated cities. It was critical that they remain focused, but he worried most about Zita. He had yet to make eye contact with her, nor penetrate her in the conventional way. He never saw her body unclothed, their sex was anonymous and always in the dark. She was truly *Nell'Ombra* in every sense of the word. He must force her into the light. Stare into her eyes to see what she was truly thinking. And he wanted to see what she hid from him. Her shoulders, her breasts, her small waist that lead to those oversized mounds she displayed only in the moonlight. He wanted to explore the folds and the depth of her womanly abyss.

"Come to my office tonight Zita. We must talk about the imminent attack. You are my sacred warrior mistress, sacrificing all that you have for nothing in return." Kahliy's selfishly desired to control her completely, to take what she had left to offer. It would be a final indulgent act of control.

Zita complied. She entered the door of his office and fell to her knees as if in prayer. She would not look up, only straight ahead. As Kahliy came up close, she reached out her hand to unzip his jeans. But Kahliy wrapped his fingers tightly around her wrist. Gripping firmly he lifted her upright to her feet. Grabbing hold of her other wrist, he pulled both arms towards the ceiling. Zita was suspended, hanging from his tight grip. Still, she did not making eye contact, a look of sheer panic erupted on her face.

"Is that fear I see, Zita? Are you not a brave warrior?" Kahliy sadistically taunted her.

Choking back tears, Zita closed her eyes tight, but her face was stained with salty drippings.

"I am you soldier." Zita mumbled.

"Soldiers do not cry, they can take the discipline. Show me your strength and commitment." Kahliy admonished. He lowered her and released her wrists.

"Take off your clothes, Zita."

Zita stood still in silence as if she had not heard.

"Do as your commander tells you. Now, Zita!" Kahliy wanted total submission.

"But please, *Nell'Ombra*." Zita softly pleaded.

"You must live in the bright light before you see the darkness. To prepare yourself for death, Zita, you must give yourself completely." Kahliy insisted but still Zita was reluctant. Kahliy unbuttoned her plain black shirt, exposing her full breasts. Taking her flesh in his hands, his mouth followed, he thought of a mother pig suckling her young. Zita remained upright, stiff, she did not react with pleasure.

"What is wrong with you, Zita? We must comfort each other before the end." Kahliy roughly pulled down her baggy summer trousers, the elastic band made it easy.

Lifting her by the waist, he sat her on the desk where others had willingly offered themselves before. Kahliy removed her sandals and dropped her bundled clothing. She sat naked, still looking down, avoiding his penetrating eyes. Kahliy disrobed, he was ready, the stripping ritual excited him.

"I command you to look at me. Look me in the eyes. Prove that you can follow orders." Kahliy pulled her tightly against him. Her body was rigid despite its deep curves. Kahliy reached for a lubricant he kept in his desk drawer, conveniently placed for occasions such as this. There was no need for condoms, Zita would be dying within weeks. Slathering a handful of jelly over himself, Zita did not offer to help.

"Are you willing to accept your own death, Zita? Look at me when you answer." He outstretched her arms, pinning her to his desk in a crucifixion pose.

Zita's brown eyes stared vacantly into his limpid green eyes, as if she were gazing at a distant sea. "I am already dead." Even Kahliy could see she had no desire to live.

She faintly mumbled and sighed in resignation, "I am nothing."

Kahliy pushed deep into her nothingness. Plunged as if swimming in a dark pool of water where you could not see the bottom. She felt so wet yet she took no apparent joy. Unresponsive as if asleep or numb to sensation.

When Kahliy finished what he had started, he stepped back, surprised to see Zita's thighs streaked with blood.

"I was saving myself for death." Zita only stated, no emotion, just a fact.

As Zita dressed, she took the small zip lock bag from her pocket and slipped it into the desk drawer that was left slightly open. Kahliy didn't notice as he wiped the desk top with paper towels, trying to remove the red tinted liquid before it stained into the wood grain.

~

The next morning Zita's body was found unresponsive.

She died shortly after being brought to hospital. An apparent suicide, Kahliy was told.

"Now there will only be eighteen." Kahliy said under his breath. In his desk drawer he found the pastille that might have been a clue to what was about to happen. Did he feel any guilt, no remorse? Or was it only his disappointment in having a soldier die prematurely, before she could accomplish her mission?

That day, he could not get his mind off Zita. How her name meant "young girl" in Tuscan. Or "little girl", a "child" as in Greek. How Zita, the 13th century Saint of Servants, served others, just as Zita served Kahliy.

He began to sob. "She was just a child. A virgin." he cried aloud. To muffle his wails, he buried his head in a pillow. Perhaps he *was* mourning her death. It had been such a long time since he shed any tears, he couldn't remember the last time.

Kahliy was too close to his goal to let an errant emotion take hold of him. His European journey had finally come to an end. With his potent pills delivered to his student soldiers, prepared for their role of human time bombs, he would soon travel south from Pisa. But first Kahliy posted his final tweet to Mei.

@YOYOYSpiko: Meet me on 8/16. Take the ferry, the sea lily. I will wait at the harbor. #tigerblake19

~

Kahliy booked an on-line room in an *albergo*, the hotel on the Isola del Giglio where he stayed with Nonno so many years ago. Many tourists visited the island in the summertime, he would be just another visitor on holiday. His check-in date at the *albergo* was Monday, August 15th.

Kahliy warned himself, "No pride, no arrogance over the power one wields." He remembered the cruise ship disaster near the Isola del Giglio, caused by the hubris and poor judgment of the arrogant *capitano*.

He reminded himself. "I am not a *capitano*, but a soldier. A David who will bring down Goliath."

37 BACK IN RHODE ISLAND

Nearly 3500 miles away in Rhode Island, Jo's mind chattered endlessly. She couldn't put the twitter-twaddle to rest. All those clues, the tidbits gathered at the Bella hotel, The Barking Dog Bar. At first they didn't seem to mean much. But on reflection, the tweeted clues and insightful stories on Skype painted a colorful picture, albeit Turneresque, still fuzzy but with patches of clarity. There were still too many details to add to the canvas.

To Jo, the human stories were of tragedy and loss. There was the obvious affection that Mel and Robert felt for their colleague, Albert, despite living continents apart. And poor Lian, the first to succumb to Tiger Flu in Seattle. Why her? Both deaths left grieving family and friends behind.

~

Now with the second case of Tiger Flu confirmed, the Partners threw their expertise into solving the mystery. Genomics genius, Mike Oman, unraveled the genetic sequences of the Tiger Flu. He found that both victims had Tiger Flu viruses with similar gene markers. The virus that infected Lian who travelled from Hong Kong to Seattle was nearly identical to the one that infected Albert traveling from Copenhagen to Boston. Both Tiger Flu viruses were unique and identical, like twins separated at birth. But how could they spring up two continents apart?

Jo thought it odd. The rest of the Partners thought the same, especially Doctor Ting from the CDC. Isolated infections like these two just didn't happen. The first Tiger Flu infection was considered a "horse", not a "zebra". As doctors are taught in medical school, "Think horses, not zebras." But now something unusual, perhaps unnatural was suspected.

The first case, Lian, was considered at the time an incident, an anomalous, unexplained, incident - merely anecdotal. Its probable origin, a "wet market", where live chicken infected with H5N1 flu virus were sold illegally, hidden in the back streets of Hong Kong or on mainland China. Thought to be just a fluke, an accidental occurrence, it could have meant nothing at all.

But then the second case of bird flu happened; Albert, contracted the same Tiger strain, the DNA sequences were identical to first case, Lian. They must have come from the same exact source. Could it have been created in a lab? Or was it a mysterious doppelganger, not natural but supernatural. One thing for sure, they could be harbingers of bad luck to come.

But Jo babbled to Jeremy, "How does the saying go? 'Once is and an incident. Twice is coincidence'?"

Then Jeremy mused, sounding more serious. "According to Ian Fleming's *Goldfinger*, 'Once is happenstance. Twice, a coincidence.' at least that is what Auric Goldfinger told James Bond."

Jeremy paused, scratching his head. "And according to Moscow Rules, three times is enemy action. Or is it enemy attack?"

Jo considered what Jeremy said. She retorted, "Twice is NOT a coincidence. No way would this bizarre Tiger Flu virus end up infecting people over six thousand miles away from each other." She shook her head in denial.

"So you have a new interpretation of Moscow Rules where *twice* is an enemy attack?"

"It *has* to be. It is not a coinkydink! That's next to impossible." In her mind, Jo was sure of it.

"Jo, I am not about to cast 'nasturtiums' on that thought." Jeremy added, pleased with his word play on "aspersions".

~

The Partners came to the same conclusion when they met up again, this time with both Jo and Jeremy. The venue, an unused basement shelter on a university campus in Rhode Island.

Mike Oman explained. "The virus that infected both Lian from Seattle and Albert from Boston most likely came from the same test tube or flask. The source of the virus was the same, most likely lab created."

He explained how no flu virus in nature had evolved this extreme virulence. There were no others ones with these unique and unusual symptoms: high fever, neurological infection, delirium and brain death.

"Nature did not create this H5N1 Tiger virus. And I want to know which lab did!" Demanded Doctor Oman.

Max impatiently tapped his foot. "So it is not the common garden-variety found in poultry farm outbreaks in China or Hong Kong or Egypt. And nothing like the recent bird flu that spread in chicken farms across the US."

Max paused. "We must find out what lab created the Tiger Flu and where it is stored!" He reddened with anger. "And just *who* has access to it!" His eyes darted back and forth between Jo and Jeremy.

Jo cowered at Max's gaze, he seemed ready to attack. "And what do you two have to offer?"

Jo and Jeremy sat at one end of the eight foot fold-out table. Six Partners crammed in together on paddled folding chairs.

Jeremy shuffled through the notecards. Jo cheeks grew red as she reported their unconventional findings.

"These are not the clues of science but they are revealing nonetheless." Jo began.

Laying out the tweets, Jo and Jeremy speculated on their meaning. No, they didn't think the tweets were lover's gibberish. Jeremy pointed out the vital piece, that a dead drop spike most likely inhabited an empty depression in the plant wall soil.

Jo described finding the plain wooden chopstick that served as a "chalk mark" for this dead drop location and the compacted earthen hole in the plant wall. "I stuck my finger into the hole." She said and blushed again.

"It is possible but unlikely that the wooden chopstick was used to test the soil depth? Or it was test run?" Jeremy quickly added. "Or maybe it was an indicator signaling a drop? Out of the three possibilities, I favor that it was a signal of something ready for pick up."

Startled looks of surprise erupted around the table.

"So you think there was a dead drop at the Bella hotel? The hole Jo found represented the place where a spike had been?" Max softened his bark to a growl. Taking a deep breath, he spewed out a string of questions: "Did security cameras pick up who planted the chopstick marker? Was it the same person who dropped the spike? What was in the dead drop spike? What secrets were hidden in it? Were there items, electronic or otherwise in it? Or something worse?"

Mike Oman interrupted, deadpan, factual. "Quite likely the spike carried microbes. Viruses. A sealed spike would be perfect to transport a deadly virus safely." He had plenty of experience investigating the Anthrax laden letters that had been sent to politicians and media people in 2001. In the anthrax case, transporting powder in an envelope was a poor idea as slight leaks made the spores easy to detect.

Max and the FBI were already investigating the identity of the woman who was seen talking with Albert the first night at the hotel reception bar. And so far "Genomics" was a reoccurring theme that linked the two victims. Both Doctor Oman and Doctor Ting thought it more than coincidental. They commented that while Lian from Seattle had toured the labs at World Genomics in Shenzhen, Albert had attended the International Genomics Conference in Copenhagen.

Rich Valens sat quietly listening. As FBI handler, he kept an ever present and all-knowing eye on Jo and Jeremy. He personally inspected every clue, every scrap of paper, every keystroke they entered into their computers and smart phones. He would now advise them at every turn. No loose lips. Absolute secrecy was paramount. All their actions would be considered suspicious. Moscow Rule number one: Assume Nothing. And its corollary: Everyone is potentially under opposition control. Jo and Jeremy's findings must be corroborated. Rich trusted no one.

38 HANDLING HANDLES

Nothing had been posted from either @XOXOXMay or @YOYOYSpiko. Not since the Bella hotel postings a week before the genomics conference.

While back in Rhode Island, Jo kept mulling over the two victims of the Tiger Flu, thinking that somehow the two had to be related. The Partners delved in, investigating how these two events were connected. Jo and Jeremy conjecture brought their intuitive thinking to the mix of expertise for a more holistic approach.

It was August 12th. Jo was cutting up a salad in the kitchen when she heard a chirrup from her smartphone. Her Twitter account was set to notify when there were any postings from May and Spiko. She dried her hands with a cursory wipe from a kitchen towel, and then pulled up a tweet. It was the first tweet in the weeks since Albert died.

@YOYOYSpiko: Meet me 8-16. Take the ferry, the sea lily. I will wait at the harbor. #tigerblake19

Jo froze dead in her tracks. She sprinted outside towards the garage where she found Jeremy sorting through his fishing reels. Smart phone in hand, Jo flashed the screen under his nose.

"You have got to look at this!" Impulsive as ever, Jo couldn't wait.

"And this is so important that your thrust your phone in my face?" Jeremy had grown used to Jo's rude interruptions. His usual response was impatient sarcasm. "Come on. Is this some life shattering event?"

Ignoring Jeremy's comments, Jo insisted. "Just maybe it is! It's a tweet from @YOYOYSpiko. And I'll bet the Partners will have picked it up too. But how will they know what to read into it?"

"Let me look at it." Jeremy grabbed the phone out of Jo's hand. "This sounds as cryptic as the rest of them. So what is the hidden message in here? Hmmm, let's dissect it."

"Exactly!" Jo read aloud from the tweet. "Meet me 8-16." So he is giving his lover, May, the date for them to meet up."

"That's in four days' time." Jeremy calculated.

"Take the sea lily, the ferry, I'll wait at the harbor." Jo read.

"So could the name of the ferry be the sea lily?" Jeremy surmised.

"A ferry...the Sea Lily...where would the ferry go?" Jo mused.

"Maybe to an island. Don't you think, Jo?" Jeremy scratched his temple.

"Yes, an island? But where?" Jo felt panic, her heart thumped faster in her chest. She was sure something was up, she could feel the menace, something ominous and disturbing. But what? And in four days, they would meet up again. The lovers. Or were they plotters? Jo's brain chattered, incessant and unrelenting.

Jeremy lay down his reel, grabbed Jo by the hand and led her into his computer cave. "I can find out."

Jeremy pecked away performing his usual hocus-pocus. He had long since conjured up the location where

@YOYOYSpiko originated.

"Spiko's account was set up in Italy, that we know. It's been traced to an open access computer at the library in the University of Pisa. The Partners think that Spiko might be a student."

Jeremy then plugged words in a Google search: ferry - sea lily – island – Italy.

The first item that came up on those search parameters was a site called the "Delightful Islands of Italy" describing a group of islands in the Sardinian sea. "There is something here about uncivilized tourists that insist on uprooting the sea-lilies in the Maddelena Islands." Jeremy noticed.

Jeremy then scrolled to the second search result on Google in Wikipedia under the "Isola del Giglio". Jo was shocked and surprised, a light bulb lit up in her head. "Jeremy, I've been there!" She took over the computer and tapped on the computer screen.

"What? That must have been a hell of a long time ago." Jeremy and Jo had been married over thirty years. "Because you did not go there with me!" Jeremy pursed his lips, thinking over Jo's youthful adventures long before they met that she had told him about. Now he smiled as he remembered the picture of Jo topless sun bathing in Greece – a particular favorite of his.

"On my summer after graduating college, you know I backpacked around Europe with my three blond girlfriends." Jo was the only brunette among them. "We took a ferry to an island north of Rome. We slept on the beach for three nights."

"You could never do that now. I doubt if that would be allowed. Plus pretty dangerous and risky for a bunch of young college girls!" Jeremy shook his head remembering what was past and gone.

"But of course, I wouldn't want my daughter doing that!" Jo agreed. "But times were different then. Safer."

"Hey, isn't that the island made famous by a fiasco, the

capsizing of the Italian cruise ship, the Concordia?"

"Yes, that was at the main port, but we slept in a cove on the other side of the island." Jo brought up a map of Giglio on Google maps. She zoomed in on street view to show Jeremy where they slept on the beach. "We slept here at Campese. See the tower on the rocks? I sketched it in my diary notebook."

Jo continued. "I remember those days as if they were yesterday. We never got out of our swimming suites. We bathed in the sea. Ate a couple of meals at the two local cafes. It looks different now." Jo was now in full random memory dump mode. "It's built up a lot since then." Jeremy was remembering the Greek island picture again, thinking Jo's tits had built up a lot since then. He decided simply nodding in agreement was a safe reaction so he didn't stop Jo's flow.

"Look at all the hotels and restaurants now, Jo. You wouldn't be allowed to sleep on that beach today." Jeremy perused the island.

"In the evening, we rolled out our sleeping bags." Jo zoomed in on the map. "Look, there is a hotel on that beach now."

"And you girls must have created a bit of interest with the local men, surely Jo?"

"We were pursued, obviously! And I had my eye on the tanned blue-eyed boy who set up the umbrellas on the beach each morning. But nothing ever became of that. He seemed more interested in my blond girlfriends."

"Oh, poor Jo, rejected again." Jeremy rounded his mouth with faked pity. Jo ignored his inevitable sarcasm.

"On the beach, there was an old fisherman scrubbing an octopus on a big smooth rock. I wondered why he was doing that so I watched for a while. An Italian woman walked past and stopped, she told me in her mixed Italian-English that he was making it tender and getting rid of its ink. When the fisherman finished rolling and kneading, he handed the octopus to me. I tried to graciously decline the offer but he was insistent, gesturing toward the café restaurant nearby."

"The woman said I should bring the octopus to the *ristorante*, they would cook it for me. I should buy a drink and a salad to go with it. So I did, and wow, that was the best grilled octopus I had in my life!" Jo gesticulated, her hands flaying like tentacles, licking her lips. "Yummy!"

"And probably the freshest." Jeremy added. "But, hey, I catch you plenty of fresh fish. All those lake trout and you remember that salt water Striper don't you?" He was proud of his thirty inch striped bass beauty.

"The best fish I ever tasted, really!" Jo exclaimed. "But it is too bad they are so full of mercury." She frowned.

"Yes, just another example of man's destructive, polluting nature." Jeremy grimaced.

"OK, but back to the island, I found it fascinating. Some very odd things struck me. Most of the people, the islanders, had clear blue eyes, unlike the brown-eyed mainland Italians. So striking in their looks, those island people with their light eyes set against their dark summer tans. And the cats…"

"What, blue-eyed cats with tans?" Jeremy ribbed Jo with a snicker, thinking of sun-basking pussies perhaps with sunglasses.

Trying to take no notice, Jo went on. "The cats were everywhere. The island was virtually overrun with them. They were incredibly mottled in color, mostly Calico markings of orange, yellow, brown, black, white. They had odd patches of grey and white stripes, like moggies. And their eyes, multicolored mixes with one eye blue and the other brown or green; di-chromatic I guess you would call it."

"OK, and the significance is inbreeding?" Jeremy prompted.

"Maybe, or just remembrances of things past." Jo mimicked a Proustian pretense. "And I also remember the white lily flowers with long spiny petals that grew in the sand on the beach. They gave off a delicate sweet odor. And the Italian word *Giglio* means lily!"

"So Spiko and May are meeting up on Giglio? Wait a minute." Jeremy looked up the ferry timetables. "There are more ferries on weekends but only a handful on weekdays. They depart from nine in the morning and the last ones come in before nightfall. And, now this is interesting, one ferry is called the Maregiglio."

"*Mare*, the sea. *Giglio*, the lily. Yes, now I remember. It was just such a long, long time ago."

"Jo, but what about the hashtag? This #tigerblake19." They both had wondered what that could mean.

Jo searched twitter for #tigerblake19. "It is the only thing tweeted under this hashtag. And it really strikes me as something foreboding."

"Me too, Jo. The "tiger". Jeremy shook his head in concern.

"Tiger Flu." Jo gulped. She frowned.

"And Blake. Well we know where that comes from. *"Tiger, Tiger burning bright, in the forests of the night."* Jeremy recited.

"Thing are getting gloomy, Jeremy".

He recited the next line. *"What immortal hand or eye, could frame thy fearful symmetry?"*

"Should we fear the worst, Jeremy? And the '19', what could that mean?" Jo asked

"Maybe it has something to do with the 19 of the 9/11 attack? Remember Jo, the 19 terrorists who attacked using planes as passenger filled missiles?" Jeremy suggested.

Jo gasped in horror at her randomized thoughts. "But, what if?"

39 WHAT IF?

Jo and Jeremy let the questions roll. The many "What ifs?" They trickled, they poured, and they overflowed. So by spilling out a cascade of questions and answers, they guessed, they imagined, they wondered just *what* it could be.

And one scenario they came up with was a parallel, a 9/11 mirror image. Perhaps 19 terrorists, human time bombs, quietly arriving on airplanes destined for who knows what cities? Leaving from who knows where? Insidious, could it be a stealth attack? An attack with a silent, deadly Tiger Flu by infected people who in turn infect others? It was the most horrific scenario Jo and Jeremy could come up with.

Jo mused. "The attackers could be like suicide bombers but with no explosives. No obvious weapons, they would be totally under the radar, beyond detection. And they would be quiet until their symptoms erupted, then spread their lethal germs by coughing and sneezing."

"Seemingly innocuous, 'It is my allergies' they would explain to anyone who showed concern." Jeremy mused, rubbing his chin.

"Until the fever burns and the bright light shines in

their eyes. And the brain is on fire…" Jo trailed off.

In what furnace was thy brain? Jeremy recited the line of Blake's verse.

Jo emoted. "But Jeremy, they could be releasing this beast on all humankind!"

"But they don't care, Jo. Whatever their motive, they are nihilists at heart."

"Heartless murderers that they are." Jo teared up. She cried in frustration and despair.

~

The implications where stark. The "what if" scenarios were ominous. As Jeremy so poignantly put, "In a world of hostile actors, anything is possible."

Expect the unexpected. One cannot predict the plans of hostile actors. The red lines were crossed when deadly microbes were manipulated, turned into potential pandemic pathogens in the laboratories of "first world" superpowers.

Whether legitimate world powers or rogue states or highly educated yet disaffected loners, anything is possible. The microbes have been created in labs, the recipes and methods published for all to read, to copy, to emulate, to rival. The instructions are stored on the laptops of terrorists and in the basements of do-it-yourself village idiots.

And with the newest technologies like gene editing, genes can be inserted into entire species of animals and plants and microbes. Custom editing of designer babies might be the sci-fi of the future, but editing the DNA of microbes has become the child's play of today.

Jo complained. "It is not a matter of "if" but "when". The technology itself has surpassed its own capabilities of being reined in."

Jeremy reminded Jo. "We must stay focused. This threat of the manipulated Tiger Flu virus must be the work of an extremist group. Terrorist threats around the world have evolved rapidly. There is a growing risk of "going dark" in their communications. And this makes the world an increasingly dangerous place."

"The Tiger Flu, out of its cage, will unleash the plague. Unless it can be stopped before it happens!" Jo uttered in angst.

"The attack could be imminent. Jo, we've got to tell the Partners, and quick."

40 GIGLIO

But of course the Partners already knew. Working at lightning speed, they mobilized the FBI and Interpol, who cloaked themselves in darkness, their agents lay in wait on the Island of the Lily. They blended in as tourists in their floral shirts and Bermuda shorts.

With the threat of terrorism at a global high, cooperation had improved since the days of agency turf battles and obstruction. The stakes were too high. World renowned scientists begged government agencies to listen, that in a world of hostile actors, bioweapons were probably the greatest threat to humankind. The capability was out there, in basement labs, in rogue nations, in the massive laboratories of world powers. The storage of bioweapon agents extended well beyond those held by the superpowers.

In a world where even the most controlled, efficient, safe and secure labs could mistakenly ship out live Anthrax, small pox and bird flu viruses to scores of laboratories around the world, what could happen in countries where protocols and procedures were sloppy?

Accidents happen. Or more accurately put,

"Happenstance happens."

As for the intentional release of biologic agents, sabotaging one's "enemies" historically happened since the days of gifting Indians with smallpox infected blankets. When new diseases infect poultry and livestock, one has to wonder where they might have come from. How easy for terrorists to attack a country's food supply. Even worse, newly designed, mutant varieties of flu could ravage the world. A ferocious strain of Tiger Flu could circle the globe devouring everyone, sparing only those wealthy enough to own their own private islands with vaccine labs in their basements.

As Jo ranted. "Don't get me wrong, people will survive even the plague of the millennium. But who wants to live in a world like that? The private biotech labs could concoct their special brews for the vaccine strain of the moment. But what about the world outside of those havens?"

"Yes, I know Jo. Plague and pestilence in a post-apocalyptic world. It's back to the Dark Ages." But Jeremy wasn't his usual sarcastic self.

~

For once, every one of the Partners was in lockstep in their thinking. Everything could be lost. All would suffer if even one agency put on the brakes or veered off course. The loss would be insurmountable. There would be no win-win but only an out-and-out lose-lose. Prevention was the directive. Not mitigation of the consequences.

So the agencies worked swiftly, they were prepared for the worst. And if by chance, they found an opportunity to prevent a hostile act, they sprang into action. And they did so with the alacrity of zealots and the passion to thwart plans conceived in malice.

The coordinated effort descended on the island along with the flock of summer tourists. And they lay in wait. *Nell'Ombra.*

~

Kahliy left Pisa early Monday morning on August 15th.

The train took less than two and a half hours to arrive at Orbetello where Kahliy boarded the bus to Porto Santo Stefano. At the port he watched the coast guard, idling their time, they seemed to have nothing to do. It was 11:45am, one hour before the ferry, the Maregiglio, was scheduled to depart.

On the one hour cruise to Giglio Porto, Kahliy reflected back in time to when he was young. It had been many years since he and Nonno scoured the rocky cliffs and hiked the walking trails up to Giglio Castello, the walled fortress that overlooked the port below. Kahliy and Nonno had strolled the sandy beach, breathed in the sweet lily fragrance and splashed in the warm Mediterranean that rippled with swirls of deep green, shades of blue, and an iridescent aquamarine. So variable in nature, its hues forever morphing in the sunlight and shadow, it was a metaphor for Kahliy and his ability to change with the moon and the tides, the currents and the winds.

Kahliy rested for one day before Mei's arrival. He checked into the same small *Albergo* he and Nonno stayed at, although it had changed some. No longer inexpensive, but still less pricey than the beach hotels. Located on a rocky outcropping, it overlooked the tower, the Torre Del Campese. He could see the umbrella-dotted beach in the distance.

The hotel had been updated, but it was simple and less touristy than others. Kahliy thought it perfect with its patio deck where he could lounge looking out at the sea, and in his room, a flat screen satellite television where he could watch the world from a distance.

Kahliy thought through his plan anticipating Mei's arrival the next morning. He would take her in a taxi from Giglio Porto to Campese, just nine kilometers away. He would indulge himself one last time. Mei would be his sex slave before sacrificing her to the gods of hedonistic pleasure, he thought in humorous irony.

The entrance to his room was private, no hotel lobby

to contend with, and the rocky cliff would provide the perfect opportunity for a lover's stroll. Mei would slip on a rocky outcropping, hitting her head on a jagged edge. He would notify the police, they would inspect the scene, and the coroner would say the injuries were consistent with the fall. It was rather a steep drop; other foolish tourists had suffered the same fate, especially after drinking too much Tuscan wine. And Kahliy would make sure Mei had plenty to drink.

Kahliy would remove her passports and cash from her knapsack before calling the *carabinieri*. A number of Asian women now made their living on the streets of Southern Italy. No one would come looking for her. It was an unfortunate accident. He would say he met her at Giglio Porto and took her back to Campese for paid sex. She had euros, a wallet with a few hundred in her knapsack filled with sexy lingerie. Kahliy knew where to safely bury the passports and large sums of money he gave her in Copenhagen. Written up as a working girl, the police would not put too much effort into the investigation. She would be just another Suzy Wong. Kahliy did not miss the irony in the name or her profession. Her final demise would be fitting for a cheap prostitute. Beautiful yes. Intelligent, very. But still a prostitute of her own making. Kahliy would fuck her then kill her.

Mei's life meant nothing. His life as a soldier had purpose. Kahliy was a nihilist when it came to the lives of others. A voyeur, whether actively involved in killing or watching people die from afar. He was elated by the control he exerted over others and the power he held over the demise of modern world. He found it exalting.

The small island of Giglio would be its own buffer against the virus. Islanders would succumb or wait for the plague to pass through. The ferries would no longer run. Kahliy could sustain himself on the *frutti di mare*, the fruit of the sea.

Giglio was an underwater paradise. Kahliy brought his

fishing rod and reel, casting out on that first afternoon before Mei's arrival. He and Nonno had done the same, catching edible fish he had never seen before. The boats going out made the big catches of tuna, barracuda, bonito and amberjack. But from the rocky shore, Kahliy and Nonno caught many varieties on their holiday all those years ago. Kahliy planned to buy his own fishing boat after Mei would meet her unfortunate demise.

Kahliy sat on the rocky ledge in his black bathing trunks, a speedo would not have been comfortable. Today, Kahliy caught only one sea bream, *Sparus aurata*, it's marking of gold glimmered between its eyes. This gilt-headed fish was the tastiest of the bream.

But, that evening Kahliy dined at a restaurant in the village. He ordered the local delicacy - grilled octopus.

41 PORTO

Kahliy stood patiently waiting at the harbor for the morning ferry, the Maregiglio, to arrive at about ten o'clock. He could see the ferry approaching in the distance. As he watched, he thought about the Concordia, now raised, floated and towed to its final resting place. The *capitano* jailed after all the international attention brought to the island. He thought the island's tranquility would have returned with the cruise ship gone and the voyeurs of tragedy no longer drawn to the scene of disaster. But the port seemed surprisingly busy.

When the last passenger and all the cars had disembarked, Kahliy lingered another five minutes before giving up on finding Mei. Disappointed but not all that surprised, he knew Mei was always fashionably late. Too busy primping and preening like a peacock, her vanity so annoyed him.

In the Porto Giglio, he found a pleasant café with outdoor seating to while away the hours before the next Maregiglio arrived. The weekday schedule was less frequent, although another ferry line also operated. He could watch from his patio table, just in case Mei missed the 9 AM ferry and she thought to take the next available.

But Kahliy was now angry at Mei, she should know better. He was very specific with his instructions and she could be precision perfect at following directions. Certainly, she would be on the next Maregiglio that arrived at 1:45PM, he had time enough for a leisurely lunch. After many cups of espresso, Kahliy ordered the *pesca di giorno*, the fish of the day. He always ate the local catch when available.

The port seemed overly active for a Tuesday. Kahliy watched the second ferry line come and go, but still no Mei. Peering out at the sea's horizon, Kahliy finally saw the outline of the ferry Maregiglio approaching. He paid up his bill and headed back to where the ferry docked. She must have missed the morning ferry, Kahliy surmised. It was quite possible her journey took longer than expected; perhaps she couldn't find the right bus at Orbetello. And of course Mei's inexperience at European travel put her at a disadvantage. He kept making up excuses; he anticipated she would have many.

Between his heavy dose of caffeine and his excited anticipation, Kahliy jittered nervously as he stood on the harbor, rocking back and forth as if swaying with the wind. With his imagination in high gear, he now had more to accomplish in a shorter amount of time than he planned. But he knew it was doable, the pace might not be so relaxed but nightfall would come sooner. Still plenty of time to ply Mei with the colorful cocktails she so loved. He would take her to a bar in Porto Giglio, Mei was a sucker for sweet multicolored drinks. They would be noticed but that was all part of the plan, his pretty prostitute would be the envy of others. His alibi would be confirmed. She was a drunken *putana* who slipped on the rocks.

They would take a taxi ride back to his room, Mei could snack if she liked, and he would do likewise. She will have brought the red lace teddy he bought her, that was part of his dictum when they were last together in Copenhagen. Do not forget it and your other fine silky lingerie. I will take you shopping for many more beautiful skirts and summer dresses. Just come with the bare essentials. His English was now powered by colloquial sayings, Mei taught him many. He mulled over Mei's bare essentials, a clever play on words. He visualized her bare nakedness, her legs spread pointing at the ceiling. He imagined, one more time, he would "take her around the world" before he would take her walking to the edge of the rocky cliff to see the sea glittering in the moonlight. But tonight there was a new moon. In China the new moon signifies the beginning, but tonight it would foretell Mei's end. It would be a perfect ending by Kahliy's calculation, in total darkness, *Nell'Ombra*.

So engrossed in his fanciful day dreams, Kahliy didn't notice the darkness thickening around him. But the day was not cloudy. The sunshine reflected off the shiny, polished black cars and the blinding flash of a wing mirror as it caught a sunbeam.

Kahliy remained focused, looking for Mei. What would she be wearing? Something cool in this heat, a short sundress, perhaps. He stepped in closer to the unloading ramp, where people filed off the ferry with their hand luggage wheeling behind them. But still no Mei. Other men stood near him. Were they waiting for a loved one too? Or like him, not a loved one, as in Kahliy's case. Maybe the passengers planned a getaway, a naughty weekend with a married woman? Or a paid lady friend? Paid escorts were easily ordered up on-line. Certainly that would be the case, he thought. But where is Mei? Where is she?! He tapped his foot impatiently. His heart beat faster; his anger now overcame his anticipation. His hands were shaking, too many stimulants played at once on his emotions.

Why did that man rub up so close? Did he just feel my jeans? Is he looking for my money? Is he a pickpocket? A thief! He thought as he elbowed the man in the gut. But the thick-necked, beefy brute grabbed his arm and, before

Kahliy could object, he clasped a handcuff around his right wrist. Almost simultaneously, a second taller man of similar build, pulled Kahliy's left arm behind his back. Kahliy struggled impulsively trying to free himself from the handcuffs; his wrists throbbed from his self-inflicted pain as he twisted to escape. His legs moved in a stationary running motion, the men were strong, experienced at this sort of thing. Holding him solid between them, they shackled his ankles preventing his every attempt to break free. Kahliy ran only in his mind, he couldn't budge a silly centimeter.

Kahliy cried out in a wailing child-like scream, the little boy that he was. "Mei, Mei, why have you done this to me?" He howled and whined a second and third time. He could think of no one else who would inform on him. After all, she was not on the ferry. Kahliy couldn't think straight, sheer panic set in. His heart beat so fast, he nearly passed out. His bladder was so full of coffee, he pissed himself in fear. Too stressed to care, he felt no embarrassment. He would shit, if he could to express his rage. After all, "We are only the product of our bodily functions. Beyond that, we are nothing." His mantra had no effect in calming or placating him.

As the ship siren made a sing-song blast in typical European fashion, Kahliy, firmly harnessed in the prisoner cabin, tried to think more rationally. What about Mei, the murderer of two victims that she infected and killed with Tiger Flu? It made no sense that she would help orchestrate his capture. He considered the possibilities. "Could the police already have her in custody?"

The police loaded Kahliy's heavily armored car on to the Coast Guard hovercraft destined for the mainland.

"I have done nothing wrong. You must have the wrong person." He complained to two guards who sat at each side silently. These were no ordinary *carabinieri*, that much he knew for sure. He knew the police must be searching his hotel room. They covered his head in an eyeless black balaclava. He could either talk or breathe through a mouth hole. He chose wisely.

Nothing made any sense to Kahliy. He thought about his students. At least they will be on their flights to America. Today!

Could he handle an interrogation? He knew he was a pro. After so many years of lying convincingly, he didn't know how to tell the truth. His entire life was a lie. He wouldn't reveal nor divulge anything.

Kahliy wondered how long they had been watching him. Did they know about his train journey? So many questions but too few answers. He began to invent the lies he needed to forestall the inevitable. They might have already pieced together too many parts. He and Mei were not the only people good with clues and mysteries and games of secret messages.

Perhaps they will torture me? Kahliy was aware of the brutal methods of American interrogation. He read the news. He had been humiliated, badgered, slapped and punched, but never truly tortured. He would kill himself before exposing the plot. And that meant Mei, too, must remain *Nell'Ombra*.

42 BLACK SLING KNAPSACK

"We need to break him; we have no time to waste!" Max snarled as he talked on his secure phone to his Interpol counterpart.

"Let's keep a lid on this as long as possible. We know who Mei Wong is. But just where is she?" Max demanded an answer. He sat in his home office in Rhode Island, he was securely vaulted. His communications highly encrypted.

Perhaps Mei Wong would still show up to board the ferry to the Isola del Giglio? They could not be certain. But with all the commotion and stories flying, it would not be long before the press made the capture of this wanted man a headline.

"University of Pisa Professor Arrested as Suspected Terrorist." Read the cover of *Corriere della Sera*.

At the Bella Hotel, the Danish and US federal authorities, alongside Interpol, viewed the security camera tapes together. No one agency trusted the other. Together, they pulled the recordings, going back in time, to when and where they first identified Mei Wong hidden under her Chinese flat cap.

They watched Mei on her first visit planting the "test"

bamboo chopstick, sliding it out from under her sleeve and measuring the depth of the Bella's plant wall. She leaves the chopstick in. Then climbing in the elevator, Mei peruses the Sky Bar, strolling the perimeter, supposedly just to admire the view. Just another student tourist.

Next on the video, Mei returns a second time. This time wearing no cap, her coiled hair is held with two tan chopsticks. She sits on the solitary lime green sofa, grasps hold of her left chopstick and impales it into the plant wall close to the original one's location. On closer inspection, each chopstick in her hair has two white bars on the ends.

Her clothing, still plain and nondescript, Mei ascends the Sky bar elevator, visits the *daman toiletten* holding her sling knapsack and emerges having transformed herself into a sexy black skirted prostitute with gold-heeled stilettos.

After curling up in a hanging basket chair in the corner of the Sky bar, she is approached by a man who checked in to the hotel with a Spanish passport. The two meet at the elevator, then video surveillance shows them getting off on the 19th floor. Later she descends to the lobby as the plain student now hidden under a Chinese flat cap and carrying the same small leather sling knapsack that she arrived with.

Unfortunately, hotel security had not scrutinized these earlier video tapes; they would have linked the mystery woman from her previous visits to the hotel.

The hotel guest on the 19th floor, now identified as Kahliy, carried a Spanish passport stolen from a tourist who traveled in Italy months earlier.

It was the third time that Mei visited the Bella hotel that she met Albert. Mei entered the hotel early that evening in her beige linen attire, her face unadorned with makeup, her hair pinned up with one large black plastic hair clip. She carried the same leather sling knapsack. That evening, she disappeared from the videotapes for quite some time while transforming herself in the toilet cubicle reserved for the disabled. This private area was not under video surveillance.

It was obvious she was not part of the Genomics Conference when she emerged, snaking herself through the crowd that had since begun to accumulate. She exuded an aura of high-end hooker, her leopard patterned skirt and the gold-heeled stilettos. But what they didn't see on the tape was how Mei, who carried nothing, hid her small black knapsack behind the toilet designed for wheel chair users. She slipped into her skirt waistband the special honey sweetie with its hard sugar coating, covered in a plastic wrapper. She also tried not to suck too hard on the honey sweetie she had tucked into her cheek.

This recorded video had originally been combed through with fine-toothed devices. But now on closer inspection, Albert's Candy Girl could be seen handing him a sweet or candy of some sort which he unwrapped and popped quickly into his mouth. Also on the video, one security agent detected Mei's sucking motions. He questioned, was it a suggestion of what she had to offer? Certainly she was a tid-bit any lone researcher would find irresistible.

The video clues from Mei's earlier visits to the hotel revealed much more about what really happened. And, like Jo and Jeremy, the investigators questioned the meaning of the buried wooden chopstick, having determined the precise time of day that she planted both.

Despite Mei's careful cover, it was the location of the green settee that gave her away. Mei's plotting and planning and execution of her ingenious murders, every move she made, was now documented and teased out down to the most intricate detail. Only her stops in the *daman toiletten* and her tryst in the hotel room were not video recorded.

From the videos, Kahliy's accomplice was also identified. A local thug, Kahliy paid him twice, once on the promise to retrieve, and a second time on the delivery of the finely tooled chopstick with its white inlay crosshatches. A petty criminal, he was rounded up in no time, but he had nothing new to offer.

43 NOTHING

Mei was nowhere to be found on the university campus. Her dorm room empty, the police busily dusted for fingerprints and gathered strands of her long black hair from the shower for DNA analysis.

The University identified her as Mei Wong without question. Yes, she was an exemplary graduate fellow in microbiology genetics who kept pretty much to herself. She had acquaintances but no real friends to speak of. She declined invitations to socialize with other graduates, both Danes and international students. Always too busy with her studies, she told them. Otherwise she was out on her bicycle, getting exercise, seeing the sights. No one even knew she owned a camera. They only knew she carried her ubiquitous backpack. Her old Chinese suitcase and most of her clothing were found bagged in the dorm dumpsters. It appeared that she disappeared with only few belongings stuffed in her black backpack.

Mei Wong never flew home to Shenzhen as was presumed by her Copenhagen University study colleagues and supervisor. World Genomics in Shenzhen were finally notified. She disappeared, but not without a trace. The authorities assembled her identity kit, but the question now was how she could travel without arousing suspicions?

A wanted felon by Interpol, her student photo was distributed at the ferry crossing from Copenhagen to the European continent. But she was seen much earlier with her backpack on a videotape at the crossing. From there, no one had any inkling as to where she would emerge.

Women like Mei were clever enough to leave no breadcrumbs behind. And, as she had already proven, she was a master of traveling *incognito*, she could easily assume multiple identities. Unlike Kahliy, Mei was not reactive, she always thought through multiple moves ahead. And she easily mutated into her next iteration.

Kahliy was not so lucky, nor as clever as Mei. Kahliy's previous whereabouts, his travels across Europe by rail, his meeting with students, were mostly revealed by Interpol who traced his multiple passport identities. Kahliy hadn't considered that his confiscated passports would pinpoint his every move on his European rail journey along with the GPS of his cell phone.

His most damning incrimination came from the revelation of his secret, *Nell'Ombra*, the sleeper cell group that Kahliy had recently awakened. The authorities knew this from Flavia, Kahliy's disaffected student "soldier".

~

Kahliy had few words when he had last met with Flavia in Pisa just weeks before. He presented her with travel tickets to her assigned American city, Atlanta, and gave her enough US dollars to last until she erupted into the "final throws of fevered brain death". He instructed her to sleep with as many men as possible, to infect them with the ferocious Tigers. But when Flavia untied her linen trousers and dropped them to the floor of Kahliy's office, offering her strawberry blonde mound and exposing her freckled breasts, Kahliy turned away, repulsed. Just two nights before, he had plunged into the bleeding Zita, on the same corner of his wooden desk where Flavia now sat spread-eagle. Kahliy angrily sent Flavia away telling her to remain focused on her final objective. Her time would come for her orgy of destruction.

The *carabinieri* had called around about Zita that very same morning, questioning Kahliy about when he had last seen her. What was her mood? Was she depressed? Zita spent a lot of time with his study groups. Was she upset about something? Or someone? Most people the police had interviewed described her as silent and strange. Even her roommates knew nothing about her; a pathetic little person with dark secrets.

But Kahliy's spurning of Flavia that evening in his office backfired. Flavia could not take his rejection. An actress at heart, she only acted out to receive Kahliy's attention. She was wildly attracted to Kahliy but the attention of other young men would have to suffice.

When Flavia joined *Nell'Ombra* it was out of pure lust for Kahliy. The philosophical allure of nihilism was more romantic to her than real. She knew she could never surrender herself to any anarchistic cause. She wanted most to surrender herself to Kahliy. She planned in his office to have Kahliy again and convince him that his ill-conceived plans would never materialize. That he was an idealist who could never carry out the plans he conceived. Their love would supersede all philosophical discourse. His plan to annihilate the world? Sheer fantasy.

But instead Flavia felt treated like a disposable napkin, with Kahliy tossing her into the trash heap of nothingness. Flavia was infuriated. She was *not* nothing. She could *never* be nothing. She *did* believe in something, an elusive concept of love that continually eluded her.

She wanted Kahliy, she could take his rough sex, and she remembered the pleasure and not the pain as he pummeled her mercilessly against his office wall. She could take it. She was tough. But not so tough as to sacrifice her life for a laughable philosophy.

And when Kahliy treated her as expendable, not even worthy of his sexual desires, she decided not to sacrifice herself for a man who would never love her as she hoped. She would say nothing, she would never take that small pill, and she would not board her plane. She just simply missed her flight. Kahliy's cruelty and rejection would not be rewarded with her obedience to his scheme of death. She flushed her Tiger pastille in its plastic packet down the toilet in her student housing.

Interpol collaborated with Italian intelligence and security services. The investigators traced Kahliy's contacts, in particular his students, their whereabouts, and their plane ticket destinations. Seventeen students departed as planned. They had already landed. The FBI and state police forces were tasked with finding these travelling biologic time bombs. If they were right in their estimation, the terrorist sleeper cell, suicidal, confirmed nihilists they professed to be, would soon show symptoms, coughing, sneezing, infecting others with the highly contagious Tiger flu after they landed.

The Pisa police brought in Flavia for questioning and handed her over to Italian Intelligence. Just why did she miss the flight she was booked on and what were the intentions of the group now known as *Nell'Ombra*? And how many others were there that she knew of?

Interrogated by needling, nit-picky interrogators, Flavia gave a different story. She told the interrogators she missed her flight to Atlanta because she never intended to carry out Kahliy's plan. Flavia knew enough to distance her involvement with the nihilist philosophy as far as possible. She spilled as much detail as she could recall at that moment but divorced herself from any radical political or philosophical ideas. Her ideals were whimsical and fanciful, not something she would ever realize in her everyday life.

Her Italian interrogators kept her for five hours. Iterating, reiterating. Checking her for consistent, rational thought. And motive. Just what were her motives for joining *Nell'Ombra* in the first place?

239

"It was merely a flirtation with the philosophy." Flavia explained in many different ways. The students read Nietzsche and other philosophical thinkers in her class at the University. It was nothing unusual for students to explore the meaning of life. It was a rite of passage.

"And was there a flirtation with your *professore, signora?*" The Italian intelligence agent asked.

Flavia admitted to her infatuation with Kahliy, explaining that everyone addressed him by his first name. He made no pretenses of being anything but one of them. She was certainly smitten by his charismatic appeal as were many of his students. But she never took any of his rants and raves as more than ritualistic play acting. It was all just for dramatic effect. Or so she thought. She never seriously thought she would even be asked to execute a terrorist plot. She was no suicide killer.

"It was all just an intriguing game for me. And I fell in love with him." Flavia broke into tears. Composing herself she added. "I thought he loved me."

44 ELECTRICIAN

Meanwhile on the Islola del Giglio, Interpol agents and the Italian investigators thoroughly searched Kahliy's room in the *Albergo* at Giglio Campese. His stack of passports were confiscated as well as his laptop. Two glasses sat ready for the chilled bottle of champagne in the refrigerator along with Italian meats, cheeses and pastries.

Kahliy's twitter handle @YOYOYSpiko and his professorship at the University of Pisa tied him to his network of people. His tweets with @XOXOXMay, when pieced together exposed their nefarious plot, but the precise details were still a mystery.

As Kahliy was shuffled blindfolded, the whir of the helicopter blades masked all other sounds. He could feel someone inject him with a drug, perhaps, he thought, a sedative or a sleeping concoction. He woke up to find himself clothed in an orange jumpsuit, lying on a cot in a large windowless underground cell. Kahliy had no idea where he was. Such were the methods of secret rendition.

The interrogation began without delay. Two guards front-handcuffed him and clasped him in leg irons. Kahliy, now propped in a lone chair, braced himself for a brutal interrogation but he never anticipated how he would react to methods he didn't even know existed.

Various pieces of equipment were brought in by the "experts". Kahliy recognized their accent; they spoke English with an American twang. He had heard about the ruthless approach and specialized expertise of the CIA. One "technician" controlled the electrical box with its variety of attachments. Kahliy thought for sure he had been transferred to American custody.

"We know who you are. And we have six fake passports taken from your computer case." An Italian agent informed Kahliy. There were no cameras but audio was recorded and translated into different languages. The audio would be transmitted to those in the "need to know" sphere of the secrets.

"You must tell us everything!" The Italian insisted.

Kahliy nodded that he understood. But the interrogation took a quick turn that he had not expected.

"We will speak to you in a language that you understand!" An American interrogator inched in closely as he looked deep into Kahliy's swollen, reddened eyes. It was an obvious threat; the interrogator was intent on extracting information as quickly as possible. Kahliy understood what he intimated.

"We will hang you from your limbs." The American lunged at him. Bullying, he punched his eye; it was a warning of impending harm.

They must be the CIA, Kahliy told himself. They must be. Who else would threaten him like this? Kahliy nervously coughed, unable to stop.

"There will be no limits to the methods we will use." The interrogator leaned in as he threatened torture beyond anything Kahliy's fevered mind could imagine .

"We have your uncle in custody. He denies any knowledge of your dealings. But we will find out what he knows." The American interrogator spat in Kahliy's face. He was skilled in the art of intimidation.

Kahliy froze in fear. When the torture began, they

poked him, they prodded him, one of the agents knuckled him hard in the eye, just common inflictions of pain to try to unnerve him. These were the techniques of gentle coercion. Just punching, pinching, squeezing, there was no brutish breaking of bones. They stretched the ligaments and battered the bones of Kahliy's calves, all to the point of intense excruciating pain but nothing that would leave any permanent impairment. But Kahliy bravely resisted divulging his Uncle's involvement with the grand plan.

But then things took a turn for the worse. With a two inch electrical wire, his tormentors beat the back of his handcuffed hands with the electric cables. When Kahliy shrieked loudly from the pain, they shifted their focus, lifting his legs and beating the bottom of his feet to the point of tearing open his flesh. But still Kahliy resisted.

Dread and anxiety penetrated his very being as the atmosphere intensified. The overhead shower in the corner was turned on. Two thug accomplices dragged Kahliy to the corner. Shoved under the rain of cold water, they gripped his hair tight, his head cocked back so far the water sprayed into his nostrils. His nose filled up, he gasped for air with his mouth now overflowing from the gushing water, and he choked and gurgled. Unable to breath, he thought he was drowning.

The tormentors stopped barely short of Kahliy losing consciousness. "Who is involved and what did you plan?"

But Kahliy, nearly asphyxiated, was too terrified to answer.

That is when the American specialists began to set up their special apparatus. The electric box. They plugged a long cord into a wall socket that had been capped with a locked cover. They had the key. The two worked in tandem testing the voltage as if they were calibration engineers. Their equipment seemed in fine working order, their first test was a quick jolt to Kahliy's left arm. He yelped. The two men let him know what he must prepare himself for, should he refuse to reveal everything.

"If you do not give a full confession, everything you know, do you know what we will do next?" The American interrogator smirked, a sadistic look of pleasure on his face; he defied Kahliy to resist. It was then that the two "electricians" produced two pair of oversized scissors and began cutting Kahliy's jumpsuit, removing it in pieces, until Kahliy stood wet and naked in the corner of the cell.

One electrician wielded a blunt instrument that looked like a cattle-prod. He plugged the cord into the electrical box, before jabbing Kahliy hard in his stomach. Kahliy buckled in pain. "You are lucky so far!" He bellowed so loud in Kahliy's left ear, that it left a ringing.

"I haven't turned the power on yet!" The electrician laughed.

The second electrician further humiliated Kahliy by unzipping his trousers and urinating on him. The ultimate thug, he laughed and sneered with a smile suggesting that much worse was yet to come. Unwinding a coil of cable, he exposed two electrode clips, not unlike ones that would be used to jump a dead car battery. He buried them in Kahliy's groin, in close contact with Kahliy's most prized possessions, his precious jewels.

"Shall we flip the switch?" The sadistic interrogator gestured with his finger toying with the lever of the electrified instrument.

"Nooooo!" Kahliy pleaded, a broken man. "Please, noooo! I will tell you everything!"

More interrogators entered the room.

At that point, nothing more needed to be threatened. Kahliy held back nothing. He told then how he was the pawn of his uncle. An orphaned child stolen form the streets of Naples by Uncle and a Romani elder. How he was forced into submission to be their servant, their soldier, their slave for most of his life. How he was coerced to enlist conscripts for the nihilist army of Nell'Ombra. It was Uncle and his cohorts that were bent on the annihilation of the West, in particular, America.

When asked about his manipulative sexual encounters with his students, he described them as simply infatuations and love affairs. No, he did not control his women with sex. They laughed and spat in his face.

"You manipulated women. You exert power with sex. We know you exploit your students. Their naiveté. Their vulnerabilities. Those who are mentally unstable. "Your sperm DNA was identified in a semen sample taken from your dead student Zita. And your student Flavia didn't depart on her flight to Atlanta."

They taunted him, dribbling out revelations that Kahliy didn't know and others he had tried to forget. After hours of sleep deprivation, one interrogator punctuated each new allegation with a series of belly punches.

Kahliy was painfully shocked. A double whammy. The revelations, allegations, and the repeated socks to his gut. How much more did they already know? Jerking at his emotions, they tortured him with the agonizing details of Zita's suicide, her labored death, bleeding out from multiple self-inflicted wounds.

And then there was the exposure by Flavia of his brutal sex, the pounding she took as he nailed her to his office wall. "An act of violent sexual submission", as defined by the psychiatrist assigned to her. Flavia had poured out her heart.

Kahliy tried to convince his interrogators that he really was a sympathetic character only doing the bidding of his masters.

"I never wanted the life of a child-soldier." He sobbed as he confessed. "It is Uncle who is the one intent on destroying the West."

Now broken, the interrogation became pure confession. Kahliy divulged everything. Almost. He held back nothing of the terrorist plans, exposing in detail how Mei lured and killed her prey with her "honey sweeties" as proof of what she could do.

He told them how Mei delivered her Tiger Flu pastilles

in the dead drop spike. That they were the lab created pathogens with all the most feared traits known to science. Highly transmissible, super-lethal and fast spreading, just a cough or a sneeze away. They were the promise of #tigerblake19. Only now there were 17 "soldiers", not the original 19 to carry out the attack.

The current vaccines, even those for Bird Flu, would not be effective. And there was no cure. But Kahliy omitted the fact that Mei vaccinated him against the Tiger Flu strain.

~

Max, listening from his secure room in Rhode Island, felt a gut wrenching reality sensing that something of indescribable horror was about to happen. The horror would not be limited to concentric circles of death like that inflicted on Hiroshima and Nagasaki. Nuclear bombs were no longer the greatest weapon of mass destruction, no longer the absolute evil of ultimate inhumanity. New technologies, in particular the biological weapons, surpassed these lethal but targeted atomic afflictions. No other weapon of mass destruction could spread, propagate, and blanket the entire globe. There had never been anything like the potential pandemic promise of a lethal, virulent, highly contagious Tiger Flu. The death rate of the Black Plaque paled in comparison. Billions could die.

And now, the United States elevated their threat level to Red, the highest possibility of an imminent attack. A weaponized bioterrorist attack was imminent on the United States for which there was no defense.

With every US international airport alerted, it was too late to stop the students from disseminating themselves around the country. But maybe they could catch up with them, scour the airline terminal videos, and the video footage at train stations and bus terminals. They would send agents to hotels most frequented by international students. Show their student photos, ask a lot of questions and most importantly have agents screen people who presented themselves at hospital emergency rooms and walk-in clinics.

Fever monitors would be used on all incoming patients to Emergency Rooms and mandated at the airports. Any international travelers with fevers, headache, delirium, vomiting, meningitis like-symptoms would be screened and isolated. Especially those within the college age demographic. And those with Italian and European passports must be questioned, especially any international students visiting as summer tourists.

But with at least ten major US cities in the mix, the mandate seemed a mission impossible.

45 EVOLUTION OF MEI

It was in Hamburg, Germany that Mei had her long black hair chopped off. The many passports that Kahliy gave her all had her old photo, one she had given him in Hong Kong. They showed Mei as a plain-faced academic, unadorned and obviously Chinese.

The first and most noticeable change to her appearance was her hair length and color. She admired the colorful hair that trendy western women wore, but she decided to keep the change subtle for the time being. She did not want to draw attention, at least, not yet. A light brown color and hair-cut above shoulder length. Different enough but no longer the same Mei who left Copenhagen.

By Mei's estimation she had a few weeks to prepare for her new life. Her Hamburg to Paris train took forever, a full eight hours, but she had her objectives: identity and beauty "manipulations". Her small breasts, which Kahliy never seemed to mind, were in her estimation not her most attractive feature. For the most part, they went unnoticed by men.

"I need embellishments." Mei told the plastic surgeon in Paris who specialized in breast enhancements. Not too large, but nicely shaped, with well-formed cleavage." She drew him a sketch. He showed her photographs. Together they chose the most perfect boobies. Full and lovely but not huge like a porn star. Two firm succulent melons exuding the voluptuousness of summer fruit, curvaceous when set against her tiny waist and rounded hips. Those of a love goddess, a Venus de Milo.

Happy with an excellent job, she asked her "breast man" for a referral to an eye surgeon, one who had perfected the art of Epicanthoplasty, surgically minimizing the epicanthic fold and rounding out the eyes. He suggested a female eye surgeon he knew, touting her skill at creating a rounder shape and exposing the eyelid without any scaring.

"Enough but not too much, retain your oriental beauty." The woman plastic surgeon suggested. They perused the photographs, the "before" and "after".

"Yes, subtle change." Mei agreed. One with the exotic look she admired but could still defy facial recognition software. Facial modification to enhance Mei's natural beauty with a softer wider eye, while preserving the curved tilt to her eye. "Pan-Asian" they agreed.

Mei paid her surgeons well, in cash, for their discretion. Her name, a fictitious concoction, invented by Mei on the fly, was nothing traceable. She showed no ID, just a name scribbled on information forms.

Within three weeks, there was no swelling, no scarring, and Mei had eyes that would invite men for any exotic or erotic experience.

Mei's faked and stolen passports supplied by Kahliy had a short shelf-life. She needed passports with new photos and new identities that could not be traced. Paris, like any big city, had its sources. She bought another handful from a gang member affiliated with the Chinese Tong. Among the passports was a French one with the surname Tran, a name common among the Vietnamese but it was a name also used in China. Ambiguous, but the name was definitely Asian. She now was no longer Mei

Wong. She could easily blend in, lost in the assimilated mass of the over three hundred thousand Vietnamese now living in France. And she had other backup identities, multiple passports with new photos of the highly altered version of Mei.

With her physical manipulations now complete, Mei next destination was Zurich. Before her departure, she tossed out her burner cell phone, no GPS would follow her from now on. From the Paris train station, Gare de Lyon, she boarded the high-speed TGV train, whizzing past the Eiffel Tower, through the French countryside, up over the majestic Swiss Alps. Magnificent, how quickly the landscaped changed. Mei thought it metaphorical.

In just over four hours she arrived in Zurich. Such a grand city, she read of the great wealth stored in its banks. Tomorrow, she would set up an account to deposit her heavy knapsack still stuffed with euros.

Mei had dressed that morning in a well-tailored black business suit she bought in Paris. She hoped it would offset the impression from her trendy new hair-cut, stylishly transformed from brown to the brightest color of red. Her recent purchase of designer roller luggage, housed her knapsack, clothes and cosmetics.

Mei chose from a list of spectacular hotels that were frequented by the richest people in the world. She was attracted most by a photo of a seductive bar with dark mahogany wood, white leather barstools, an old-world elegance and the old-world money that drinks in it. She checked into the Baur au Lac Hotel that afternoon under a new French identity. In the evening, Mei emerged.

Mei sits now perched like a mermaid on her bar pedestal. She lounges resplendent in an iridescent blue-green wrap skirt draped high on her thighs, poised with her elongated legs and upturned feet sheathed in faux green snake skin with gold stiletto heels. Under a black lace blouse protrude two exquisitely sized and shapely breasts with a strong hint of cleavage. Her Asian fusion eyes more rounded yet tilted in perfect exotic indeterminate ethnicity. One chopstick hair ornament threads through her softly spiked carnelian hair glowing in the overhead hanging lights as if her head were on fire. Her red-orange flames erupting wildly. The perfect look that Mei so desired.

Mei orders a cocktail from a long list. "A Jewel of the Nile, please. On the rocks."

The bartender looks at her room card to make sure she is a client and not a sex worker. He delivers an exotic mix of Green and Yellow Chartreuse served on crystalline ice cubes in an elegant cocktail glass. A small red stirring straw lies against the rim. The Yellow Chartreuse is sweetened slightly with honey but the Green is still too sour for Mei's liking. But it is the perfect swirls of yellow and green cut by icy shards that Mei admires and the iridescence that matches so well with her special attire.

Mei grips and slowly glides the ornamental chopstick out from her hair, careful to not disturb her French styled red-orange coif. She twists the top end of the chopstick, unscrewing the sealed metal container. Slowly, carefully, she pours in six pastilles from the same batch she delivered to the Bella's bamboo wall. She stirs them gently with the little red straw.

She takes a small sip. "Ahhh, perfect."

Under the luminous glow of the overhead light, a radiant, almost angelic smile beams on Mei's pan-Asian fusion face. Her evolution complete from human to reptile to genetically engineered mermaid, now fully transformed, Mei has mutated into the post-modern woman of her own making.

ABOUT THE AUTHOR

Joann Mead is a writer, teacher and researcher. Her fiction is inspired by her published research on disasters and emerging threats. She brings her unique perspective from teaching science in four countries (United States, England, Russia and Zimbabwe), working in biotechnology and in medical research.

Joann Mead's "Tiger Tiger: Underlying Crimes" is the second novel in her series, "Underlying Crimes".

www.UnderlyingCrimes.com

30256546R00165

Made in the USA
Middletown, DE
18 March 2016